Illusions

Spirian Saga Book 5

Rowena Portch

Illusions

AEON ENTERPRISES, FEBRUARY 2013

www.Aeon-Enterprises.us

Cover illustration and book design by
Aeon Enterprises

ISBN-978-0-9886275-4-3
V2.0_r1

Printed in U.S.A.

ACKNOWLEDGMENTS

To my lifetime mate and best friend, Gregg—I am honored to share your life. You make me so proud and rarely fail to amaze me with your wisdom and wit. Thank you for teaching me what love and trust is all about.

To my parents, Eve and Arcadie, and stepfather, Bob— thank you for putting up with me and all my odd and crazy quirks. You have been supportive, loving, and most of all, the best parents a creative, free-loving soul could ever hope for.

My dear friends and adopted siblings, Dave and Evelyn, you are God's Angels, I'm certain. Your hearts are as pure as they come. Thank you for always being there even when life becomes hard to endure.

To my readers—thank you for your fabulous feedback and loyalty. My sincere gratitude goes to those who have emailed me, visited my blog and have sent me letters. You are the reason I continue to write and are my driving force to keep going. May the Spirit bless you with unconditional love. I couldn't make it without you.

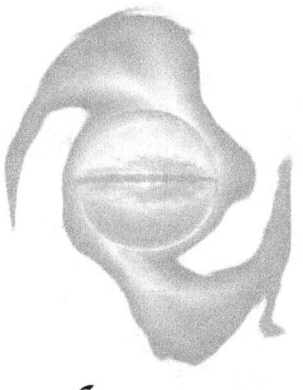

Chapter 1

Illusions alter our perception of reality and offer glimpses of what is possible, leaving us to ponder what is truly real and what is an illusion.

- I a n -

A LOW GROWL RUMBLED DEEP in my throat, vibrating all the way down to my gut. The man sitting next to Erika reached for her hand.

A strong grip on my shoulder halted my advance to the gardens toward the too-cozy couple. "Easy, Ian." Erika's father, Arcadie, had a calming yet commanding voice.

I glanced ahead to where Erika still sat. My mate-to-be's face did not show alarm or interest toward the man's advances. I forced myself to breathe, reminding my over-protective instincts that she was not yet my mate, nor had I any claim to her. She had a right to court other men, but damned if I was going to be happy about it.

"Let them talk," Arcadie added.

"I jus' want t' let 'er know I'm 'ere," I said, my Irish accent more thick with emotion than I intended.

Arcadie guided me away from the pair, leading me to the study on the far side of his house—a large mansion on a private island in Brazil. It was the main dwelling in the center of his clan. Arcadie owned the island, accessible only by plane and a narrow bridge that was secured by a gate. His clan consisted of over thirty families, all living in close proximity.

Kitta, his mate, greeted us in the corridor. "Ian, we were not expecting you."

I glanced behind me toward the gardens. "Erika asked me to come."

"Let's talk," said Arcadie. He looped his arm around Kitta's and led us all to a spacious room down the hall and to the left. It offered no view of the massive gardens that dominated the house.

I took a seat across from the formidable man and his lovely mate. Arcadie's silver hair and blue eyes looked so much like his father, Shanuk's that I felt as if I were staring at the old man who had died nearly ten years ago. Arcadie was a very powerful Spirian and governed the largest territory of any leader. He was not a man to be taken lightly.

His mate Kitta was a tall elegant woman with dark features and a will that rivaled that of a mother bear. She was not keen on me courting her only daughter and never failed to demonstrate that fact.

"What is this about?" I finally said.

Arcadie poured us all a glass of brandy. It was not my favorite. I preferred Irish whiskey, but right now I didn't care. I needed something to ease my nerves.

"I have asked Jazen to court our daughter," Kitta stated, almost as a challenge. She even lifted her chin a bit to emphasize her position.

"Ah, yes," I said, hiding the daggers behind my voice. "The son of Thonel, leader of the Taru clan in New Zealand. Powerful choice."

"You, too, are a good choice," Arcadie added, as if trying to tame my anger.

"But," Kitta added, "Jazen can offer Erika stability, a good home, and status."

"I have status."

"You are not a leader, Ian, nor will you ever be."

My jaw pulsed with tension. I stood and started to pace. "I am a good man for her, Kitta. I can take care of her."

She smiled. "I know you can, Ian. And yes, you are a good man with strong gifts and fine blood. You are also very popular with the ladies." The last remark sounded like an exclamation disguised as an afterthought.

"I have not been with another since the day I met your daughter."

"Ian," she pleaded. "Please do not think I'm judging you. I know you have a good heart and unquestionable integrity. I just want Erika to explore all her options before settling on a mate."

I looked at Arcadie, hoping to glean his perspective. The stone-like expression on his face told me little if anything about his opinion on this matter. As Erika's father, he could trump his mate's decision, but it was clear he would let the situation run its full course without intervention.

"I will not give up," I assured them, raising my glass and downing the warm, amber liquid.

Arcadie smiled. His eyes sparkled with a knowing as he raised his own glass. "I would be disappointed if you did."

"Promise me this," said Kitta. "Do not influence her with your illusions. I want her decision to be made in earnest."

Again, my jaw clenched. "You have my word."

As an illusionist, I had the ability to make someone see what I wanted them to see, and feel what I wanted them to feel. It was my gift. I was good at it, almost to a fault. I wondered if Jazen was asked to curb his gifts as well.

If I remembered right, he was an energy bender and could change the shape and function of any object. His gift was strong and rivaled my own. In a practical sense, I could see how Kitta believed he was a better choice for her daughter. My heart knew better.

"May I see her now?"

"Ian," Erika's sweet voice filled the room. I turned to see her smile at me. Jazen stood behind her.

"Ye asked me to come," I said, holding my hands out toward her. "Your requests are something I will not refuse," I glanced over at Jazen. "Ever."

Jazen's eyes narrowed, changing their sienna color to hints of red. He was slightly taller than my six-foot-two-inch frame and styled his honey-brown hair like the cover-model of a GQ magazine. Not a strand of it was out of place. He wore a cream-colored silk shirt and pressed brown slacks that equaled the compulsive pride of my clan leader and good friend, Khalen.

Erika took my hands, making the gesture seem as comfortable as touching a brother or a good friend. I kissed the backs of hers, keeping my green eyes fixed on her delicate face. She was remarkably beautiful in that cobalt-blue dress. It matched the color of her eyes, perfectly. Like her mum, she was tall and slender. Her hair, however, was the color of spun honey with golden highlights. She took after Arcadie in that respect.

"This is Jazen," she said, gesturing to the man now standing beside her.

I nodded. "So I've heard."

Jazen smiled and extended his hand toward me. "Erika speaks highly of you," he said, gripping my hand like one would grasp the throat of a threatening snake.

I matched his fervor with the strength of my own. "Jazen."

My attention returned to Erika. "I understand ye helped solve another case?" I smiled. She had the uncanny ability to talk to deceased humans. The gift seemed useless until she helped the police solve a missing persons case several years back. Now they used her often as a consultant.

She nodded. "Yes, that is why I called you. I was hoping we could celebrate tonight. There's a—"

"Jazen is taking you to a dance, darling, remember?" said Kitta.

"Perhaps another time," Jazen said to Erika.

"This dance is important," Kitta explained. "It is the gathering of all young Spirians who have come of age."

"Mother, I came of age years ago. Must I attend each of these gatherings?"

"Until you are mated, yes."

"I am not ready to mate with anyone."

Erika had the spirit of an eagle and the heart of a lion—the very traits that intrigued me about her. Crossing her mother, however, was not wise.

"Go to the dance," I told her. "You and I can celebrate later." I smiled, trying to assure her that our time together would be well worth the wait.

She vehemently stated, "Honestly, this tradition of dance is going to be the death of me. Do I not have a life of my own?"

"Not until you are properly mated," Kitta retorted.

The hum in the room escalated and I knew Arcadie had reached his level of tolerance.

"Do as your mother wishes."

Erika immediately looked down and took a deep breath. "Yes, Father." She had only argued with him once. It was something I never wanted to witness again.

She looked at me apologetically. "You came all this way. I'm so sorry."

The ten-hour flight from Bremerton, Washington was something I had done often just to see her again. "For a glimpse of yer smile, lass, I'd do it again for the askin'."

"Will you stay?"

I glanced over at Kitta, who casually looked away.

"No. I'm returning home."

The sadness veiling her blue eyes weighed heavy as lead on my heart.

She lowered her eyes. "Oh, I understand."

She really didn't and I wasn't in a position to explain things to her. The distance between our clans made it impossible to connect as close clansmen. I was not part of this clan. My place was in Washington State. Kitta and Arcadie shielded their daughter's thoughts from me. I understood their reasons, but it made things difficult for us.

"Will you be back soon?"

I looked at her parents. "Perhaps." I smiled at Erika.

"All ye have to do is ask."

"Can you come to the dance tonight?"

"You already have an escort," said Kitta.

"There will be many fine women there," said Jazen. "I'm sure Ian will not be alone for long."

Kitta grinned. "I believe you're right. That's a brilliant idea."

Arcadie smiled at me with an understanding that stood only between us. I had fought many battles beside the man and he knew me better than most. "I agree," he said. "Join the celebration."

Erika's eyes sparkled once again. "Do you have something to wear?"

"I'll manage," I said.

She flashed me a brilliant smile that nearly undid my restraint to embrace her. "I'll see you there, then?"

I nodded to her. "I'll be there."

Jazen's glaring eyes felt like daggers dipped in poison. His intention was not lost on me. The warning was as palpable as the walls around us.

THE CLOTHES I'D BROUGHT WERE inappropriate for the formal dance that evening, but a quick illusion could change that. I conjured a black suit with dark-green silk trim. Erika always commented on my eyes and I knew the color would make them stand out. I never liked these formal gatherings, but they were important to her mother.

When Kitta visited our clan, she traded her formal gowns and fancy dresses for blue jeans and casual shirts. They looked good on her and she always seemed to relax more around the camp in them. Here at home she was far more stuffy and formal. Arcadie attributed it to her upbringing and duty as the leader's mate.

I had witnessed the pressure that clan leaders endured and felt relieved to know I would never be placed in that position. Though my status was high within our clan, I did not carry the blood of a leader. In truth, if it were not for Khalen, my brother, Aidan and I would be considered misfits and would most likely end up in a Shadow clan.

I finished combing my hair and giving myself one last inspection. "What are ye doing, Ian O'Dougherty?" I was treading deeper waters than I was prepared to swim. Erika and I were good for one another, but we came from different worlds. She was the princess and I was the pauper.

Doubt shadowed my confidence like a dark, damp shroud. The image staring back at me was a man with a mission—a man who knew what he wanted and was willing to die trying to obtain it. I shook my head. "Yer a stubborn, foolish bloke."

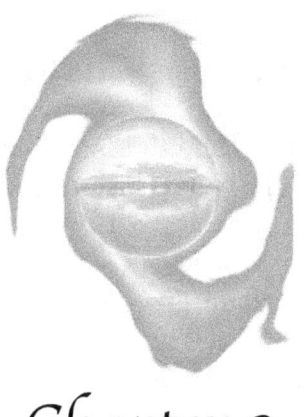

Chapter 2

-Ian-

THERE SHE WAS, LOCKED IN the vise grip of Jazen's arms. He was making sure that Erika never left his side. Again a growl rumbled deep in my throat. An image of snakes constricting his throat began to manifest in my mind. I shook it off, remembering my vow to Kitta. Powerful as my illusions were, I had agreed not to use them around Erika or to influence her decisions.

My brother, Aidan, would say that I'm a leopard trying to disguise myself as a giraffe. Perhaps he was right. I had set my sights on a débutante when I should have been targeting someone more in my league. Somehow, that didn't matter. I wanted Erika, débutante or not.

I straightened my illusory suit and made my way toward her.

"Ian."

I turned to see Kitta walking toward me. She looked radiant in her emerald green gown decked with more finery than my mother had seen in her lifetime.

"Kitta."

Her smile beamed and the sparkle in her eyes seemed out of place. "I want you to meet some acquaintances of mine." She took my arm and led me toward a group of young women.

"Ladies," she said, interrupting their conversation. As the mate of Arcadie, she was one of the most powerful female Spirians alive. She pretty much had carte blanche over all forms of etiquette and no one would dare question her.

"I want you to meet a very dear friend of ours." She gestured me to step forward. "This is Ian O'Dougherty of the Gradhun clan."

A pretty little sprite with long blonde hair smiled sweetly. "That's Khalen's clan in Washington, correct?"

"Aye it is," I confirmed, offering a curt bow.

She extended her white-gloved hand toward me. "I'm Susenna, daughter of Jamiel and Chloe."

I took her hand and pressed my lips to the back of it. "Delighted to meet such a well-informed young woman." I emphasized the word, "young," hoping she would get the hint. The girl was nearly half my age if not more. Granted, age did not mean much to Spirians after maturity, but I preferred to have someone with a bit more wisdom and experience—like Erika.

The young female giggled.

Kitta continued her introduction before explaining my presence. "Ian is visiting us and is not currently mated." I didn't miss the way she raised her brow as an invitation. "He is a very gifted illusionist who has fought many battles. Khalen sees him as a brother."

That last part was added to emphasize my status in

the clan. By blood, my status was fairly low. When my sister, Valerie, mated Khalen many years ago, we joined his clan. Our parents had died when the Shadows attacked our camp. Valerie was the eldest, but she turned against Khalen and became a Shadow. He was forced to kill her. The feat nearly undid him, even though Aidan and I supported his decision.

It took years before he was able to take another mate. Skye was good for him and a much better match than Valerie could have been.

Satisfied with her introduction, Kitta took her leave, allowing what she considered 'nature' to take its course.

Judging by how the ladies were dressed, I assumed they were from lower-ranking families. I had dressed according to my assumed status that Khalen offered. Good enough for these ladies, but not for Kitta's daughter. The message was loud and clear.

So there I was, stuck in the midst of five lovely ladies all vying for my attention while the woman I wanted stood next to a man who held an obvious advantage over me.

Erika's eyes narrowed as her mother pointed me out. Perfect. This couldn't look good.

Erika broke away from Jazen and made a beeline toward me and the ladies.

When she approached, her arm wrapped possessively through mine. She smiled and planted a long, lingering kiss on my lips.

"Ian, I have been waiting for you." She eyed each of the ladies as a warning.

The young blonde began fanning her face. "Forgive us, Erika. We didn't know you had sights on him."

"Now you do," she replied sharply, leading me away.

"Thank you," I said.

"Just like my mother to pull something like this. Ugh! She makes me so angry!"

"Down, lass," I quipped. "Nothin' would'a come of it."

"I should hope not. I'm counting on you to keep it together, Ian O'Dougherty."

I bowed. "As y'wish, m'lady."

Jazen approached, Reclaiming Erika's arm. "Everything all right?"

I smiled down at Erika. "It's perfect."

She returned the smile. The notion was not missed or appreciated by Jazen.

He tugged her arm. "Come," he said, rather sharply. "The music starts and I would like to dance."

Erika hated dancing; she always had until I showed her how the Irish danced at Aidan and Sunjia's union ceremony.

I watched as she glided over the dance floor like a feather on the wind. She was beautiful, refined, and—

"Still in your league," came a voice from behind me. It was Arcadie. His large hand settled on my shoulder. "I remember looking at her mother the way you look at her. She was well sought after and had every high-status buck rutting for the rights to have her, including me."

I laughed. "Our blood is slightly different," I reminded him.

He removed his hand. "Blood has little to do with it, my boy. Integrity, heart, and loyalty rise above anything that flows in our veins. In my opinion, you have what it takes to win that girl's heart."

"What about her mother's?"

"She's already taken, dear boy," he bantered. "Besides, it is not her you need to impress."

I met his eyes. He smiled and walked away.

Arcadie wanted me to prove my worth for his daughter—perfect. To this day, I'd never had to prove anything to anyone. Women were abundant and finding one for a night's pleasure was not an issue. Earning a mate of worth, however, was nothing short of a challenge. A slow grin started to form on my face. I love challenges.

I noticed a few blokes by the bar chatting over pints of warm beer. A set of pipes, a drum and two flutes rested beside them. A thought sprang to mind. I walked toward them.

"Evenin', lads," I said, striding up to the bar beside them. I ordered a Scotch, allowing my Irish accent to bloom.

"Ah, an Irishman," one of them said.

"Aye." I extended my hand. "Ian of the Grahdun clan."

The tall, lanky one with flaming red hair extended his greeting. "Shawn of Praduk, and m'brothers, Tahl, Grenden, and Penn."

The lot of them nodded as their names were mentioned.

I gestured to the pipes, flutes and hand drums on the floor. "Ye play those things?"

"Like bloody bards," the younger one said. He was a handsome lad with dark brown hair and hazel eyes that sparkled with mischief.

"Ye think ye c'n play me a song?" I gestured to the methodical band playing a slow waltz. "Somethin' I c'n dance to?"

"Aye, I think we c'n. Arcadie asked us to come an' play durin' the other band's breaks. Do ye 'ave a song in mind?"

"Do ye know Glacier's Spring?"

"Oh, aye," said Shawn. "We play a lively version o' it. I think y'll find it dandy enough."

"Perfect," I said, smiling. "Keep the beat goin' throughout the break, eh?"

I placed a bill on the counter. "Buy yourselves another round on me."

Shawn spied the bill and raised a brow. "Bloody generous of ye, lad. We'll play our best fer ye."

I nodded. "Appreciate it."

I took my Scotch and meandered my way through the crowds. An older woman with cascading dark hair touched my arm.

"Care to dance?" she asked in a charming British accent.

I kissed the back of her white-gloved hand. "I'm sorry, miss, but m'heart is taken with another." I glanced toward Erika.

"Lucky woman," she said and then worked her way through the crowd.

I leaned against the stone wall and sipped my drink, observing as Erika endured one dance after another. It was almost painful to watch.

Finally, after my drink was drained, and the crowd settled, the band took their break.

Jazen led Erika back to a table in the far corner of the room where Arcadie and Kitta waited with two other couples. I followed them over.

"Ian," Arcadie announced. "Come and meet some friends of ours." He gestured to the two couples. "This is Brig and Tamrin." The couple nodded and smiled. "And this is Thonel and Lindi."

I extended my hand in greeting. When I reached Jazen's father, my smile broadened. We had met many years ago when I was a younger lad, though I doubted he would ever remember.

"Thonel," I said. "It's a pleasure to see you again. Your son is an impressive dancer."

"Many years of training," the man added. "You said, 'again.' Have we met before?" His thick New Zealand accent was as refined and polished as his son's.

"Many years ago, when I was very young."

The man nodded, his expression skewed between confusion and embarrassment.

"Ian comes from the Gradhun clan. He is Khalen's brother," Arcadie explained.

Thonel raised his bushy dark brow. "Brother, you say? I heard he had only one; a twin if I remember."

"Yes," I confirmed. "Traeger. He walks the next world now. M' brother and I are Khalen's in-laws."

Thonel smiled. "Then you come from Shanuk's line?" He obviously thought we were Skye's brothers.

Arcadie cleared his throat, clearly annoyed with the conversation. "Ian and Aidan are Khalen's first mate, Victoria's, brothers. She passed away many years past."

"Yes," said Lindi," "I remember now." She touched her mate's arm and telepathically filled him in on the details of Victoria's demise.

Thonel's expression grew solemn. "I'm sorry, mate," he said.

"It happened long ago."

Arcadie pulled out a chair. "Come join us, Ian."

I saw the band begin setting up on the stage. I had a few minutes.

Arcadie ordered me a Scotch and two glasses of wine for him and his mate.

Jazen ordered a glass of Sauvignon Blanc for himself, and a cognac for Erika. It angered me that he knew her drink of choice.

"Erika is a wonderful dancer," Jazen commented.

The drinks came and I downed a good portion, trying to keep my emotions in check. The illusions I conjured in my mind were leaning on the edge of an abyss. I quickly cleared them away before they manifested into something I would regret.

The band announced their presence and began playing a song to set the mood. It was a short version of I Useta Lover.

I stood and walked around the table. Extending my hand to Erika, I smiled. "Care to dance, love?"

Jazen's grip on her arm tightened. "I'm sure she's tired and needs to rest, man."

She gently pulled her arm away and stood. "I'd love to."

"Kick yer shoes off, lass."

She giggled and flung them under the table.

"Erika!" her mother scorned.

"Leave 'em be," Arcadie said.

I led her out to the dance floor and began moving to the lively rhythm of the song. When Glacier's Spring began to play, the smile on her face broadened.

"You're full of surprises, Ian," she said.

"More than ye know," I replied, leading her into a dance that rivaled the play of fire on aged pine.

We breathed hard, laughed, and spun along on the floor as if we were the only couple dancing. I felt several eyes upon us but it didn't matter. I was in bliss with my heart's mate, dancing as if life had stood still.

The break was over too soon and Erika was whisked away by an angry and determined Jazen.

Arcadie slapped a hand on my shoulder. "Well done, lad. Impressive display."

"Yes," Kitta commented. "You looked very commanding out there."

I followed them back to the table and swigged my Scotch. My heart still pounded from the exertion of dancing, but more so from the anger welling inside.

Erika was nowhere in sight. The bloke was purposely keeping her from me.

"Come," said Arcadie. "Let's walk."

- E r i k a -

THE PAIN OF JAZEN'S GRIP on my arm stung clear to my bone. "Jazen, slow down. You're hurting me."

He led me to the barn several hundred feet from the main hall. The music could not be heard, only the sounds of night and resting horses.

"You waste your time with that bloke," he said, pinning me against the dusty wall.

"I don't appreciate your temper," I replied, meeting his gaze. His sienna-colored irises were nearly swallowed by the blackness of his pupils.

"Perhaps you should not rile me then by dancing like a harlot." He dangled my shoes by his fingers. "Put them back on."

"You do not intimidate me, Jazen, nor do you claim my heart."

"In time, you will change your mind. By year's end, you will be my mate."

"This is not something you have the power to force."

I felt the hum of his anger increase. I had underestimated his power and will. With little effort, he rendered me helpless. I couldn't move as he strapped the shoes back on my feet.

"If you ever embarrass me like that again, my dear, I will issue a harsh reminder of the respect I deserve."

With that, he pressed his lips to mine, willing me to return the affection with equal ardor. My stomach twisted inside while my thoughts reached out to Ian. They bounced back like shards of a shattered mirror.

"He won't help you."

~ I a n ~

SOMETHING WAS WRONG. I COULD feel it. Arcadie and I froze and then hurried toward the barn.

When I saw that bloke with his lips on Erika's, my body stiffened like a bolt eager to find its mark.

Arcadie stilled me with his hand. "Easy, lad. My daughter is not without her own defenses."

A wave of energy rippled out from her, slamming Jazen against the far wall. He sat, holding his ribs. Before he could retaliate with what would be a destructive blow, Arcadie rendered him helpless.

I hurried toward Erika, struggling to keep my need for vengeance in line. "Are you all right?"

She nodded and then pressed her forehead against my chest. I wrapped my arms around her.

Arcadie stood over Jazen. "You're lucky to still be conscious, my boy."

Jazen's eyes met mine and then fixed on Erika. "She has no respect," he seethed. "She does not recognize my position."

"Your position?" Arcadie inquired, extending his hand.

Jazen gripped it, holding his aching side as he painfully

hauled himself to a stand. "She broke my ribs."

"They'll heal," said Arcadie.

"I am her future mate, and yet she flaunts herself over this bloke of questionable blood."

Arcadie displayed an impressive calmness toward the cocky spike. It was clear to me now how Arcadie obtained his high status—he earned it. That position had little to do with his blood and everything to do with how he conducted himself in the heat of turmoil.

"She is my daughter, Jazen. Currently, her heart remains unclaimed. You are not her mate until she agrees to be so. It will be her choice."

Jazen's jaw flexed into sharp lines that betrayed his temper. Like myself, he struggled to tame the beast that lurked within. A sliver of me felt sorry for him.

"My status equals her own," said Jazen, fixing his eyes on mine. "You, Arcadie, give her too much power," he growled. "She should be—"

He fell to the floor, his face skewed in pain, his words choked.

"Do not tell me how to raise my daughter, young man, lest I remind you of my status."

"My father will hear of this," he rasped.

"I'll make sure that he does," Arcadie replied, releasing his bind.

Jazen slumped to the straw-laden floor, gasping for air.

Arcadie wrapped his arm around Erika. "Did he hurt you, my dear?"

She arched her brow. "Do you really think I would let him?"

Arcadie laughed a hearty roar filled with relief and pride for his eldest daughter. Erika's spirit rivaled her mother's. She would be a challenging catch for any man, including myself.

Her dress was ragged and marred with dust. With a quick thought, I restored its brilliance with an illusion.

Arcadie shook his head. The illusion crumbled as I recalled the promise I had given to Kitta—no illusions, period.

Having read her father's mind, Erika smiled. "It's all right, Ian. You need no illusions to impress me."

She brushed the dust from her dress and brushed back the stray strands of hair that had fallen from her coiffure.

Before we reached the dance hall, I stopped. Arcadie gave me a knowing grin before continuing into the hall leaving Erika and me to talk.

"Aren't you coming in?" she asked me.

"No, I'm headin' back to my room, then leavin' for Washington tomorrow."

Her smile faded, but her eyes shone with understanding and strength. "Will you be back here soon?"

"I'm never far from ye, lass." I leaned over and pressed my lips against hers. The power in that kiss surprised me. It was a claiming, possessive affection that held an unspoken promise. I half expected her to back away. Instead, she pressed into me, matching my desire for more.

"I wish you didn't have to go," she whispered.

"Our time will come, but my life is in Washington, as are my duties. Yours are here."

She lowered her head. We had this discussion before. Arcadie had opened his clan to me, but my loyalty was with Khalen. He had agreed to release me of that vow, but it was not an option I wanted to consider. Khalen had given my brother and me new lives. I was not willing to let that go—not even for love.

"I understand," she said, raising her chin with mock strength and courage.

"That's m'girl," I said.

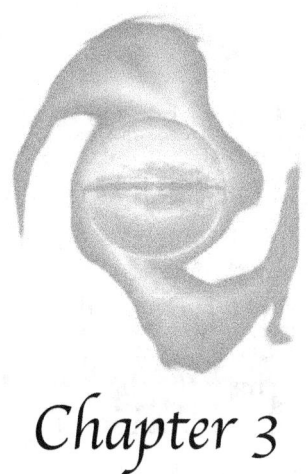

Chapter 3

-Erika-

THE NEXT FEW DAYS WERE filled with work, helping Detective Gray with a few cases involving missing children. I enjoyed the challenge, but contacting the children who had died or were murdered played havoc on my soul. I wasn't sure how much longer I could do it.

Seeing the relief of closure on their parents' faces made things worth the pain of revealing their children's demises. My father was uncomfortable with me using my gifts in the presence of humans, but seeing I was aiding them with a gift that many humans possessed, the risk seemed minor. I made certain not to show too much of my Spirian side, but it was rather draining. I couldn't wait to come home at the end of each day.

The glass of tart Petite Syrah I enjoyed now in the quiet of the study provided a relaxing reprieve. I had a lazy fire burning in the small hearth and a plate of fresh-baked peanut butter cookies beside me. The house was quiet.

I hadn't heard from either Ian or Jazen and wondered if I had bleeped completely off their radar. I couldn't blame them, really. My mother had become quite the tyrant and my father had made it a point to Jazen's father that he keep the boy tamed.

Jazen was a strong male, typical of high-blood Spirians. He was in line to be the next leader of the Australian borders, something his father had recently obtained when their leader passed on. Jazen would make an excellent leader and a strong mate and father. I would need a strong mate. My mother knew it as well. A lesser man would bore me to tears in less than a year.

Ian had a more gentle spirit, yet he was strong in his own right. I could feel the struggle he had with keeping his temper leashed this past weekend. It both frightened and excited me at the same time.

Until now, he had been a good friend; someone to have fun with. His kisses were sweet and gentle. The last had been more possessive and filled with a hunger Ian had never revealed to me. I knew his reputation with the ladies and never considered it—until now.

A smile stretched over my face.

"There you are," my father said from the doorway. "You've been rather absent these past few days, my dear. Is Detective Gray keeping you busy?"

I scoffed. "You might say that."

My father poured himself a glass of the Petite Syrah and sat across from me. "Keep your boundaries, dear, lest others define them for you."

I sipped my wine and stared into the flames licking misshapen maple roots like the long tongue of a forbidden lover. The roots burned long and hot. They were my father's favorite wood source, though they were expensive and hard to find. I loved the sweet smell of them.

"Your mother worries for you," he said, admiring the flames with vivid blue eyes.

"As well she should for meddling in my affairs as she does."

"She believes it is for your own good."

I sipped my wine, giving him a half-baked smile. "And what do you believe?"

He returned the smile, his eyes glistening with a knowing that only years of wisdom could claim. "I believe you know the truth of your heart, my dear, but cannot see it through the webs of your own misconceptions."

I thought about that for a moment, my brows pinching together as if the gesture could shed light on my father's obscure logic. "Care to expand on that?"

He shook his head.

"I didn't think so," I said.

He finished his wine, set the glass down on a small marble table and then patted my leg as he stood. "I will send for your mother. You two must talk."

There was no sense in disputing him. When her father made such a statement, his decision was final. "She won't want to," I said, quietly as if to myself.

He stepped out of the small dark room without reply. There was no need for one. I knew as well as anyone that mother would not deny his wishes. Not many Spirians did—at least not more than once. I often wondered what it would be like to have his power. I shuddered at the thought.

As I took the last sip of my wine and contemplated heading for bed, my mother walked in with two snifters of cognac in her hands.

"Your father sent me to talk to you," she said, smiling and handing me a drink.

"Thank you." My first sip of the amber liquid flowed down my throat like a welcoming flame, torching back the words sticking in my throat. What I wanted to say and what I had a right to say were in conflict. Years of painful reminders warned me to mind my place.

She took a seat across from me. "I know you are unhappy with me," she began, "and perhaps you have a right to be so."

I watched as she turned the glass in her hand and stared into the fire. "You are my first, Erika. I want the best for you."

"And what is the best for me?" My words had an edge to them. She noticed, but chose to ignore it.

"A strong man; one who can take care of you."

"Do I need to be taken care of?"

She smiled, but still did not meet my eyes. "Not in the traditional sense."

That piqued my interest. "Explain."

"You're a strong woman. The man you choose to mate must be stronger or you will soon grow tired of him." She looked at me with a seriousness that typically followed a tragedy. "Imagine spending a lifetime with a man who holds you back. Can you do that?"

"You don't think Ian is strong enough," I stated, keeping my voice low and respectful.

"I believe he can be."

My mother was talking in riddles. I sipped the fiery liquid and practiced having patience. After a few deep breaths, and waiting for her to continue, I concluded that I was simply too tired for this game. "Do you care to expand on that?"

"Ian has never had to prove himself to anyone, dear. Women come easy to him. He's followed in his brother's footsteps from day one. Khalen has taken him under his wing. His only status comes from a union that was never meant to be. In his mind, he knows he is out of your league, but his heart won't listen."

I fought the need to roll my eyes and feigned patience.

She reached over and held my hand. "Give him something to fight for. Give him a chance to prove his worth. I know he's strong. Now he needs to find that strength and let it flourish."

I thought about that for a moment. Until the night he left, his kisses had been sweet, tender—uneventful. That night, however, the kiss nearly undid me. I felt something I had never felt around him—yielding, and perhaps a bit excited.

"Now you're starting to understand," she said, smiling. "Nothing is worse than having a man you can rule over. Strong women need something more."

"Perhaps," I said. "But what if Ian decides he is not good enough for me and gives up?"

"Then he doesn't deserve you."

I frowned. "Do you think he will give up?"

Her grip on my hand tightened. "I hope for your sake, dear, he doesn't. Jazen is a good man, and the perfect choice to stoke Ian's fire."

My eyes widened. "That's why you're pushing Jazen and me together."

"Ian needs something to fight for. I'm merely giving him the opportunity to prove himself. The rest is up to him."

I sighed. "Jazen will be angry if I choose Ian over him."

Mother shrugged. "Jazen will be leader of a fairly large

territory. He must get used to disappointment."

"So you really don't hate Ian?"

She smiled and released my hand. "No, child. I just see something more in him that has been dormant for far too long."

I studied the woman sitting across from me and saw a side of her that I had overlooked for too many years. We had been close once, and she had been somewhat of a mentor to me. I had always admired her strength, but until now, had failed to see her wisdom. I smiled inwardly. "You are much wiser than I have credited you with, mother."

She nodded. "You can thank my mother for that."

"Let me guess. She put you through a similar hell with father?"

"Oh, it was much worse, I assure you. Poor Arcadie. He dealt with several men vying for my attention. My mother cut him down at every chance she got."

"But he never gave up."

She shook her head. "No, he never gave up."

I finished my drink and then placed the glass on the small table beside me. "Thank you," I said.

"For what, dear?"

"Explaining your actions and the reasons behind them."

"You're welcome, my child." She scanned me from head to feet. "You look exhausted."

"I am. I need to be at work early tomorrow." I stood and offered her a lingering hug. "I love you, mother."

Her hold around me tightened. "Thank you."

"Good night."

"Good night, dear."

I took a long hot bath and settled into bed as my phone started to vibrate. It was Ian. What was he doing calling me at midnight? "Ian," I answered. "Are you all right?"

The silence that followed was unnerving. "Ian, it's nearly midnight. What's wrong?"

"I wasn't expectin' ye t'answer," he said. His accent grew thicker when his emotions were roused. At times, he was difficult to understand.

"Why?"

"I was goin' to leave ye a message."

"Talk to me, Ian. What's going on?"

"I had a nightmare, that's all."

"Do you want to talk about it?"

Again he was silent. I waited.

"No. Ye sound tired. Go to sleep. I'll talk to ye later."

"Um, very well. Call me tomorrow, yes?"

"Aye, love. Good night."

"Good night," I said. The call terminated with a click. I stared at the phone, half expecting it to ring again. It didn't. I settled it in the charger and turned the light off. Tired as I was, sleep did not come easy.

It was unlike Ian to call like that. He said he wanted to leave me a message. Why? There had never been anything we couldn't tell each other. He didn't sound right.

I rolled over, took a deep breath, and forced my mind to calm. Whatever it was, Ian would tell me tomorrow.

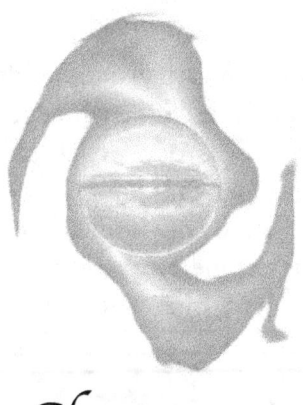

Chapter 4

-Arcadie-

OUR ELDEST SON, DIRK ENTERED the garden room where Kitta and I enjoyed our afternoon tea. His face was pale.

Kitta sat up. "Dirk, what is it?"

His eyes focused on me. "Someone is here to see you, father."

I quickly read his thoughts and stood. "Wait here," I told them.

Tanen, the Shadow leader of the Scotland territories, waited for me in the front foyer. I didn't much care for Shadows in my home and my energy spiked with an audible hum.

When the old leader felt me, he immediately built a shield around himself. Pitting myself against him now, in my own home, would have adverse effects and anyone around us could die in the wake of it. I pulled my energy back.

"Forgive my impromptu visit, Arcadie, but this matter won't wait." His polished Scottish accent resonated with strength. This man was dangerous and clever, and had power that rivaled my own.

"What brings you to my home, Tanen?"

"A situation has earned my attention."

I walked closer to him, keeping my guard up. "I'm listening."

"Baru seems to be missing," he said, shielding his thoughts from me.

"Am I keeper of your wards now?"

He smirked, his gray eyes glowing. "Something tells me you know where he is."

I said nothing.

"He's been missing for quite some time," Tanen added.

"I fail to see how this concerns me, Tanen."

"Your name is the last one he spoke to me. Can you tell me why?"

"No, I can't," I said, purposely giving him nothing to consider.

"Your son's thoughts tell me otherwise."

I tapped into Dirk's mind and extracted what I needed. Tanen was correct, he knew everything.

"There was a battle," I told him. "Baru perished in it."

"The battle was not in your territory. What business did you have interfering?"

"Khalen is family. The battle involved his clan and I was asked to help. No laws were broken, Tanen."

Tanen's eyes grew brighter. "You formed an alliance with the Archangels."

"Yes, we did."

"Then a law was broken, was it not?"

"There are no laws that prevent such an alliance."

His jaw grew tense along with his stare. With a violent wave of his hand, the room was filled with black smoke. When it cleared, he was gone.

I quickly dispersed the lingering energy that stifled the air before returning to my waiting family.

"Father, I'm sorry," said Dirk, noticing my grim expression. "I should have shielded my thoughts from him."

I met his eyes, not really wanting to state the obvious. Dirk was an intelligent man in many ways, but his occasional carelessness would be his undoing one day, I was sure of it. "I'm afraid we have a problem," I said.

Kitta read my thoughts and gasped. "Erika," she said. "We have to find her."

"She's safe," I assured her. "I have warned her to stay alert. She will not be harmed where she is. I will escort her home tonight when she is done."

"I should call my father," said Kitta, picking up the phone.

I telekinetically removed the receiver from her hand and hung it up. "I'm taking you to Khalen's."

"Khalen's? Heavens why? The Shad—"

"He will be able to protect you."

"So can my father," she protested. "Arcadie, Khalen is in the thick of this as well as you. Do you not think his clan will also be under attack?"

"I do," I said. "But his wards are strong, and if anything happens, Skye will be there with you."

"Where will you be?" she asked.

"Here, protecting my territories."

For the first time in many years, perhaps decades, I saw terror in my lovely mate's face. It didn't become her. "Have faith, my dear."

She rushed toward me and wrapped her arms around my waist. "Tanen scares me," she said, trembling in my arms. "He is vindictive and strong."

"The Source is stronger, love. His will cannot be thwarted."

"How can I help, father?" Dirk asked, straightening his shoulders like a young soldier preparing to forge the front lines in battle.

Knowing how hard he had been practicing his fighting skills, I knew how important it was for him to be able to prove himself. He had been slow in developing and his gifts were finally gaining some momentum. Denying him this right to stand by my side would destroy him. "Do you feel you are ready?"

His chin lifted a notch. "I do."

"Very well. You will fight." I looked over at Kitta. "Pack our things, dear. We leave tonight."

Dirk shifted his feet.

"Prepare the jet," I told him.

"Yes sir," he said.

There was a subtle shift of energy around me. I held my hand up, indicating I needed silence. Both of them stared at me as if I had lost my senses.

"Damn!"

"What is it?" asked Kitta.

"Listeners. They heard everything we've said." I couldn't sense their location. They were shielded, but I could feel them. Their energy was like heavy fog laced with copper—subtle, but present nonetheless. Using sign language, I told Kitta and Dirk to keep their thoughts closed and not to converse using words. Sign language was considered a powerful tool in situations such as this, and every child was taught it at a young age. Our techniques were rather crude, but effective enough to communicate simple thoughts and ideas.

I PICKED ERIKA UP FROM WORK, encouraging her to wrap things up earlier than she had planned.

"Where are we going?" she asked, sliding beside me in the Rover.

I made sure there were no listeners around before speaking. "I'm taking you and your mother away."

"Away? Where?"

A shimmer stilled the air. A Shadow was close. I shook my head, indicating that now was not a good time to speak of it.

She pulled her cell phone out of her purse.

I placed my hand over it and shook my head again.

"Jazen is supposed to meet me tonight for dinner. I can't just leave him hanging."

"Make the call quick and brief," I said.

She nodded with understanding.

"Jazen," she said into the phone. "Something has come up. I'm sorry, I cannot meet you tonight."

I heard the mumbled vibration of his reply.

"I'll tell you later, okay. I have to go." She pressed the END button, tossed the phone into her purse and then stared out the window.

I tapped her shoulder and reminded her with sign language to keep her thoughts closed.

She nodded.

As we crossed the gated bridge that connected our island to the mainland, I felt the Shadows' presence. They were everywhere. I telepathically communicated to my immediate clan, issuing a warning they were very familiar with. We would not leave the island without a fight. My gut tightened. How the hell did the Shadows get on the island without my notice? Even now, their numbers were hidden from me.

Jazen's Mercedes was parked in the driveway as we drove up. He met us at the doorway.

"Kitta filled me in. I want to help."

"Good, we can use it," I said, ushering Erika into the house. "We're leaving in five minutes, get your essentials."

Erika ran upstairs.

Kitta came around the corner placing two more bags next the other five that were already lined by the door.

"Crimeny, what are you bringing, woman?"

"The last time this happened," she said, "we lost almost everything." She gestured to the bags on the floor. "These things I intend to keep."

"Where's Dirk?"

"Readying the jet."

I pinged him with my thoughts. There was no reply.

Using encrypted telepathy that the entire clan knew, I warned the elders and told them of my plan. I received many replies and was ensured of their support. We were a small clan on this island, but the elders' gifts would be a challenge to any Shadow.

"Jazen, pack the Rover and wait for the women. Meet me at the jet as soon as you can. Toss me the keys to your car, quickly! And Kitta, keep your thoughts open to me only, understand?"

My mate nodded, wringing her hands together the way she did when things were uncertain.

"It will be all right," I told her, rushing out the door.

The Shadows were drawing in on us. The hum of them rattled my gut like a worn-out chain saw. I sped toward the hangar where Dirk should have been, but it was void of anything except the two jets. The lights were on and the hangar smelled of jet fuel.

"Dirk," I called out.

A flash of a thought found my mind, followed by another. The Shadows had my son. By the images he sent me, I knew they were at the rear of the hangar behind the workshop.

"Nice of you to join us," said a familiar voice. The ex-leader of the North American continent stepped out from behind the workbench.

"Victor."

"You didn't really think we were going to just let you fly out of here without saying goodbye, did you?"

I heard the Rover pull up just outside the hangar. I told Kitta to stay in the car before placing a shield around it.

Shortly after, I felt it being tested.

Let me out, Jazen communicated. *I can help you.*

Victor smiled, having heard Jazen's thoughts. "Go ahead, Arcadie, let the buck play."

A stronger hum entered the hangar. I was being surrounded. The Shadows knew that my shield would weaken during a fight. They were counting on it. I told Jazen to stay with Kitta and Erika. Things were about to get interesting.

My clan was gathering to help. My goal was to free Dirk, get Kitta and Erika on that plane and buy them all time to fly out of here.

This clan was seasoned and experienced with Shadow wars. Of all my territories, this one contained the greatest number of elders with strong gifts. It was time to get this party started.

I started walking toward Victor. "Tell your blokes to release my son."

His face visibly paled as my energy increased. But like a typical fool, he stood his ground. I was well aware of his energy-bending gifts and quickly diffused them. He was strong—I was stronger.

With encrypted thoughts, I told Dirk to ready himself against the energy blast I was about to project. Once I felt his shield, I released the energy I had gathered from the earth.

Victor slammed back against the far bench, his back snapping like green twigs in a hurricane. The three men holding Dirk spun away from him. I grabbed my son and flung him toward the plane.

"Hurry, Dirk, get her ready."

He stumbled forward, quickly recovered, and then ran toward the jet. Two blokes stood in his way. Using the skills he had been honing, he made quick work of them, keeping his head and control calm and precise.

The three men on the floor rebounded from the blast and worked their way toward me. Taking advantage of their weakened state, I focused on their chests, bursting their dark hearts with precise, concentrated energy.

Dirk started the jet's engines. I released my shield on the car and instructed Jazen to get the women safely to the plane. It would not be easy; the hangar was infested with Shadows.

Victor's back was definitely broken, but his mind was dangerously sharp. He transformed tools on the workbench into deadly snakes and flung them toward me. It was a clever distraction from the Shadows closing in on my flanks, but I was aware of the ploy.

Energy blasts were effective, but they would weaken

me too much if overused. This battle would be long and I needed to conserve my strength.

The way transformations worked was by invoking fear in the one being attacked. The snakes flying toward me were real enough; however, they were really nothing more than tools made to resemble something far more formidable.

Using Victor's own thoughts, I redirected his assault toward the Shadows closing in on me. Their fear and screams fueled the illusions and resulted in death of pure terror, nothing more.

A quick energy blast ended Victor's attack. Tanen knew that Victor would be no threat to me. He was nothing short of a pawn on this chessboard, along with the other young Shadows swarming the hangar. Tanen's plan was to weaken my territories slowly, with agonizing precision. He had a larger plan, and that truly frightened me.

Shadows were notorious for distracting the men of a clan in battle. This often left our women vulnerable. The young would be killed and our women would be claimed. The thought of it twisted my gut until rage nearly overtook my reason. I had to keep it together or get lost in anger and vengeance. That was the Shadows' strength—the ability to turn a soul into a destructive mass of negative emotions.

When my clan arrived, I immediately felt energized by their presence.

Dirk, get the plane out of here, I told him in thought. The building energy of the battle would destroy the plane's electrical system and render it useless. Bolts of energy flew through the air like shrapnel. Getting caught by one would render me useless against a Shadow's attack.

Jazen fought back several Shadows, allowing the women to board the plane. His techniques were polished and impressive. He would make a fine leader one day.

Go with them, I told him. *Keep them safe.* I watched as Jazen killed two more Shadows, and then boarded the jet in one fluid motion before closing the door behind him, his eyes meeting mine in what looked to be a final farewell.

Dirk rolled the plane out of the hangar and sped toward the runway. His impressive ability to keep the plane from attack did not escape my notice. I just prayed I would survive this battle to relate that pride to him.

Battling thousands of zombie minions did not compare to the energy required to battle gifted Spirian Shadows. The casualties were countless. In the end, we were the victor; however, the loss was nothing short of devastating.

Danu, a clan elder nearly twice my age, stumbled toward the ground, clutching his gut.

I rushed toward him, catching him before he collapsed. "Danu," I said, forcing him to look at me. His dark eyes were dilated and dull.

"Save the clan," he said, before surrendering to the peace of death.

"God keep you, old friend," I said, closing his tired eyes.

Looking around, I saw many of my clansmen suffering serious injuries. If I didn't get help, many of them would die.

I needed a skilled healer who could heal from a distance—my niece, Skye Dunning. With shaking hands, I dialed her mate's number.

"Arcadie?" Khalen answered.

I quickly filled him in and warned him about Tanen's threat. "I need your mate's help."

"She's here."

"There are many injuries," I said, fighting the threat of passing out. Looking down, I saw a steady flow of blood oozing from my side. My words started to slur.

"Arcadie, you're not making any sense," I heard him say, then nothing. Darkness consumed me.

~ I a n ~

"ARCADIE!" KHALEN SCREAMED INTO THE phone before stuffing it back into his pocket. "Bloody hell!"

"What is it?" I asked.

"Arcadie's clan was attacked. Dirk is bringing Kitta and Erika here. I think Arcadie's injured."

"I can't feel him," Skye said. "I need a way to connect to him."

"We need Elle," I said. "She can contact the Angels."

We tried calling to her telepathically but she still did not have the gift to receive it.

Khalen growled the way he did when his patience hung by a fragile thread. As the clan leader and Elle's templar, he was able to sense her location. "She's sitting on the log by the lake. Bring her here," he told me. "Quickly!"

I ran toward the lake, trying not to startle Elle as I approached. She had a wicked shield and I didn't much care to find myself flattened against a tree. "Elle?"

She turned to face me. "Ian. What's wrong?"

"You need to come with me, quickly."

She stood and hurried around the log before running to catch up to me. "What's the hurry?"

Illusions

"Something's happened. Khalen needs your help."

She laughed. "Khalen needs my help?"

I was impressed at how well she was able to keep up with me. My legs nearly doubled hers in length. I ran a little faster. Still, she kept pace.

When we approached, Khalen grabbed Elle's arms. "Call the Angels," he ordered.

"Why? What's happened?"

"Please, Elle," Skye pleaded. "Do it quickly. Arcadie may be injured. I cannot connect with him."

"Raphael," Elle called. "Come quickly."

In an instant, the Angel manifested. "Elle."

"Raphael, we need you to help Skye connect with Arcadie. He may be injured."

The Angel looked between Elle and Skye. "Hold hands," he told them. He vanished in a blue haze.

Skye's eyes glowed silver. "I feel him," she said, gripping Elle's hands firmly.

Elle's face paled as Skye began her healing.

"I can't hold on," Elle cried. "The vibration is too much." She started to shake.

I placed her into an illusion that focused her mind on something else—a beach with rhythmic waves. Her trembling stopped.

Case came running up along with Aidan and Eve. Case assessed Elle's weakened condition and placed his hands on her shoulders. "I can't ground her. Khalen, shield them both; bind them to the earth."

I felt my illusion waver as Khalen formed his shield. It was difficult to hold a person in an illusion while they were conducting for another. Doing it through a shield was doubly so.

Aidan combined his power with mine, a technique we

had mastered long ago. It strengthened our illusions and enabled us to form longer and more complex deceptions.

"The healing is slow," Skye said. "Arcadie's spleen is ruptured and bleeding badly."

"Can you help him?" asked Case.

"Not fast enough. Raphael has called other Angels for help."

Case fumbled with his cell phone as he pressed a series of numbers. "Tetris, you old fool, pick up your bloody phone."

Eve placed a comforting hand on her mate's arm. Her other hand covered her mouth as if trying to hold back the storm of emotions that welled in her eyes.

Case dialed another set of numbers. "Deran, where is Tetris?" He closed his eyes, lips firm with forced control. "Interrupt him. Tell him I need him here now! Understand?"

Moments later, the old wizard manifested before us, dressed in ceremonial garb. "I was told this was an emergency."

"It is," said Case. With a thought, he quickly filled the wizard in. "Can you dematerialize Skye and bring her to Arcadie?"

Tetris frowned, clearly uncomfortable with the notion. "I've never tried, Case. It is not safe. She may not survive."

"Do it," said Skye. "It's the only way."

"No!" Khalen shouted, his eyes focused on Tetris. "Not unless you can ensure her safety."

"I canno' do that," Tetris sadly admitted.

"He's dying," Skye announced. "We have only minutes."

"Take us both," said Khalen.

Tetris' eyes widened. "Do ye have a death wish?"

"We'll survive, Tetris. Do it now."

Tetris made the sign of the cross over his chest. "May God give me strength," he said. Then, with a dramatic wave of his hand, the three of them dematerialized.

Elle collapsed.

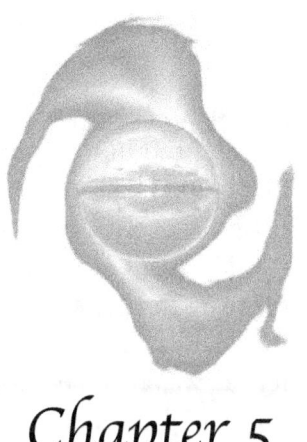

Chapter 5

-Skye-

I FELL TO THE GROUND, FIGHTING the urge to vomit. The feeling passed after a few moments. Khalen lay ten feet away from me. I crawled toward him.

"Over here!" Tetris yelled.

Khalen was groggy, but breathing. I rushed over to where Arcadie lay in a pool of blood. "Check on Khalen," I told Tetris. "Where are the Angels?"

I placed my hand over Arcadie's side. He had lost a lot of blood and his vitals were weakening. Quickly I stopped the flow of blood and healed the wounds. It was all I could do for now. Without blood, he could die. We had to get him to a hospital soon.

The hangar was cold, the air heavy and nearly suffocating. I had difficulty breathing.

"We are not alone," said Tetris.

Khalen stumbled to his feet. "Shadows."

"Aye," Tetris confirmed. "Many o'them by the feel of

it."

Khalen shook his head. "I see two of everything."

"It'll pass," Tetris assured him. "Feel lucky to be alive, both of ye."

"I feel tingly," I said.

I felt Khalen's shield form around me, dispersing the sensation of needles pricking my skin.

"Skye, don't move," he said. "Stay very still."

"Okay," I replied. It was too dark for me to see much of anything, but the smell of fuel and stale smoke was evident. The room was cold—too cold for this time of year.

"Get him out of here," I heard Raphael say to Khalen. "Take the Rover."

A trail of light lit a path outside. Khalen grabbed my hand while telekinetically lifting Arcadie over his shoulder. "Tetris, let's go."

The old wizard followed us out of the cold dark building. "Dun't have to ask me twice," he mumbled.

Raphael led us to the Rover. Khalen lowered Arcadie into the back seat.

"There's a hospital in town," Raphael said. "A mile from the bridge. Archangel Michael will guide you. Make haste."

Khalen slid in beside me and turned the key. We followed a trail of light to the bridge. After we crossed, the darkness lifted.

Michael's light faded when Khalen pulled up to the Emergency Room doors. We were greeted by two EMTs and a nurse.

Khalen shouted orders to them all, requesting blood and a slew of other acronyms that didn't make sense. We followed a young orderly to an empty room where the supplies were to be brought.

"Sorry miss," a woman said, holding my arm. "You must stay out here." She gestured toward a waiting room full of people.

"No," Khalen countered. "She stays with me and this man."

"Our doctors will ta—"

Khalen's eyes glowed brightly. "I am his doctor."

The woman released my arm and took a step back, one hand over her chest. She looked close to hyperventilating. The other workers left with her, leaving us alone for now.

Tetris was with us, but he had made himself invisible. I sort of wished I had that gift as well. The attention we had drawn made me feel like a mouse in a room full of cats.

"It'll be all right," Khalen assured me. "I just need time to give him some blood."

"What about the authorities?"

"I'll take care of it," said Tetris.

Khalen nodded his appreciation. He worked quickly setting up the IV. I had forgotten how skilled he was as a doctor. He'd given up his practice years ago to take on the role of leader. It was nice to see he had not lost his touch.

I placed my hands on Arcadie's chest, offering him strength. I felt the draw of energy his body immediately took and it made me gasp.

"Mind yourself," said Khalen. "I need you to be able to walk out of here."

Using the skills that Case had taught me. I grounded myself to the earth and allowed my spirit to connect with the Father. The course of energy that flowed through me felt warm—almost intoxicating. My hands hummed with it. Arcadie pulled upon my vigor like a hungry child latching onto its mother.

There was a commotion outside. The door flung open revealing two policemen and an old man in a white coat. "Where are they?" the older policeman said.

The nurse who had asked me to wait outside peered into the room, stared directly at Khalen and me and then shrugged. "They came to this room," she said. "The supplies are gone."

"Search the floor," the policeman ordered. "They can't be too far."

They left, leaving the door open. Khalen closed it with a thought. "Almost done." He checked Arcadie's vitals. "He's stronger. Keep working on him."

"Best hurry, Khalen," said Tetris, still invisible. "I can't hold this veil much longer."

"Are they watching the car?"

"Oh, aye."

"Is there another way out of here?"

"Too far," said Tetris. "We'll have to leave the way we came in."

"Go for the closest car out of sight," said Khalen. "Can you hold the veil until we get there?"

"Aye, but we must leave now."

Khalen handed me the bag of blood. "Hold this high," he instructed while lifting Arcadie into his arms. "Let's go."

Tetris led the way, making an invisible wake that people instinctively avoided without knowing why. He made a beeline to a van and opened the far door.

"Get in," Khalen told me. "Keep the bag held high." He lowered Arcadie beside me. "You got him?"

I nodded.

He and Tetris got in. Khalen touched the steering

column and the van roared to life. Sometimes my mate still surprised me with his gifts. At times, it seemed there was no limit to what he could do. I felt the shimmy in the air around us as Tetris allowed his veil to fade. He was shaking from the effort.

"Nice work, wizard," said Khalen with a grin.

Tetris held up his hands and studied them. "They say your gifts grow stronger with age. Sometimes I feel I'm fading away a little more each day."

Khalen's smiled broadened. "Then I best have you train my son before it's too late."

Tetris' eyes lit to a brilliant purple. "I—train your son?"

"Gabrihen shows strong promise of becoming a wizard. I would be honored if the best were to train him."

I saw the old wizard's aura ignite and glow with the intensity of the sun. It made me smile. The man thrived on having a purpose—the way we all do, I supposed. Even though Tetris was given the responsibility to run Case's clan in England during his absence, he was the kind of man who needed a challenge.

I continued to channel energy to Arcadie's body, hoping it would give him strength. The bag of blood I held high over his arm was beginning to get heavy.

"Take a break," said Khalen. "I'll take over."

The bag lifted from my hand and hovered above Arcadie's body like a ghost in a cheap B-rated film.

"Thank you," I said, rubbing my aching arm.

Arcadie stirred a bit.

"I think he's coming around," I said.

"Keep giving him energy, love. I think it's working."

I opened myself between Heaven and Earth and felt the Father's power flow through me.

Arcadie jolted and nearly broke my hand as he flung it away from his body.

Tetris turned around, assessing the situation. "Easy, Arcadie. Yer safe now, lad."

I felt a weak pulse of energy expand from him, then quickly collapse.

"You're weak," I told him. "You need to rest."

"The others," he groaned. "Help the others."

"We need to get him out of here," said Khalen.

"I can't dematerialize all of ye, lad. I barely hung on to you and the lass."

"Can you take us one at a time?" I asked.

"Only one of ye. I'm weakened from the veil and dematerializing two bodies at once is risky as it is."

"Take Arcadie back," Khalen said. "Skye and I will take a plane."

"We don't have our passports," I said.

Khalen pursed his lips as he thought of an alternative.

"Go to Ghandoltes," Arcadie moaned. "He has a jet. He will take you home."

He sent both Khalen and me an image of how to find Ghandoltes clan.

"Got it," said Khalen. He pulled over. "Take him," he told Tetris. "We'll be all right."

In a flash of blue and violet, the wizard and Arcadie vanished.

"Come sit up here with me," Khalen said, opening the doors telekinetically.

I slid in beside him. He waited for me to fasten my seatbelt before pulling back onto the highway.

"How long before we get there?" I asked, not really knowing the area.

He reached for my hand and gave it an affectionate

squeeze. "About two hours."

"Will Arcadie be all right?"

"Yes, his mate and daughter will be there soon. Knowing Arcadie, he will find his strength for them."

"He is a strong man," I said.

"Frighteningly so. I pity the poor scum who targeted his clan for attack."

"There was an odd energy in that hangar," I said. "An unfamiliar one that was not entirely from Shadows."

"Yes," he said. "I felt it too."

"Did Archangel Raphael seem off to you at all?"

"Off?"

"His aura was dull, not as bright as is typical of him and his cohorts."

"Weakened perhaps?"

I frowned. "What could possibly weaken an Archangel?"

Khalen pulled left onto another highway and the car picked up speed. "Something tells me we will find out soon enough."

"Do you know this Ghandoltes character?" I asked, changing the subject to something less disturbing.

"I met him once, when I was very young. He leads the Leek clan, on the southern tip. It is a small clan, but highly skilled."

We rode in silence for a while, the scenery quickly changing from a flat, colorless landscape to a lush wetland. Ahead of us rose an impressive display of green hills and jagged mountaintops. He pulled onto an unpaved road that wound itself through thick forests of exotic hardwoods.

I could feel the energy shift as we entered the clan's territory. The vibration was akin to what a wolf would sense when entering another pack's enclave. The feeling was familiar, yet different enough to cause concern.

"They know we're here," said Khalen.

"Yes, I feel it as well."

"Open your thoughts to them," he said. "It helps establish trust."

As we rolled up to a gated area, Khalen waited. He could have easily opened the gate himself, but that would have been rude. Instead, he sent his intentions to Ghandoltes, requesting an audience.

I felt the old man gauging my thoughts and weighing my emotions. There was a hint of mistrust as a response.

The gate started to swing open. Khalen drove slowly through. I felt the hum of his shield around us. "Something is wrong," he said.

Ghandoltes met us in front of a large building that resembled an old church. With a wave of his hand, he killed the engine. The windows rolled down.

"State your business," he said, his voice as gruff as that of an old priest who had given a few too many sermons.

In the distance, I heard the wail of a woman in pain. There was no one outside. The place looked deserted, yet I could sense the presence of many.

"Arcadie sent us. I am Khalen and this is my mate, Skye."

Another scream pierced the air.

The old man closed his eyes and relaxed against the window frame. "I heard of his clan's demise," he sighed. "Many of the women found their way here. Some of their children are missing."

"Are there wounded?" I asked.

"Many," he replied. "Our medical supplies are dwindling."

"We can help," said Khalen. "I'm a doctor and my mate is a healer."

Ghandoltes' eyes widened and sparkled with renewed hope. "You are a gift from the Father," he said. "Our prayers are answered."

He willed opened the van's doors and gestured for us to follow him into the large structure. I could not see much inside. Most of the lighting came from chandeliers and fancy sconces that graced the walls. Judging by the sharp echoes, I assumed the floors were covered with marble and there was not much in the way of furniture.

"Hold my hand," Khalen said. "The floors are littered with cots and people."

"Is the lighting poor in here?" asked Ghandoltes.

"Skye is blind. She cannot see in this light."

"I can turn the lights up if that will help?"

"No," I said. "I require bright sunlight to see shapes. Thank you, though."

"Who is the most critical?" Khalen asked.

Ghandoltes stopped before a small figure lying on a mat. "This young girl is badly burned. Another, lying by his fading mother, bleeds internally."

"Take me to him," I said. "I will heal this small one next."

Khalen guided me around, letting me know when I had to step over objects by tapping my hand. He could have let me see through his eyes but that took energy and he was wise to conserve it.

"Here," Ghandoltes said. "His name is Will. He is the son of Banderson. His clan was hit the hardest."

"Where is Banderson?" asked Khalen, as I hunkered down beside the boy.

"He died shortly after bringing several wounded here.

His mate is still unconscious, as well as his son."

I centered myself and felt the flow of energy course through my body. My hands tingled and hummed with a vibration that mimicked that of an ultrasound machine— fast and subtle. This vibration changed depending on who I was healing. I did not choose it; the person being healed did. I was simply a vessel through which their body could draw the Father's energy.

As a result, I could see the injuries heal and feel the flow of a life force that could only come from the joining of Heaven and Earth.

The young child's breathing grew stronger. His pulse pounded beneath my hands as the bleeding ceased. He would be weak until his body could restore the blood.

"He will need fluids," said Khalen. "What supplies do you have?"

Ghandoltes led him away. "Come, I'll show you."

They returned and Khalen began setting up an IV. "Find me something to hang this from," he instructed the old man.

Next I healed the young girl with burn wounds. Khalen followed, offering what he could to ensure full recovery.

Several hours later, we retired to a small room. A fire burned in the hearth and there were drinks and refreshments arranged along a narrow table.

"Can I pour you a drink?" asked Ghandoltes.

"Red wine if you have it," I said.

"Brandy," Khalen replied, fixing us both a plate of various cheeses, meats and fruit.

The old man returned with our drinks before returning to the table to pour himself a portion of Scotch.

"Why was your clan spared the attack?" I asked.

Ghandoltes smiled and shook his head. "Because

technically, we are not part of Arcadie's territories."

"Explain," said Khalen.

"Arcadie supports us financially and provides us protection, but he has cleverly excluded us from his territories for situations such as these. Because we are neutral, our clan becomes a safe house for any surrounding clan that requires protection."

"The Shadows don't respect their own territories, why would they care if you fall under Arcadie's or not?" asked Khalen.

"We are small and insignificant. The Shadows are after mass destruction. We offer little in the way of women and children."

Khalen took a bite of goat brie, chasing it down with a sip of his brandy. "Any idea what caused the Shadows to challenge Arcadie?"

The old man shrugged. "Damned if I know."

"Well," I added, "I doubt it will take long for the Shadows to find the women who fled their camps."

"No doubt," said Ghandoltes. "If they do strike, we don't have the numbers to stop them."

"Move everyone underground," Khalen suggested.

"Yes," I agreed. "The earth will mask your energy and the Shadows will think you have left."

"It will be tight. Our underground storage areas are small and full of supplies."

"Consolidate what you can and bury the rest. Skye and I will help you."

Ghandoltes raised a hand in protest. "You two have done enough, my friend. I'm sure you are eager to return to your own clan."

"We have no way to get back," I said. "Arcadie sent us to you. He said you had a jet."

The old man sighed. "I do but I fear leaving my clan."

"Understood," said Khalen.

"Can you fly?"

Khalen shook his head.

"I will call my good friend, Liam. He's human, but he understands our ways. It will take him a few hours to get here, if he's able to leave right away."

"In the meantime, we will help you secure your camp."

Ghandoltes raised his glass. "A solid plan."

Khalen and I were able to move most of the supplies to one shelter with the help of a few others who were not injured. The clan was small in comparison to our own, perhaps a quarter of the size with a few young children. Most of the members were middle-aged and unmated. I concluded that these people were not as gifted as most Spirians are and had little to offer when it came to finding mates.

Ghandoltes did a good job at leading the clan, but the members seemed inherently lazy and sloppy in their duties. Khalen's patience was tried nearly beyond his tolerance. It was not his clan, however, and he kept his opinions to himself.

Liam arrived several hours later. He was a strange man, reminding me of an old hippie that never moved past the free-spirited times of the sixties. He wore a tie-dye shirt and torn jeans with hems that dragged on the ground. Long, brown dreadlocks hung from his head beneath a knitted cap sporting rainbow colors.

Ghandoltes went to meet Liam. They exchanged a few words that caused the man to peer over the old leader's shoulder to look at us. Liam nodded, took something from Ghandoltes' hand and then strode alongside the old man toward us.

"I'm Liam," he said, extending his hand.

Khalen shook it, keeping eye contact. Impressively, the man held Khalen's chilling stare with the warmth of a Jewish mother. Liam was tall and a bit lanky. I assumed he was in his sixties, but he was in great shape. The streaks of gray hair on his head gave him a hint of sophistication that didn't quite fit his overall appearance.

"I'm Khalen, and this is my mate, Skye."

After the exchange, Ghandoltes shook Khalen's hand and then offered me a bone-crushing hug. "Thank you both," he said. "God speed to you."

"Are you going to be all right?" Khalen asked.

"I have faith that we will."

"You have my number. Give me a call if you need support."

The old man gave a courteous nod, before turning to leave.

Liam started walking. "Well, let's get you two home, shall we?"

"You're not from around here," Khalen commented.

"Nope. I'm from southern California—San Diego to be exact."

"What brings you here?" I asked, following him across the camp toward what looked to be a clearing.

"Doctors Without Borders," he said. "I come for a month every six months or so, when I have the money to do so."

"You're a doctor?" Khalen questioned with a raised brow.

"A surgeon, actually. I specialize in brain traumas."

"You don't say," Khalen said, and he laughed.

"Hard to believe, I suppose, based on my appearance."

"A little," I said. "But I think it's wonderful what you

do."

He smiled. "Ghandoltes tells me you two are quite the healers yourselves."

Khalen squeezed my hand and silently asked me to remain conservative. We knew little about this man, and revealing our gifts was not something we did before humans. "We do what we can."

"Understood," Liam replied, not pressing the issue.

"It's been a while since I flew this bird, so our trip might be a bit bumpy," he said, opening the door to the hangar.

Khalen helped me into the plane before offering to help Liam prepare for takeoff.

"Looks like we have just enough fuel to get us there," said Liam.

"We have an open account at Bremerton Airport," Khalen replied. "You can top off the tank for your return trip there."

"Good to know," Liam said, smiling. "Better settle in."

The engines fired causing the entire plane to rattle.

Khalen and I exchanged glances. He knew that flying made me uncomfortable. I would rather take my chances on having Tetris poof me back home, but that was not an option. I sat back and took a deep breath, trying to calm my fears.

"Is this jet used often?" Khalen asked.

"Not often enough, judging by the sound of the engines," Liam replied.

"Perhaps we should have a mechanic work on it in Bremerton."

"Might be a good idea. She's idling kind of rough."

Like a cold wind blowing in from the north, the presence of Shadows drew near. I could sense the conflict in my mate as he questioned his decision to leave the old man.

"Stay, if you need to," I told him. "I'll be all right."

"No," he said. "I want you with me and this situation is dire enough as it is. Ghandoltes is prepared. The earth will shield him. The Shadows will not take time to look for them."

I smiled. "Are you trying to convince me or yourself?"

Liam eased the throttle forward, and the plane rolled out of the hangar. The Shadows were closing in.

"Make haste," Khalen shouted. "We're about to have some dangerous company soon."

"Shadows?"

"Yes—many of them by the feel of it."

Liam urged the plane forward toward the runway. "Damn!"

"What?" I said, gripping the chair arms.

"Khalen, you'd better come up here."

Khalen unbuckled his seat belt. "Stay here," he told me.

Reading his thoughts, I knew we were surrounded by a legion of Shadows. They were blocking the runway.

"Keep going," Khalen instructed.

"How? I can't blast through them."

"Keep going," Khalen roared again. "I'll take care of the cars."

Liam shook his head. "It's a good day to die, I suppose." He pushed the lever forward and the engines screamed in what sounded like protest.

"If you have a plan," said Liam, "you had better put it into action quickly."

Khalen waved his hand. Metal and rubber screeched with an agonized pitch as cars and trucks flung sideways left and right out of our path.

"Day-amn!" Liam drew out. "Nice gift." The jet picked up speed, and in a few more seconds, left the ground.

After tucking the landing gear and leveling our course, he looked over at Khalen. "Dude, you're shaking."

"I'm fine," Khalen said, his voice wavering on the edge of exhaustion. He released his seat belt and made his way back to me. His energy had been drained.

"Come here," I said.

He collapsed in the chair beside me. I reached for his hands. They were cold and clammy.

"Take what you need," I told him. His breathing fell into a slow and steady rhythm of deep sleep. I waited for the hum to calm in my hands before pulling away.

"Is he all right?" Liam asked.

"The energy he used to push those vehicles aside drained him. He'll be fine after he rests."

"That was pretty impressive."

"Yes," I agreed. "I've been mated to him for many years and he never fails to surprise me with the feats he can accomplish with merely a thought."

"I hear he can take a man's life."

My gut wrenched and I didn't answer right away. "Only when necessary," I clarified.

"Of course," he stammered. "I wasn't implying that he was frivolous with that gift in any way. I was j—"

"It's all right," I assured him. "You seem to know a lot about him. I'm sure all that information was not obtained from the short conversation you had with Ghandoltes at the camp."

"We spoke earlier on the phone. I have an issue flying people when I don't know much about them."

I nodded. "Fair enough." I checked on Khalen. His

breathing was deep and rhythmic. His head hung at an odd angle so I removed my sweater and tucked it between his neck and shoulders, offering him some support.

"How's he doing?"

"He will need to rest for some time to recover."

"Does this happen often?"

I removed my seatbelt and moved up front to sit beside the odd surgeon. "When we use a condensed amount of energy at one time, our bodies become drained. It's kind of like a fire hose under pressure. Once the pressure is released, the fire hose collapses."

"Interesting," he replied. Looking at the gauges, his brows furrowed. He tapped one a few times and sighed.

"Is something wrong?"

"Well, either our gas gauge is flaky or we are burning far more fuel than expected."

"Do we have enough to get home?"

His expression reflected doubt mixed with a response to sour lemons. "Not according to this gauge."

"Perhaps we should stop?"

He looked down over an endless view of water. "Last time I checked, this bird was not equipped for water landings."

The fear squeezing my innards threatened to take control. I concentrated on breathing and staying calm. Already, my minimal sight was closing down—a typical response to stress. "How long do we have?"

Again, he looked at the gauge. "Ten to twenty minutes, tops."

I looked back to my sleeping mate. I would have to awaken him.

The engines sounded rough and the plane began to shake.

"Turbulence," he said. "Better strap yourself in."

I moved back to Khalen's side and jostled him awake. "Khalen, wake up."

His eyes snapped open as he sat bolt upright. "What is it?"

I rubbed his back and shoulders, giving him time to adjust. "We have a problem, love."

"Shadows?"

"No. We are low on fuel and may not make it to land. Can you help?"

He rubbed his eyes and sat forward. The plane jolted up and down; an engine sputtered.

"We lost the left engine," Liam shouted.

"Khalen, can you do something?" I asked, trying to keep the panic from my tone.

He squeezed my hand reassuringly. "Secure your belt," he said. "I'll see what I can do."

Taking a seat beside Liam, Khalen assessed the situation. "What do you need me to do?"

"Keep our speed up," said Liam. "With any luck, we can make it to Costa Rica."

Khalen gathered the energy from above and below, harnessing it with the grace and skill of a seasoned master. He made it look easy, but I knew better. Harnessing that amount of energy was akin to reining the ocean during a storm. If it got away from him, the plane and everything within a fifty-mile radius could disintegrate.

"Damn!" Liam exclaimed as the jet kicked into a whole new gear under Khalen's power. "Too bad you can't keep this up for another five hours."

He picked up the radio, called in a series of numbers and code words that could have been a foreign language for as much as I understood it.

We were given some coordinates and vague instructions for landing. In an hour, we arrived at a small airport.

Khalen looked pale.

"Um," Liam said. "Looks like we have company."

Khalen looked out the window. "Bloody hell."

"Let me guess," said Liam. "You don't have your passports?"

"No, and I'm too damn tired to scramble their minds."

Liam stood and hurried toward the rear of the cabin. I was curious about what he was up to when he lifted a square board concealing a hidden compartment. I doubted I could fit through the small hole. Khalen was twice my size.

"Get down there," Liam said. "Hurry."

I squeezed myself through the opening, then watched as Khalen followed, barely making it through before Liam slammed the board shut.

We heard voices. Liam replied in fluent Spanish. Footsteps echoed above us.

"What's down here," a man asked. The door above us cracked open.

Khalen willed it to stay closed.

"It's locked from the inside," Liam explained. "I'll have to crawl into the cargo space to free it, if you want to take a look."

"What do you carry?" a man asked.

"Nothing yet," Liam said. "I'm on my way to pick up some mucky muck from Los Angeles."

"Okay," the man said.

Khalen released his hold on the door and collapsed against me. I placed my hands on him and began channeling energy. What he really needed was rest—undisturbed rest.

After what seemed like an hour, Liam flipped the door open. "Stay low," he said. "I need to pay for the gas."

I held Khalen against me. He was in no condition to move right now, and staying in this hole provided an odd sense of security. My hands hummed against him as he continued to pull energy through me. It was a peculiar sensation—water flowing between my skin and muscle. As was typical when sharing an energy flow, our hearts were synced and pumped a steady rhythm of one beat per second.

I closed my eyes and took comfort in the sound. Khalen's soft breath brushed against my hands as I held him close. He was a strong man, but draining his life spirit so low was dangerous. There was a point of no return, a point when the spirit leaves the body and cannot find its way back.

Khalen and I were connected, and perhaps I could guide him back, but I didn't want to test that theory—ever. Life without Khalen was not something I wanted to consider. It was unfathomable. He was so much a part of me now that I felt certain my body would perish without him.

Liam returned and closed the cabin door. "Hey, you guys okay down there?"

"We're okay," I answered.

"Well, come on up," he said. "I need to seal that space."

I jostled Khalen and helped him to his feet. Wearily he climbed up through the hole tearing his shirt in his effort to squeeze through the cramped space. He didn't seem to notice.

I followed him up and then helped him into his seat before securing his seat belt. It took more effort than I had expected to close the trap door. It hissed as Liam pressed a button that sealed the space.

"Belt yourself in, Skye. You're going home."

With all the excitement this day had to offer, I was ready to return home without further mishap.

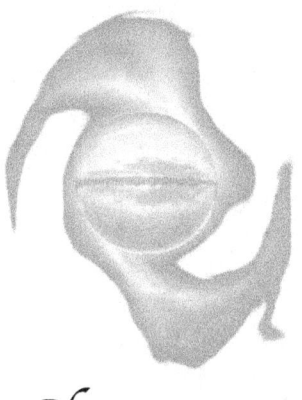

Chapter 6

~ I a n ~

I RECEIVED A CALL FROM **KHALEN.** He had asked me to meet them at Bremerton Airport. His voice was clipped and had a razor's edge to it. When Khalen's emotions were raw as they were, it was best not to ask a lot of questions.

I had just returned with Erika, Jazen and Kitta when my phone went off. I didn't want to leave Erika in Jazen's care, but by the looks of it, I had little choice. The bloke had his hooks in her and it would require hefty extraction to remove them.

Arcadie believed I was up to the challenge. Perhaps I was. Part of me believed that Jazen was the best choice for her but my heart believed otherwise. Bloody hell, life was far more simple without the complications of love.

I thought about that for a while as I passed through Belfair. Love, I laughed out loud. It was never something I wanted. Now, it's all I think about. When no one else vied for Erika's attention, I was content to have fun with her. Now, I wanted her more than life itself. I wasn't sure I liked that feeling. It gripped my chest like wet leather bindings shrinking under the heat of the sun.

I pulled into the airport and proceeded out to the area where Khalen and Skye would disembark. I offered to share my hangar for the night so that my mechanic could service their plane tomorrow. Khalen mentioned it was in desperate need of maintenance. He didn't go into details, but by the sound of his weary voice, I gathered he did most of the work at keeping the bird in the air.

As the plane rolled in toward me the left engine sputtered and skipped. The right engine didn't sound too great either. The pilot looked haggard sitting there in the cockpit with a very weary-looking Khalen beside him.

Skye also looked tired when the three of them exited the plane.

"Rough trip?" I asked.

Skye shook her head and silently pleaded with me to stay quiet. The tension was thick.

"How's Arcadie?" asked Khalen, his voice clipped and tense.

"Good," I cleared my throat. "He's resting."

The pilot extended a shaky hand. "I'm Liam."

The man had an Irish name but looked nothing of the like. I steadied his trembling. "Ian," I said. "Give me the keys to yer jet. I'll have my mechanic take a look at it tomorrow."

The man tossed me the keys. "I could use a drink."

"It looks like ye all could," I added. "Get yerselves in the Jeep. I'll drop these keys off at the office."

I returned to find Liam in the front seat and Khalen and Skye snuggled in the back. Khalen's eyes were closed, his body shivering.

"Is he all right?" I asked her.

"He's drained," she said. "He needs to get back to the clan—quickly Ian."

"Understood," I said. As I had suspected, Khalen had used his power to keep the plane in the air. God only knew what else he had to do to ensure everyone's safety. He was a strong man—one of the strongest I had the pleasure of knowing, but God help him, he was a martyr and would give his own life to save another's, especially Skye's. "Care t'tell me what happened?"

Liam cleared his throat. "We were attacked at the airport. The Shadows had the runway blocked with trucks and cars. Khalen blew them away with a wave of his hand. It was quite an impressive display of telekinesis, let me tell you."

I had seen Khalen's power first hand. Impressive was an understatement. "Ye're human. How is it that ye know so much about us?"

"I was working at a village when Ghandoltes, the leader of a nearby clan, brought me a small boy who had fallen from a tree. The boy's head was swollen with fluid. I drained it and he recovered. Long story short, Ghandoltes and I became friends."

"You're a doctor?"

"Yes," he replied. The exasperation in his voice indicated he had been questioned about that many times. Given his frumpy appearance, I'd believe it. He looked nothing like a doctor.

"Somethin' tells me ye have a story to tell, eh?"

"Put a glass of Scotch whiskey in my hand, friend, and I'll tell you anything you want to know."

"I have somethin' better waitin' fer ye, lad."

A hint of a smile curled the man's lips.

When we arrived back home, Skye ushered Khalen back to their yurt where he could rest. I brought Liam back to my cabin to indulge him in a glass of good Irish whiskey.

We clinked glasses and he took a long, appreciative sniff. "I'm not an Irish whiskey fan," he said, but his expression did little to hide his surprise.

He sipped the golden liquid, allowed it to float in his Mouth, and then swallowed. His lips curled into a smile that rivaled that of a child in a chocolate factory. "What is this?" he asked, holding up his glass.

"Bushmills," I said.

Doubt faded his smile. "I've had Bushmills, my friend. This does not compare."

"This is Bushmills Malt, aged 21 years in bourbon barrels, sherry casks and then Madeira drums for final agin'. It's a rarity, lad, and nothin' ye'll find in yer average store."

He took another long, slow sip. "Damn, this is good."

"I'll make an Irish man of ye in no time," I said, holding up my glass.

A knock sounded on my door. I knew who it was. Erika had an energy about her that roused my libido whenever she came near. I willed the door open and smiled. "Ah, the love of my life," I said, gesturing her to come in.

The blush on her face only added to her beauty. "Am I interrupting?"

"No," I said. "I'm merely introducin' our new friend, Liam, to some fine Irish whiskey."

Her eyes glistened with interest. "Is there any left?"

I poured her a glass. "A woman after m'own heart," I said, placing the glass in her delicate hand.

The woman was a master when it came to appreciating

a fine drink. My chest ached with the need to take her in my arms and make her my own, but I fought it. I wanted her to choose me.

Liam looked at her and then at me with speculation before pursing his lips with a knowing that was laced with a smirk. He extended his hand toward her. "I'm Liam," he said, sporting an overly exuberant smile.

She returned that smile with one of her own. "I'm Erika."

His brow arched in recognition. "Arcadie's Erika?"

"Yes. Have we met before?"

"Not in person," he said. "I heard about you from other circles."

She looked to me for clarification.

"Liam is acquainted with Ghandoltes' clan. He's a brain surgeon who frequents the small villages in Brazil."

"A brain surgeon who flies?" she questioned.

I knew the entirety of his story from gleaning his thoughts, but it was not my place to tell it.

I gestured to the couch and chairs in the living space, knowing this conversation would not end quickly. I grabbed the bottle of whiskey and joined Erika on the couch. Liam sat across from us in a chair made of leather and logs. Drew had made all of my furniture, giving the cabin the rustic look that I wanted.

"I flew in the war," said Liam. "My plane was shot down. Next thing I knew, I was lying in a hospital with gauze wrapped around my head."

I poured us all another glass of whiskey before settling back and wrapping my arm around Erika. She wiggled in closer to me. My body reacted in kind.

She must have read my thoughts, because a teasing smile stretched across those beautiful lips, red and alluring as ripe berries.

"What made you decide to become a surgeon?" she asked, her voice hiding the thoughts she had brewing in her own head.

Liam cleared his throat and wiggled uncomfortably in his chair. Apparently, our body language did nothing to hide our physical attraction to one another. His next swig was not savored quite as much as his first.

"I had problems at first. I suffered from double vision and my memory was limited to only long term." He shook his head and laughed. "God, I couldn't even hold a conversation."

"What went wrong?" she asked, sipping her drink.

"There was a blood clot. No one would operate because they claimed it was far too risky."

He took another swig of his drink and set his glass on the table beside him. "Then came Nicholas Darby, brain surgeon extraordinaire."

"He fixed you," she said without question.

"Yes. Against everyone's judgment, he did what he knew he could do. It inspired me." His eyes shifted between Erika and me. "I should go."

"Will you be staying with us for a while?" she asked him.

He offered a sad smile. "Just long enough for my plane to be serviced. Khalen offered me a spare cabin to stay in. I thought I'd settle in before dinner."

I stood and walked toward my liquor cabinet to retrieve another bottle of whiskey. I held it out to him. "Thank you," I said, "for helping my friends."

He took the bottle and his smile broadened. "This is a very generous gift for such a small deed, but I accept."

"We'll see you at dinner, then?" asked Erika, her voice

hopeful.

"Yes, I'll see you then."

With that, he turned to leave, closing the door behind him.

"He seems so sad," she commented.

"He harbors many shadows in that heart of his," I said.

"Yes," she agreed. "I sense that as well."

I stepped closer and wrapped my arms around her. "It's good to have ye here," I whispered.

A knock sounded on my door.

Erika sighed. "You must keep your thoughts closed."

"Why?"

"Erika?" Jazen's voice called through the door.

"That's why," she seethed.

I released her and eased the door open partway. "Erika and I are havin' a moment together," I said, in a challenging tone. The weasel was always on my flanks and he was beginning to rub me the wrong way.

"I understand that," he said with a smirk, "which is what brings me here now." He tried to push through, but I had the door blocked with my foot. His head slammed against the hard wood that failed to yield to his momentum. "Bloody hell!" he swore. With a thought, he blew the hinges off my door and pushed his way through.

I felt my anger build as I pushed Erika behind me to protect her. "I will have my time with her, Jazen, without yer interference."

"I don't trust you alone with her," he said. "It's inappropriate."

"Who appointed you her guardian?"

"I did. Care to challenge that?"

I wanted to wipe that cursed confidence from his face with a well-thought illusion—one that would mimic his worst nightmares.

He laughed. "Your Shadow side is showing, old man."

Old man. I was merely twenty-nine nine years his senior, hardly a difference to gain notice. Granted, Erika was closer to his age, she being fifty-three. The hum in the room elevated.

"Um," Erika murmured, knowing this situation was about to get way out of hand. "Let's gear this conversation down a few notches, shall we?"

"Outside," Jazen ordered her. "Now!"

Her eyes widened. "I most certainly wo—"

With a sudden wave of his hand, Erika flew through my door and landed unceremoniously in the dirt three feet beyond my threshold.

To hell with gifts, I thought. This required a good old-fashioned fist fight. I grabbed his shirt and planted a solid blow to his jaw, following it up with another to the back of his thick skull. The bones in my left hand crunched as I felt the sting of the blow.

Jazen quickly recovered and offered a counter punch to my midsection. It was a solid hit, causing me to lose wind. Unable to stand, I rolled onto the ground, swinging my legs and catching him at the knees. He fell hard to the ground.

I jabbed my knee into his chest and pressed a spot an inch from his hipbone to hold him down. It was a technique Drew had taught us in training many years past. So long as the person didn't move, the pain was tolerable. Movement could make most men pass out. Jazen was not like most men. He struggled to free himself of the hold until finally resorting to other more destructive measures.

Flames began to climb the walls of my cabin, quickly devouring all that they touched.

I tried to extinguish them the way Khalen could, but had never really developed that gift to the point where I could compete with Jazen.

Something smashed against the back of my head. I fell into darkness.

~ E r i k a ~

I SAW THE FLAMES. THE DEEP resonating tones of anger rattled my bones. I shook the dust from my clothes as I ran to find my father.

He was still resting, my mother sitting tenderly by his side.

"What is it?" she asked.

"Jazen and Ian," I stammered.

My father's eyes opened as he sat bolt upright. "Get Khalen," he said, staggering to his feet before rushing for the door.

Khalen was already there with Skye at his side. The flames were extinguished. Ian lay on the ground, still and dusted with ash.

"What happened?" my father asked Jazen.

Jazen ran his trembling fingers through his hair, tainted with smoke and ash. "We had an argument. It got out of control." When his eyes met mine, I looked away.

My father must have tapped my thoughts. In an instant, Jazen fell to the ground, gripped by the pain my father was apt at delivering.

"If you ever treat my daughter with violence, I will ensure it will never happen again."

Jazen looked up at my father, his veins swollen and his eyes glazed over in pain. "Understood," he gasped.

Ian groaned. He tried to sit up, but Khalen held him down.

"Easy, Ian," he said. "Your head's a bit of a mess right now."

I saw the blood covering the back of his scalp and stifled my urge to gasp. Skye and Khalen were helping him, I thought. He was going to be all right.

Aidan came running. He plowed into Jazen with such force that both of them tore through the smoldering cabin wall.

Arcadie pulled them apart. "Enough! There has been too much fighting already."

Khalen helped Ian stand. "Skye, help him to our yurt where he can wash up." He then turned his attention to Jazen.

"Clean yourself, and then come to me."

Jazen nodded, glancing back at Aidan and Arcadie as he left.

"Something is wrong," Khalen told Arcadie. He sent a telepathic message to Case, asking him to come to his yurt.

Khalen's temper was calm—much calmer than I remember him being. He had grown into an impressive leader. I was sure that Skye had something to do with that. She had a way to balance him. They were good for one another.

That thought made me consider my own choices for a mate. I had Jazen, an overpowering potential leader, and Ian, a playful friend who was not exactly a take-charge sort of man—the type of man I needed and wanted.

Jazen was a leader but he rarely considered my feelings. Ian considered my feelings, but never took control. I sighed inwardly, wishing I could combine the men into one who filled my needs.

My mother's arms wrapped around me. "Are you all right?"

I brushed more dust from my jeans. "My pride's a bit injured, and my heart is frustrated beyond belief, but other than that, I'm fine."

She shook her head. "Lord, you're a mess. Come to our cabin. I'll draw you a bath."

"That sounds wonderful."

"So," she said, smiling. "What's it like to have two men vying for your heart?"

"Horrible."

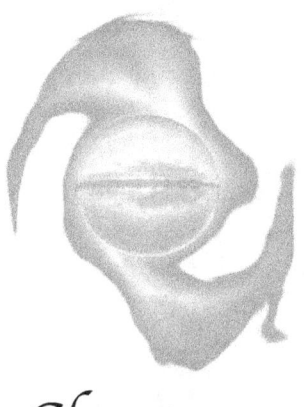

Chapter 7

-Elle-

MY SON, CONNOR'S SHRILL GIGGLE lured me out of the greenhouse that had been erected for me last spring. Drew, the clan's carpenter, and a major thorn in my side, insisted that the structure be large enough to grow way more herbs than I could possibly manage. He included a huge shed equipped with stainless steel counters and sinks where I could create my tinctures and salves.

Making medicines was one of my gifts, or so I was told. I had other gifts as well, some more powerful than others. Apparently, I had a shielding gift that packed the same force as a hurricane.

Khalen and his father, Case, had trained me to control my gifts—somewhat—but they still got the best of me at times, especially when Drew got too close. His insistent affections never failed to spark the darker side of me until a wave of destruction followed. Khalen had since

Illusions

dampened my gifts, rendering them nearly useless.

I was all right with that. I never wanted this life anyway. Five years ago, I was touched by an Archangel. That brief encounter turned me into something I didn't want to be—gifted and somewhat immortal.

Before my mate, Avel, died, he arranged for me to live with the Spirians so that I would be safe from the Shadows. I have since discovered the ironic similarity between protection and imprisonment.

I piled the sheep sorrel and burdock that I harvested into separate containers. Later, I would prepare them to dry.

Connor giggled again as Drew showed my four-year-old the trade of carving wood. Though Drew was not my son's father, he raised the boy as his own.

He insisted on taking care of us after Avel passed away. I had prayed for Avel's spirit to be there for Connor's birth and thought I had felt his presence. More than anything, I wanted to hold his hand. Drew's was there, instead, offering strength and comfort.

It felt wrong, almost like betrayal the way I relied on Drew. I wanted Avel. He was my mate. He would always be my mate. Drew refused to believe that, despite my constant reminders.

Khalen and his mate, Skye, helped deliver Connor. Khalen had been a doctor before assuming his charge of the clan and the surrounding regions. He was also my templar, a role I knew too little about before agreeing to the arrangement. His mate was an impressive healer. If it were not for her and Khalen, I would not have fared well during the birth. Connor came late and had grown too large. For a brief moment during labor, I thought I had seen Avel's face. His eyes were so clear. I remembered crying out to him just before he faded. God, I missed him. I wondered if he could feel how much.

I removed my gloves and smacked them together to remove the dirt. The noise drew the attention of my son and his self-imposed stepfather.

"Mummy, come see," called Connor.

As my templar, Khalen was responsible for finding me a new mate—he chose Drew. It had been a long four years of warding off the man's advances and convincing Khalen not to force the union. I feared my time had run out.

I walked toward my little one, smiling. His face was covered in sawdust. Like his father, he had straight black hair and brilliant hazel eyes that were more green than gold today.

"Look," he said, pointing at the sign that he had been helping Drew create. "Drew says it's for your greenhouse."

The carved and burnt sign read: "Elle's Herbal Alchemy."

"We still need to finish it," said Drew. "Right, little man?" His violet eyes sparkled with pride. If my heart was not already spoken for, I would find him rather attractive.

"Right," Connor agreed, grinning. His two front teeth were missing, but the gap in his smile did not diminish his sweet charm.

"It should be ready to hang tomorrow," Drew said, focusing on me.

I shook my head. "Honestly, Drew, you have done enough for me. You must have other projects needing your attention."

"You are important to me, Elle. And the sooner you realize that, the better we will be."

"I'm a waste of your time. I've told you that numerous times. What will it take to convince you that I am not interested in becoming your mate?"

"More than you can imagine," he said.

"Ugh," I groaned.

"Khalen has made his decision, Elle. You and I are to mate."

"Khalen does not own me!"

"No, but he sure can make your life unbearable."

I rolled my eyes. "He already has."

Drew remained kneeling on the ground, still holding the sign. "Am I so horrible that you cannot see a life with me?"

Lord, the pain in those words loosened the stones I had carefully packed around my heart. I knelt down beside him to purposefully look into his eyes. "No, Drew. You are not horrible at all. I'm just not ready."

He reached over and gripped my wrist. "It has been nearly five years, Elle. Khalen is talking about performing the ceremony this summer." His eyes changed to a deep amethyst, something that happened when his emotions were roused. "I don't want to have you by force."

"Even if he forces the union, I will not be your mate."

He shook his head. "You clearly do not understand the Spirian ways. Once the union takes place, you will be my mate, whether you're willing or not." He pulled me down to sit beside him.

Connor came and crawled upon my lap. I held him close as he rested his tired head against my shoulder.

"Why do you waste your time with me?" I asked. "You are a good man and can have any female you choose."

"I have chosen you."

"No, Khalen chose me for you."

"Only after I asked about you. I was intrigued the day we met. Your strength draws me. No other female has affected me the way you do."

There it was, his soul bared before me like a tempting secret I had no right to know. Closing my eyes, I breathed in the familiar scent of my son. My hold on him tightened.

"I will not take Avel's place with you, Elle. That's not what I'm asking."

"Why is it so important that I find another mate?"

"Unmated females are a commodity. The Shadows are a cunning, ruthless lot. The moment you leave Khalen's protection, they will sink their claws into you and poison your soul with darkness you can only imagine in your worst nightmare."

I rolled my eyes. "Nothing escapes Khalen's cursed notice."

Drew smiled, showing a brilliant display of perfect teeth that accented his mouth—alluring and sensuous. I looked away.

He laughed. "I find your thoughts of me—encouraging."

Connor slumped against me, fast asleep. "Hmm," I replied. "I'd best lay this little one down for a nap."

He stood and helped me stand as if I weighed no more than the small child I held in my arms. "I'll finish your sign before I start rebuilding your steps."

"My steps are fine," I assured him, "so long as I stay on the right side."

"That cabin is a temporary shelter. Why not come stay with me. My home is large enough for all of us."

"Absolutely not!"

His mouth tightened. "Then I will build you a new home."

"I don't want a new home."

He picked up the sign and followed me back to my

cabin. "You have spent some time in my home. Do you find it uncomfortable?"

"No," I said.

"Then perhaps you don't care for the location?"

"The location is fine." I climbed the short three stairs leading to my front door, making sure to stay to the right where the wood was still strong. They creaked loudly as he followed me up and into the cabin.

I laid Connor down on the bed and pulled a soft blanket over him.

Drew pulled me against him and looked down into my eyes. I tried to look away but his grip on my chin was too strong. The scent of him was something I had begun to crave, but I would never let him know it.

"Look into my eyes, Elle, and tell me that you want nothing to do with me, ever. Tell me to leave this camp and never come back."

"Don't be stupid," I huffed. "Where would you go?"

"A neighboring clan," he replied. "Say those words in earnest and I will stop my pursuit of you."

I had spent so much time with him during the last four years that the thought of not having him near left me speechless. I opened my mouth. All I would have to do is say those words and he would leave me alone—forever.

"Say the words," he growled.

My throat strangled any trace of sound that tried to escape.

Slowly, he pressed his lips to mine, claiming me with a possession that left me raw and weak. "Don't," I said, my voice barely audible.

"Say the words."

I could feel my shield amp up and then fizzle with Khalen's cursed constraints. I resolved to do the next best thing. I swung my arm in an arch with the intent of knocking Drew senseless for daring to snare me like some timid rabbit.

He blocked the blow and had my arm twisted in a painful joint lock before I realized my efforts had been thwarted. He was fast and elegant in his defense. I tried stomping on his instep, but he knew my intent and countered with a sharp twist to my arm and a kick to the back of my thigh.

He flipped me onto my back, then pinned me to the floor with his massive weight and size.

"I allowed you to fell me once. Be assured, it will not happen again," he warned.

The amethyst glow in his eyes emphasized his point. For the first time since I met him, I was concerned. The man had a strength that surpassed my own. Even if Khalen hadn't dampened my gifts, I wasn't sure I could match Drew when his temper was flared.

"Good," he said, having read my thoughts, "that's a start."

He pulled me to a stand. "Khalen expects us for dinner tonight."

"I'm not feeling particularly sociable tonight," I said, straightening my shirt.

"I'll pick you up at five," he said.

My eyes narrowed. If I didn't show up, Khalen would come get me; I could read that much in Drew's eyes. "I can find my own way there."

His mocking smile didn't hide his frustration. I sensed the tidal wave building inside him. Part of me wanted to stay and see how the destruction played out, while another part knew it was best to run for higher ground.

"Elle," he said, his voice even and forcibly controlled.

"I will see you at Khalen's fire." He turned and headed for the door, fists clenched.

Spirian men, I determined, were an overbearing lot, especially those who were of age. Seth, Sunjia's son, was very sweet. He was only in his twenties, though, and still very young. Spirian men typically didn't come of age until sometime after the age of fifty, or so I was told. It made me wonder how old Drew was. His arrogance was nearly as intolerable as Khalen's.

Seth continued displaying his attraction to me when Drew was not around. I enjoyed the young man's company and the many conversations we had by the lake. The Spirian life was still very new to me and Seth had made it his duty to tame my confusion. Unfortunately, the more I learned, the more confused I became.

I freed my laptop from its power cord and carried it over to the couch to do some writing. I was ahead of schedule on my next novel and wanted to keep the momentum going. I entitled the story *Aeon Pneuma*, the Latin translation for eternal spirit. The book, of course, was about my mate, Avel—a fearsome Spartan warrior who returned to this life several hundred years later to save the world from an evil necromancer. Most of it was true, with a few improvisations to make it more interesting.

After pouring myself a glass of burgundy, I settled in and started writing. As was typical of me, time flew by while my mind soared through the imagery playing in my head.

My wine glass was still mostly full when I glanced up at the clock—5:10. My heart slammed in my chest as if I had missed something very important—dinner with Khalen. More like a summons, really.

Connor was still fast asleep on the bed. He'd hardly

stirred at all after I had laid him down. He must have been exhausted after spending most of the morning with Drew.

I took a sip of my wine, saved my work and then closed the lid to the computer. My body was stiff as I stood from the couch. Typically, I liked having my shower before my evening meal. No chance of risking that luxury tonight, however. With my luck, Drew would come looking for me and he would not hesitate to enter the women's shower hut to find me.

The hut was used mainly by guests and those who had no showers in their cabins or tents, such as me. I rarely saw anyone in there. Tonight my shower would have to wait.

I walked over to the bed and jostled Connor. "Hey, sleepy head. Time to wake up."

He squinted his eyes, rubbing them with the backs of his hands. "I'm hungry," he said, trying to sit up.

I laughed. "Yeah, you should be. You slept right through lunch."

"I have to potty," he said, scooting off the bed.

"Me too." I grabbed our coats from the pegs by the door. "Come on."

Skye walked toward our cabin as we closed the door and trotted down the steps. No doubt she was sent by her impatient mate. The sullen look on her face seemed out of place for the woman I had grown to love as a sister.

"Skye, what's wrong?"

"Are you coming for dinner?" she asked.

"Yes, just as soon as we hit the privy."

She fell into step beside us.

"Where's Maiyun?"

Though Skye was a very capable blind woman, her

service dog was rarely far from her side.

"She is with Khalen. He's having a rather heated discussion with Drew."

My throat started to constrict. "About?"

"Khalen is tired of waiting for you two to set the date, so he has set it for you."

"He's what?"

She stopped and placed her hand on my arms. "Two weeks from now, on August 3rd, you and Drew will be united."

"No!" I said. "I'm not ready. He can't do this. I won't go along with it!"

I started walking again to the privy. Connor ran ahead.

"I'll wait for you here," said Skye.

I rushed toward the feeble seclusion of the privy, contemplating my response to Khalen. I had stood head to head with him once before. My reward was unbearable pain, a week of hard training in the proper way to address a leader, and the loss of my gifts. What more could he do to me?

A lot, I reasoned. He could force this union whether I participated in the vows or not. I had no question about that possibility.

As promised, Skye stood where I left her, chatting with Connor.

"Hurry, mummy. Zhentu is waiting for me."

Zhentu was Skye's youngest son. He was seven now, but held a special affection for Connor. Zhentu's older brother, Gabrihen was a year older. He was more like his father and demanded to have the upper hand in all situations. He and Connor did not play well together for some reason, similar to Khalen and me.

"Go on," I said. "We'll catch up."

Connor ran toward the smaller fire where the children tended to gather, governed by the elders whose fire was in close proximity.

Skye and I walked toward the leader's fire, much larger in diameter and occupied by the key members of the clan. I saw Case, his mate, Eve, Caleb, Aidan and his mate, Sunjia, and Seth who sadly met my eyes before walking away. My stomach suddenly felt full of rocks.

Khalen and Drew were not in sight but I could feel the strong hum emanating from Khalen's yurt.

"You best go inside," said Case, following my gaze toward the leader's yurt.

My heart pounded, anticipating the friction that was sure to burn me in the end. I sauntered up the stairs and positioned my fisted hand before the door. I was just about to knock when it opened by Khalen's will.

"Come in," he said, his voice clipped and sharp.

I stepped inside and noticed the dismal look on Drew's face. How horrible it must feel to be forced to take a woman before she was ready and willing I thought.

Khalen held out a brilliant crystal hanging on a silver chain. It looked similar to the one that Skye wore; only it did not have the same blue tint to it. This one almost had a lavender hue, a direct reflection of the amethyst glow of Drew's eyes.

Drew took the crystal from Khalen's hand. The pain on his face was evident as he walked toward me with the pendant.

"Our time has run out, my dear. Khalen has ordered us to unite in two weeks." He began slipping the chain over my head. I stepped back.

"This is not what you want," I stated. "Nor is it what I want."

I looked over at the determined leader. Using the most respectful tone I could muster, I said, "Khalen, if two people are not ready to unite, do you really think the union will be successful?"

His reply nearly floored me.

"Perhaps you are right." He walked over and took the pendant from Drew's hand. He stared at me for a moment before adding, "I will find you another mate that is better suited."

Drew's hands started to fist as Khalen headed toward the door.

"Wait!" I said. "Please."

Khalen turned to face me.

"I don't want a mate," I said, "but if I am forced to take one, I choose Drew."

"You don't have to do this," Drew whispered. "I have agreed to leave if you choose another in my stead."

"I don't want you to leave."

He walked over and took the pendant back from Khalen. He turned toward me and held the chain open. "Make your choice, then, Elle. Either agree to unite with me in two weeks, or say goodbye."

"That's it?" I said. "I'm forced to decide now?"

Both men looked at me in silence.

I closed my eyes and breathed in air that felt like lead to my lungs.

Slowly, I nodded my head. The thought of Drew leaving loomed as a black hollow void in my chest. "Okay," I choked. "Just don't leave."

I felt the chain slip over my head and the heaviness of the crystal pendant rest over my heart.

"With this pendant, I vow to take you as my mate." He kissed my forehead, lingering until the warmth of his breath moistened my skin.

God, what was I doing?

"It is done, then," said Khalen. "I will make the announcement."

Drew and I watched as he turned and left the yurt.

"Thank you," he said. "I'm not sure what I would have done if you had refused me."

"You said you would leave."

He nodded. "I would have to."

"Why?"

He smiled. "Do you honestly think I could stay here knowing you would soon be another's mate?"

I said nothing.

"The feelings I have for you would cause strife within the clan. Your mate and I would be in constant conflict."

"Like you and Seth?"

He shook his head. "Seth is not of age. If he were, you would feel the turbulence between us. As it stands, he has no claim on you and never has."

He took my hand. "Come, Khalen will make the announcement soon and he will want us present."

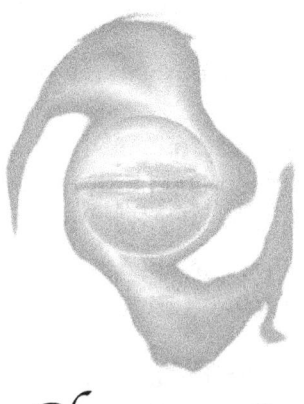

Chapter 8

- E l l e -

THE CAMP WAS HUMMING WITH activity. The pendant that Drew had placed around my neck hung heavy and low before my heart. It was a constant reminder that I wasn't ready for this union with him.

Part of me hoped that Khalen would be so busy with all the new situations that he would forget about uniting us. I occupied my time in the gardens with Eve. Joining Skye on long walks was also a good distraction from the handsome man who had been trying to get me alone with him.

A strong arm wrapped around my waist. I squealed, dropping the bundle of chickweed I had been collecting for tinctures.

"You have been avoiding me," he purred in my ear.

"I'm surprised you're not in Khalen's yurt with the other men. Ian's cabin burned down," I said, trying to change the subject.

"I'm aware," he purred again, his warm breath sending tingles down my neck.

I tried to twist away but his hold was firm. My heart beat faster. I was sure he could feel it.

"I'm still unable to hear the other's thoughts," I said, my voice sounding a bit sadder than I had intended.

He turned me around to face him. "You will, after we unite."

My breath caught in my throat. I gestured toward Khalen's yurt. "By the looks of it, our fearless leader is knee deep in alligators. I'm sure he has better things to think about."

His eyes drew together in what looked to be a menacing frown. "Do you not want this?"

I tore my eyes away from his gaze and pushed back the lump restricting my voice.

"Ceremony or no," he said, "I intend to make you mine tonight."

Panic flooded through me like a tsunami, destroying all my reserves and better judgment in its wake. "No!" I shouted.

His arms fell away from me. His eyes grew dull and surprisingly dark. With a swift wave of his hand, the pendant fell from my neck to the soft dirt at my feet.

"I release you, Elle Alder. You are free to find another."

"I don't want another."

"And you don't want me," he added, turning and walking away.

"It's not like that," I called after him. He didn't seem to notice.

I did want him. I just wasn't ready to love him—not in the way I loved Avel.

The pendant, still lying in the dirt at my feet, looked

dull and lifeless as Drew's eyes before he left. I sighed, picking up the stone. The chain that had held it in place was severed as if it were cut with a very hot torch. My fingers curled around it. I would talk to Drew this evening and tell him that I just needed more time.

THAT EVENING, THINGS WERE EVEN more tense around camp.

No one had seen Drew, not even his brother. Khalen was preoccupied with his own drama, and the women seemed unconcerned. A tremor of panic ran through me at the thought of him leaving camp.

It was not uncommon for him to be gone for days on end, but he typically said goodbye first and he always called now and then to see if I was all right. I hadn't heard from him all day.

Connor played with the other children. I wandered over.

My son smiled up at me, holding a string bean between his thumb and forefinger. "Want a bean?"

I shook my head and smiled. "No thank you, sweetheart. Have you seen Drew today?"

Connor nodded.

"Do you know where he is now?" I asked.

He shook his head. My son was not big with words. Most children his age were rarely quiet. Connor, on the other hand, was content with silence and spoke only when it was necessary.

"When did you see him last?" I asked, leaning down to meet his eyes.

"This morning," he said.

I smiled and ruffled his hair. "Okay." Walking back to

the other campfire, I felt a tinge of relief. Drew would never leave without saying goodbye to Connor, even if it was temporary.

Skye walked toward me. "You seem off. Are you all right?"

"I was looking for Drew, that's all."

Her reaction was subtle, but telling all the same. "Why?"

"I wanted to talk to him." I looked down. "We had a bit of a misunderstanding earlier and I wanted to explain."

She gestured toward the log that overlooked the lake. "Want to talk about it?"

I nodded and walked with her toward the familiar log.

She patted the spot beside her where she wanted me to sit.

As was typical with our relationship, Skye would wait patiently for me to start talking without prompting or hinting of any kind. Sometimes we would sit or walk for hours without speaking a word. Of course, she could tap my thoughts, but I was always deaf when it came to telepathy.

I inwardly sighed. She sensed my discouragement with a smile and a slight shake of her head.

"What?" I asked.

"You are your own worst enemy, my dear sister."

Sister was her affectionate name for me. She claims that we became sisters the moment her mate agreed to be my templar. I liked being her sister, but I certainly did not like having her mate as my charge.

"I have been told that before," I agreed. It was time to change the subject. "How's Ian?"

"His head was hit pretty hard, but he'll be all right."

"Does this sort of thing happen often?"

She shook her head. "No, it is very rare."

"Khalen did not seem happy about it." When she didn't respond, I continued. "Ian and Jazen looked concerned when they were escorted to Khalen's yurt."

"Yes, they should be," she said. "Khalen will strip them of their gifts for a period of time, leaving them vulnerable beyond camp."

"He can do that?"

Her blue-gray eyes met mine. "Oh yes. He is a regional leader and harnesses more power than every member of his clan combined."

My eyes widened. "Even more than Case and Arcadie?"

She shook her head. "They, too, are regional leaders. They are also his elders and have more experience. If a battle would arise between the three of them, Arcadie would come out on top."

I stopped myself from rubbing my hands raw by tucking them under my arms. It was a nervous gesture that I had developed many years past, and it was a real nuisance.

"What about Khalen's ability to take life?"

Skye frowned as if I had hit a sore spot in the center of her heart. "If Khalen choses to take the life of Case or Arcadie, two stronger Spirians than he, his life would also be spent."

"How does that work?" I asked, too sarcastically.

"When Khalen takes a life, an equal part of his life is spent. So long as the life he takes is less powerful than his own, he is able to restore that part of himself in short time."

I nodded, understanding. "How long will Ian and Jazen be without their gifts?"

She shrugged. "Khalen has not yet determined that

time." Her frown returned. "He is in turmoil and is genuinely worried."

"What's it like to read minds?"

"It is akin to loving someone with all your heart and hiding nothing from them. It's as if you are a part of the person you read. A bonding takes place and sharing comes as easily as talking to one another."

I looked down at the ground, watching an insect as it scampered over and around tiny grains of soil as if they were boulders. "Why don't I have that gift?"

She placed her hand on my shoulder, sending a wave of energy through me that felt like a comforting heated breeze. "Because you have trust issues, my sister. You keep your heart wound so tight that any amount of light threatens to blind it completely."

"I open my heart to you," I said in defense.

She shook her head. "No, you don't."

I sat up, staring at her as if she were the one with the issue. Could she not see how much I trusted her?

"You trust me more than most, Elle, but that trust has limitations and conditions."

"Like?"

"What is your son's primary gift?" she asked.

"What does that have to do with it?"

"There," she said, pointing at my chest. "Do you feel that? Your heart closed tighter than a clam on its way to the steaming pot."

I stood and started to pace.

"Answer the question," she said.

I racked my brain and tried to discern my son's greatest gift. "He's loving, brave and intelligent."

"Yes," she agreed. "He's all that but there is more, something deeper that you have chosen not to see."

Again, I pictured my young son. She was right. When I looked at him, interacted with him, everything was on the surface. I didn't want to know him, not in the sense that mothers really knew their children. Tears started to well in my eyes.

I collapsed on the log beside her, pressing my head against her comforting shoulder. "God, I'm truly damaged," I sobbed.

"Only on the surface," she said.

I half laughed and sobbed at the same time. "Can you heal me?"

"Open your heart to me, Elle, and I will share mine with you."

I shook my head. "I don't know how."

"I am going to send you a thought. I want you to feel that thought with your heart, not with your mind. Understand?"

I sat up, wiped my teary eyes and sniffled, nodding my head. Nothing, I felt absolutely nothing.

"Breathe, Elle. Breathe deep into your belly as if the air came from the Earth and Heavens."

I did as she instructed, trying to imagine air being sucked in through the top of my head and the soles of my feet. A strange, electrical sensation hummed in my spine and then immediately dispersed.

She started to giggle.

"What's so funny?" I asked.

"You got scared."

"I did not."

"Then why did the tingling stop?"

I looked away from her, my hands working diligently to remove the outer layer of skin. Again, I tucked them under my arms. "It was a weird feeling, that's all."

"When you are a Spirian, that feeling is essential to survival."

I took a deep breath and tried to pound my ego down long enough to try again. The tingling down my spine fluctuated and then grew stronger with every breath. My breathing slowed and became more rhythmic. Images flashed in my mind in the form of emotions.

I saw my son, but not as a human. I saw his soul. God, it was beautiful. I reached out to it, feeling its warmth and glow beginning to merge with me. The sensation was so odd and foreign that it felt surreal. Like a child immersed in the magic of a fairy tale, I observed without expectation.

"Good," Skye whispered.

Another feeling came forward. Connor knew me—not as a son knew his mother. He knew me at such a deep level that it was as if we were one. I just thought he was a good kid.

I continued to watch as fire danced around him like a loving hug. He was not afraid. Water came and cooled the flames. I watched as the ash soaked into the earth, making it stronger as if it were some kind of super food.

Next, a strong wind blew around him, taking the ash and earth in its wake and revealing a light so bright, it hurt to observe it. Avel's face stared back at me. I gasped and everything vanished.

I struggled for air, feeling as if the wind had been stripped from my lungs.

"Now you know the truth," said Skye.

I stood and walked toward the lake, stopping at the sharp descent that led to the water's edge. "That was not real," I said.

"It was very real. How much time do you think has

passed just now?"

What a strange question, I thought. "Why?"

"How much time?" she repeated.

"Ten, twenty minutes?"

"Fewer than three," she said.

"No," I said. "It felt longer."

"When we communicate telepathically, we do so in images. These images reveal their truth and meaning with emotion that only the heart can discern. Our minds are merely the receptors."

I turned to face her. "I saw Avel."

"Yes, I know. He has never left you. A part of him lives in Connor."

"Which is why I cannot love another," I seethed, feeling angry and frustrated.

"These feelings you have are normal," she said. "But they don't serve you. Avel never asked you to love no other. In truth, he asked you to find another."

"Then why do I feel as if I'm cheating every time Drew looks at me?"

"Drew cannot replace Avel in your heart, Elle. Drew will claim a part of you that Avel hasn't touched."

"How is that possible?" Again I sat beside her.

"I was married once, to a human." Her eyes glowed silver at the memory. "His name was Derrick and he was my world. When he died, I swore I could never love another and pushed anyone who dared to get close far away from me. My heart belonged to one man, and that man was gone."

I knew that feeling so well that my chest constricted with familiarity as if it embraced the pain Skye's words revealed. "How did you learn to love Khalen?"

"I pushed him away so many times; he felt I didn't

want him. He offered to give me to Aidan, believing in his heart that Aidan was the man I wanted."

"I'm guessing that wasn't the case?"

She smiled. "Aidan was attractive, true enough, but he wasn't the man my heart yearned for. Even after acknowledging that fact, I still could not bring myself to love Khalen. I loved to be around him, but the thought of being intimate with him left me cold in here." She pointed to her chest.

"What happened to change that?"

"We almost killed each other," she said coldly. "I was mad because he tried to give me away, and he was mad because I was too blind to see the truth of things."

"How could that have almost killed you?"

"You have not seen us angry. Remember what happened with your karate instructor, when he tried to pin you down?"

"Only pieces of it," I said, remembering more of the shocked faces of my friends around me.

"When a Spirian's emotions are roused, that power combines with their gifts and produces a wave of destruction strong enough to rival a tidal wave."

"What saved you?"

"Case. He severed our energetic bond and sent Khalen far from camp."

I looked away, sensing the pain in her eyes. I knew that what she was telling me tugged at her heart. She was sharing with me something that she didn't want to share. Why?

"That must have been hard," I said, at a loss for more intelligent words.

Skye bit her lip and struggled with her next phrase. "Khalen sent Drew away."

I couldn't swallow or even breathe for a few moments. The words she spoke hit me like a sledgehammer straight to my soul. "Why?"

"Drew refused to join with you, against Khalen's wishes. In doing so, he severed his ties to the clan."

"Drew didn't refuse," I said. "I pushed him away. I wasn't ready. I told Khalen I wasn't ready. Why must we rush this?" Again I stood, pacing the earth as if I had somewhere to go.

"Drew explained the consequences to you, did he not?"

"No—I mean yes, but that was so long ago. I didn't put much weight to it." My eyes darted back and forth, trying to search for sense and reasoning to all this.

"I need to talk to Khalen and explain."

"He won't listen," said Skye. "This was Drew's choice. He does not need your permission to join with you. He chose not to let it happen."

"It's not his fault!" I shouted. My legs started to move as if of their own volition.

Skye did not follow. She no doubt already knew what I would do. There was no stopping me. I was beyond listening now, beyond reason or even fear. This decision of Khalen's was unjust and he needed to know it.

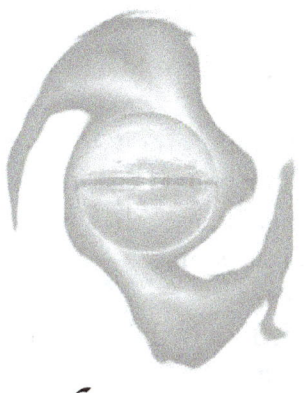

Chapter 9

I PACED THE GROUND SURROUNDING Khalen's yurt for what seemed like hours. There was no sound coming from inside, no movement, or even signs of life. With a deep breath, I walked up to the entrance and knocked on the door.

It opened revealing a somber group of men all staring into the flames in the hearth.

"I know what you have to say," said Khalen. "The decision has been made."

"Bring him back," I demanded. "I need to speak with him."

His golden eyes met mine. "Come back when you are in a better frame of mind and we'll talk. Until then, mind your tongue."

I started to open my mouth. The intense pain coursing my body forced my words to a strangled whisper.

Skye came in behind me. "Elle, come with me."

"No!" I rasped out. "I have something to say."

Skye glanced up at her mate as if pleading him to stop.

"You are out of place," she told me. "This is not conducive to what you want."

My eyes were blurry now with pain. I wanted to curl up on the floor and weep, but not a thread of my stubbornness would give that audacious leader the pleasure of my submission.

The pain stopped.

"Go with Skye. Talk with her. When you have calmed yourself, we will speak."

I was being dismissed. "How d—"

Skye clamped her hand over my mouth. "Don't say it," she warned, pulling me along with her.

Once we were outside, I shook myself free of her. Part of me wanted to march back in there and give that man a piece of my mind. The stable, more life-loving part of me urged me to continue walking.

"You nearly pushed him too far," she told me. "I would not have been able to stop him."

"He is sworn to protect me. What's the worst that could happen?"

I immediately dropped to my knees and grabbed my gut. It was hard to breathe.

"He is asking if you really want to learn the answer to that question."

Unable to speak, I shook my head. The pain stopped.

"You really make it difficult for me to help you," she said.

"Help me?"

"Yeah. If I hadn't come to get you, Khalen would have you in tears by now, begging him to forgive your insolence."

"I would have died first."

"That would have been a neat trick considering you're

immortal now."

"Ugh!" I screamed, walking faster toward my cabin.

Skye ran to keep up with me.

"Leave me alone," I said. "I need time to cool off."

"Fine," she said, still keeping pace with me. "I'll not say a word unless you ask me a question. In the meantime, I'll pour us both a glass of wine and sit with you by the fire."

"I don't want you with me."

"Tough!"

My jaw ached from being clenched so hard. "You are as stubborn as your mate," I said, not even trying to hide the scorn from my tone.

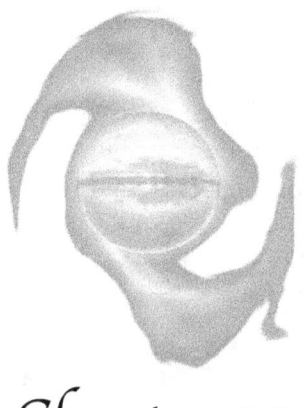

Chapter 10

-Ian-

I COULD FEEL THE AMPED-UP energy humming from
Khalen. He had been pushed too far today and struggled
now with keeping control.

"You both know what must happen—what you have
forced me to do?" he said.

"Aye," I answered.

"I do," said Jazen.

My face and head pounded from the effects of
whatever hit me. My vision was still a bit blurred but at
least my stomach no longer threatened to purge lunch.

"Two weeks," said Khalen. "Without gifts. And, the
two of you will rebuild Ian's cabin together."

The two weeks without gifts was tolerable.
Rebuilding my home with that cheeky bugger was bloody
unreasonable. "I prefer to ha—"

Khalen raised his hand. "I don't want to hear it, Ian.
Go now, before I make things worse for you both."

I didn't see it coming, but I felt the void as my gifts vanished. A dead silence fell over me as if I had been placed in solitude under one hundred feet of earth and stone. I was telepathically deaf. It was an odd feeling not having my gifts—like losing a major appendage.

Aidan came running after me. He placed his hand on my shoulder. "I'll help you rebuild," he said. "Stay close to camp, my brother."

I glanced over at him and smiled. "You sound worried."

"Something's brewing, and it doesn't feel good. I'm concerned and I believe Khalen is as well."

Jazen approached from behind and Aidan immediately tensed.

"Easy, brother," I said. "You and I have had many skirmishes over women; this battle is no different."

His jaw remained tense.

Jazen's dark eyes roamed between me and my brother. "This isn't what I wanted," he said. "I never meant to hurt you."

"You didn't," I agreed. The statement would have been more convincing if my house remained standing and my face wasn't swollen.

"Leave us!" Aidan demanded.

Jazen smirked as a lion would at an ant crossing his path. Again, his eyes rested on me. "The sooner we rebuild your cabin, the better. I would like to start now by removing the debris."

"I'll help," said Aidan. Then he stiffened and clenched his jaw even tighter. Khalen must have told him not to help.

"This is not your lesson to learn, brother. It is my own hole and I will dig my way out of it."

Aidan glanced back at Khalen's yurt. "I need to go to

him. Promise me you'll stay in camp?"

"To the best of my ability," I said, knowing that was all I could offer.

He gave Jazen a token look before turning toward Khalen's yurt.

Jazen laughed. "Big brother looks after you," he jibed.

"I don't need looking after," I growled.

~ E l l e ~

I WATCHED INTENTLY AS SKYE stared into the flames. She was tapping into her mate's thoughts, listening to the conversations between the men. Her expression changed between sadness and concern.

I sipped my wine, feeling awe at how easy she made it seem. Doubt had convinced me that I would never experience that gift with such grace.

Holding true to her promise, she said absolutely nothing since we returned to my cabin. As sisters go, she was the best. I would never admit it, but I was grateful for her company and I knew she sensed it.

"What are they saying?" I finally asked.

"Khalen is concerned about the building aggression in camp. Everyone feels it. We are all on edge."

"What do they think is causing it?"

"Tetris believes the barriers between dimensions have been torn."

"And translated into English, that means?"

She sipped her wine and then added another log to the fire. "Before the Angels helped us in battle with Avel, the lines between our worlds had never been crossed. Forming an alliance with them created a gateway between our dimensions."

I waited for her to continue. She apparently thought her explanation was thorough. "Is this bad?"

"Yes," she said, looking at me as if I were denser than mud. "If the Angels helped us, the fallen could help the Shadows. Before our battle, that alliance was forbidden. By opening the door between our worlds, we have condoned the alliance."

"That sounds bad. Really bad."

"The anger we feel is the presence of the fallen. We are being surrounded and slowly consumed by their darkness."

She reached over and grabbed my hand. "Come with me."

I walked with her back to her yurt. In the distance, I heard the children play and saw Connor wrestling with Maiyun. They were oblivious to the drama unfolding. I prayed it would remain that way.

She opened the door and pulled me through behind her, as if I would resist.

"She can help," Skye explained to the stunned-looking men. "She can call upon the Angels."

Khalen motioned for us to join them. "Do it," he said.

I called Raphael, the Archangel I was most familiar with, and my only link to Avel. The Angel never spoke of him, but somehow having Raphael near made me feel closer to my lost mate.

Raphael appeared before us, making himself visible to everyone. "Elle," he said, addressing me as if I were his master.

Blood warmed my face and constricted my voice. "We need your help," I choked out.

"Archangel Raphael," Khalen said, bowing his head.

"We sense the dark fallen ones around us."

"Yes," said the Angel. "They aid the Shadows in war." His golden eyes looked directly at Arcadie. "The fallen ones attacked you and your clan."

"They are strong," said Arcadie. "I haven't experienced such weakness in many decades. They made me feel adolescent in their presence."

"Their numbers build. The dimensions are merging."

"Merging?" Case confirmed. "God Almighty, that could have disastrous effects."

"As you have already sensed," said the Angel.

"What can we do?" asked Arcadie.

"What you have always done—fight them with all you have. Don't allow their darkness to consume you and drive your will. You and your clan will be tempted to battle amongst yourselves. This must not happen. Fight only to defend the light, not to destroy the darkness that surrounds it. Remember, darkness relies on darkness to survive. Remove the darkness, and evil will soon follow it." His image started to fade. "The Angels and I are with you." A white hazy mist expanded around him and then he vanished.

Tetris cleared his throat. "The ancients have talked about this day. It is long overdue."

"The humans will suffer the most," said Case.

"Aye," Tetris agreed. "They will also benefit the most."

"What do you mean?" I asked, finding all this to be just short of a nightmare.

Tetris frowned. "I don't really know."

He was a strange man. I shook my head. "I suppose none of you have lived through this type of experience before?"

Arcadie shook his head. "Nor have our elders, so far

as I know."

"We'll work our way through it," said Case, "or die trying."

"That's comforting," I added.

"And a bit exciting," said Skye, surprising everyone, including me.

The only one who didn't look surprised was her mate. He smiled at her as if he knew what she was about. Given the closeness of their relationship, I had no doubt that he did know her at a much deeper level than the rest of us.

"Hey," Skye added, obviously noticing everyone's confusion. "It's coming, we all feel it. We cannot change or stop it, so we might as well enjoy the ride."

Tetris started laughing. "God help us all."

Eve, being the constant jovial soul that she was, entered with a tray of goodies and a steaming pot of tea. Skye and I jumped up to help her settle the precarious ensemble onto the coffee table.

The rest of the conversation involved the men strategizing their next move regarding the Shadows, while Eve, Skye and I talked about our children, herbs, and upcoming meals. Deep down, I missed Drew and felt the need to be close to him.

Skye must have sensed it and offered me a smile. "Eve and I were going to take the children on a nature walk. Would you and Connor like to join us?"

"Yes, I think I would." Anything was better than listening to war plans and thinking about Drew.

-Erika-

I SLEPT UNTIL EARLY AFTERNOON THE next day. After a hot bath I was beginning to feel better and a bit less achy. Mother made me a pot of tea and sat with me now as we watched out the window. I nibbled on the cheese and cucumber sandwiches she had on a tray.

Ian and Jazen worked in silence as they piled the burned debris in a neat pile of usable fire fuel. Other debris that couldn't be burned was tossed in the back of a horse trailer. Both men tried to outwork the other, proving their strength by carrying larger loads or heavier items.

I shook my head. "Men can be so irrational at times."

"Especially when it comes to love," Kitta added. "I remember when your father pitted himself against another of my suitors in a battle of labor."

"What happened?"

"They were building a barn for my father—under his watchful eye, of course. I believe he was entertained with the young men's display. He watched them work and chuckled as each of them tried to out labor the other with acts of impressive telekinetic skills. Both of them were shaking toward the end, neither of them willing to concede to exhaustion."

"And your father allowed this?" I knew that if a Spirian exhausted himself energetically, it could be life threatening. I couldn't imagine an elder allowing this to happen.

"To a point," she said, sipping her tea. "When things became dangerous, he asked the young men to cease and rest. That's when it became really interesting. They ignored my father's suggestion, and continued their antics. My father came between them. Energies clashed, shingles, nails and debris went flying and then a fire erupted below."

My eyes widened, having difficultly imagining my father in the midst of such a predicament. "What happened?"

"They all got down from the roof just in time before the entire structure fell in a heap of flames."

"I bet your father was mad."

"Furious," she laughed. "Both of them were forbidden to see me for two months."

"Wow, that seems harsh."

"And they were stripped of their gifts for the same duration."

I remembered my father stripping my gifts after I had used them to avoid his punishment. That was only one week—enough to make me never want to use my gifts inappropriately again. I couldn't imagine being without them for entire two months. "How did you feel about all this?"

"Part of me was relieved, while another part felt deprived. I especially missed your father's company." She blushed a bit, something I rarely witnessed in her.

We sat there quietly for a moment, watching the two young men work, both quiet and wrapped up in the task.

"You look sad, sweetheart, what's wrong?"

"Frustrated, actually."

"Hmm, let me guess," she said, tapping her finger to her lip. "Jazen intrigues you because he is strong and commanding, yet his insensitivity repels you. Ian is fun to be with and understands how to make you happy, yet he never takes control of the situation so you're concerned that your strength will overpower his own. Am I right?"

I smiled, genuinely impressed at my mother's observations of me. I never would have guessed she had paid that much attention. "How did you know?"

She laughed. "Because I had that same disconcerting look on my face when trying to decide which man to choose."

"Was father the strong one or the sensitive one?"

Kitta looked down. "The strong one, but in time, he did become more sensitive. His commanding ways were wearing me down and it undid him to see me upset. Our first few years together were not pleasant by any measure. I honestly thought I had made a mistake."

"Who was your other suitor?"

Kitta's eyes looked distant. "His name is Tomen. He is several years older than your father and nearly as strong in gifts and blood."

"I've seen that name before," I said.

Kitta laughed. "Ironically, Arcadie asked him to be my templar."

"Really?"

She nodded. "Yes. He wanted me to be cared for by someone who dared to challenge him for my hand."

"Challenge?"

"Oh yes. After three years of courting and my inability to make a decision, my father suggested the two men fight it out. Tomen eagerly agreed—too eagerly according to your father."

I adjusted my position on the couch so that I could face her directly. I had never been told these stories before and listened intently—like a child hearing an adventurous tale for the first time.

"Who won?"

She smiled with remembrance. "Your father, of course."

I frowned. "Is that why you chose him?"

"I didn't choose him. He chose me. Directly after his victory, he marched over to my father and asked for my hand. He then made an impressive promise of all he could offer me and why we were a perfect match."

"Did you want him?"

"Yes, because he was so commanding and no, because he never considered my wishes."

"What did your father say?"

"He accepted the union pendant from Arcadie and slipped it over my head. That was his way of saying the matter was closed and the decision was made."

"And you accepted that?"

She looked at me with surprise and a hint of insult. "Before the two of them, I removed the pendant and tossed it into the flames in the hearth."

"Ooh, that couldn't have ended well."

"Arcadie extinguished the flames, retrieved the pendant through sheer will and then clenched it in his hand. I knew it had to have been hot from the fire, but he wasn't about to show it."

"Then what did he do?"

She smiled, obviously enjoying my interest. "He said, 'the next time you wear this, you will be begging me to do so.'"

"He didn't!"

"He did."

"And?"

"He ignored me for nearly a year."

"A year?"

Having finished our tea, she reached over and grabbed

the open bottle of wine. Before pouring us each a glass, she spoke under her breath. "It was the longest year of my life."

"I'm assuming you asked for the pendant?"

"No."

I sipped my wine and savored the smooth balance of fruit and spice with a kick of pepper. A proper Zinfandel was hard to find. My mother, however, had a knack for picking out the best. "But, you're united."

"Having grown tired of waiting for me to give in, your father graciously asked me one last time to be his mate."

"Asked you?"

"On his knees." She laughed. "Holding out the pendant that I had tossed into the flames."

"And you said yes?"

"Lord, how could I have said no? He was the one I wanted, not Tomen. I just didn't want to be forced into something I had no say in. I wanted it to be my decision. Your father sensed that and he never gave up, even when most men would have."

"That's a great story."

"Yes," she agreed. "As will be yours."

I sighed, looking out through the window. "I hope so."

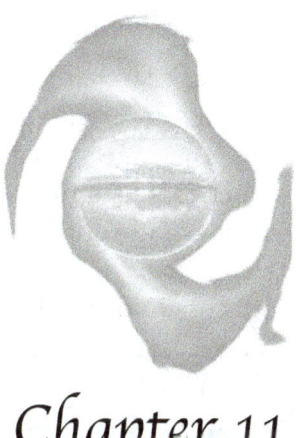

Chapter 11

~ I a n ~

TOGETHER, JAZEN AND I MADE quick work of removing the debris. Each of us was trying to outdo the other and my energy was spent. Damned if I would show it, though.

Sweat beaded over Jazen's forehead and his color looked pale.

"Perhaps we should take a break?" I suggested, sending a mental thought to dear Eve for some iced tea and lemon. Then, I remembered she would never hear those thoughts. Khalen had made sure of that.

I didn't blame our leader, though in truth, I wasn't happy about his decision, either. There had been numerous times when he had lost his control. His only discipline was to be sent away. Case had been more than merciful.

Jazen continued to work, tossing lengths of wood as if they were mere splinters. I had to admit, for a well-bred, he certainly was no stranger to hard work.

"Rest before you collapse," I said, handing him a cloth to wipe his face with. By some strange miracle, half my house remained standing and unmarred by smoke and flame. My bedroom and bathroom were spared, leaving me with towels and clothing.

Jazen took the cloth and dabbed his forehead. "Sit it out if you must, old man, but I prefer to push through."

He tossed another piece of wood onto the burning pile, stumbling with the effort. Another few steps brought him down onto the earth like a sack of wet grain.

"Crimeny," I groaned, making my way toward him.

Maiyun came running and then nudged her face against me. "Find Skye," I told her. She pricked her ears, stared into my eyes for a moment, and then darted toward the lake.

A few moments later, Skye came running along with Khalen, Case, Aidan, Eve and Elle. Kitta and Erika also came, all crowding around Jazen.

"He's overheated," said Khalen, looking over at me. "Did you not have the sense to stop and rest?"

I shrugged. "I tried."

Khalen growled as if doubting my effort. "Let's get him out of the sun," he said, lifting Jazen's upper body while Aidan grabbed his legs. "Eve, get some cold water and towels. Case, get an IV kit and a bag of electrolytes."

I watched as the clan hurried to help, feeling useless and far too tired to care.

Skye touched my face and stared into my eyes. "You're overheated, Ian. You need to drink something." She turned her attention to Erika. "There's some lemonade in our refrigerator. Could you get it for him?"

She nodded and ran toward the yurt.

"I'm fine," I said, my voice sounding distant and slurred.

She struggled to help me stand. "Come on, you need to get out of the sun."

Erika returned with a pitcher of lemonade and a glass. She poured with shaky hands and then handed the glass to me.

"Thank you," I said, but she refused to meet my eyes.

"Drink slowly," Skye instructed.

I did as she suggested, fighting to keep my hands steady and suppressing the urge to gulp the cool sweet liquid. "I'll be all right," I assured them. "See to Jazen."

Erika set the pitcher down beside me and left to check on her other suitor.

Kitta sat beside me.

"She looks disappointed," I said, gesturing to Erika.

"Then she probably is." Kitta never was one to dance around a subject. If she was going to strike a nail, it would be on the head. In this case, it was mine.

"Because of our behavior?" I asked.

She looked toward the bustle around Jazen. "Among other things."

"Care to expand on that?"

She smiled shyly and patted my hand. "You'll figure it out."

I watched perplexed as she stood and walked toward the others. Women could be confusing at times and even a tad irrational, but this was downright bizarre. I wanted to shout and ask her what she meant by that statement, but buried my aching head in my hands instead.

Jazen began mumbling something about getting back to work. Aidan shook his head and came walking toward me.

"The man's an idiot," he said.

I watched as Erika tenderly stroked Jazen's forehead. My gut twisted at the sight of it.

"Dun't give up on 'er," said Aidan. "It is you she wants, not him."

"I'm not so sure."

He followed my point of focus and shook his head. "I've never seen you back down from any challenge, brother. Dun't disappoint me now."

THAT EVENING, THE FIRES WERE crowded with activity and conversation. The women played games with the children while the men strategized a counterattack on the Shadows.

My head still pounded from the overexertion of the afternoon and I had difficulty keeping up with the conversation. Khalen had given Jazen something to make him sleep. I rather wished he gave me something as well.

Case's camp in England had been hit a few days ago, as well as some in Scotland and Ireland. The casualties were low, but extensive damage had been done and quite a few women and children were missing.

Khalen heard that five other clans on the peninsula had been attacked. One of which suffered the most, leaving several men dead and only three surviving elders.

"Something must be done," said Arcadie. "They're targeting our smaller clans."

"Yes," said Case. "They expect our larger stronger clans to come to their rescue, thus lessening our numbers."

"We need to band together," said Khalen. "Bring them all here."

Tetris turned in a circle, surveying the camp. "Ye have

room, Khalen, but not enough to house thirty plus clans."

"If we go to help them," said Aidan, "we leave our own clan at risk."

"I spoke with Lenore and Darius," said Khalen. "They were hit hard but suffered no deaths. They have asked the neighboring clans to join them."

"Perfect," said Case. "I will band my lot together in Eastborne."

"And I will ask mine to band together with Ghandoltes' clan," said Arcadie.

"We have room for the peninsula clans here," said Khalen. "I will send word to other leaders to arrange a similar strategy."

He looked over at Caleb. "Any word from Drew?"

"The training goes well," he said. "There have been no threats so far."

"Where is he?" asked Elle, slowly approaching the group.

"It's beyond your concern," said Khalen.

"I want to know," she insisted, entering our circle as a rabbit would enter a den of wolves.

Caleb looked at Khalen, then at her. "He is safe."

"Will he be back?"

Caleb looked away. "I don't know."

"I need to speak with him," she said.

"Now is not a good time," said Caleb.

She looked over at Khalen. "Why did you send him away?"

"He left on his own accord."

She looked between the men and then rested her eyes on me before turning and walking away. I could feel her pain even without my gifts. Khalen had told her the truth. Drew had left on his own volition with strict orders to never hear her name again.

The men continued to strategize the best way to gather the clans. I watched as Elle walked toward the lake alone. There was no sign of Erika. Kitta said she wanted to be alone. I knew how she felt and made my way back to my dilapidated cabin. It was a clear night and I wanted to sleep in my own bed.

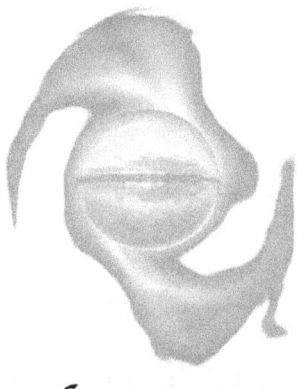

Chapter 12

-Elle-

I HAD TO FIND DREW MYSELF, that much was clear. Skye said that if I opened my heart I could feel the others, especially those I was close to.

Sitting on a large boulder with my knees tucked in close to my chest, I concentrated on Drew and tried to imagine his location. Nothing happened.

Frustration crept in, closing my heart with the cruel fact that some things never change. "Ugh!" I groaned.

A cold wet nose pressed against the back of my neck. "Hi Maiyun," I said, reaching back to scratch the dog's head.

"Whatever you're thinking," Skye said from behind me, "get it right out of your head."

"The only thing I was thinking was how I'm doomed to stay telepathically deaf."

"I was that way for forty-five years. I don't remember it being that bad," she countered, sitting beside me on the dirt.

"I need to find him, Skye. I have to explain my decision."

"Some things are best left unsaid."

"Will you help me? Please?"

"What can I do?"

"Find him for me. Your gifts are strong. You can sense him."

"Drew and I are not that close, Elle. He is too far for me to feel him."

"Khalen knows where he is."

She sat very still, staring out at the water. Her hand mindlessly brushed through Maiyun's coat as the dog sat beside her, panting softly."

"If you knew his location," she said, "what would you intend to do?"

"Talk with him," I said.

"And how do you envision his reception?"

I tried imagining his face when he opened the door and found me there. His expression was hard and grim. "I'm sure he won't be happy, but I think I can convince him to hear me out."

"Consider his feelings. He is hurt, Elle. I was there when he asked Khalen to never speak your name in his presence again. He was dead serious."

"I don't blame him," I said.

We sat in silence for a moment

"Hey," she said. "The women and I are going to the movies tomorrow. Did you want to join us?"

A day out of this camp sounded much too tempting to resist. "What are you seeing?"

"Tower Heist, or something like that. It's playing at the V.I.P. lounge in Gig Harbor."

"Who's watching the kids?"

"Seth and the elders have agreed to watch them. The women and I have not spent time together outside this camp for much too long. It is well overdue."

"And Khalen is fine with it?"

"Khalen is too wrapped up in this war to think about us. Besides, we cannot just sit here and wait for something to happen."

"So, I take it he doesn't know?"

She sighed. "He will by tonight."

"ABSOLUTELY NOT!" KHALEN ROARED. "Our clans are being attacked at all angles and you want to have a girls' day out?"

"Aidan will come with us," I explained.

Aidan's eyebrows shot upward as he turned toward his mate. Apparently she never asked him.

"Aidan's coming with me tomorrow," Khalen countered.

"Then we'll ask someone else," said Skye. "Honestly, Khalen, you think we are more at risk in a movie theater than we are here?"

"I'll accompany the lassies," said Tetris, stroking his long white beard littered with braids and beads.

Khalen studied the old man. "Do you not see the danger in this?"

"With due respect, young Khalen, your mate is right. The women who were taken from the other clans were taken from their camp."

Khalen closed his eyes and shook his head. "Very well. Keep a close eye on them, wizard."

EMBER AND JADE AGREED TO MEET us at the Galaxy Theater in uptown Gig Harbor. When Liam heard they were joining us, he decided to come too. I was certain he had a thing for Ember, given the way he looked at her the other night over the fire. They never spoke, but Skye and I both sensed the attraction.

Skye, Eve, Sunjia, Tetris, Liam and I piled into Eve's Outback and were well on our way by noon. The tension was so thick in camp that it felt good to get away for some down time.

We met the ladies outside a quiet Mediterranean place called Fondi's. The fireplace was burning outside and the weather was perfect for outdoor dining. After placing our orders, we sat at a large table by the fire, making sure to leave a place for Liam next to Ember.

It had been many years since her mate had died and it was time she found another. Predictably, Jade sat beside Ember between her and Liam. Ember didn't seem to notice or care, but Liam certainly did.

"Would you mind if I sit between you two lovely ladies," he said, pulling his chair out for Jade.

I admired his charm and diplomacy as he left Jade little room to argue against the request. She returned his radiant smile and accepted the chair he held out for her. Despite the way she flaunted her ample chest and backside, Liam kept his eyes indifferent.

I enjoyed watching the play between them, and especially liked the way he looked at Ember. She was not as flirtatious as her younger sibling, nor did she have the assets. What she did offer was intelligence, loyalty, and a beautiful smile.

Our food was delivered by a radiant young black man with a pleasant South African accent. I returned his smile as he placed my salad before me along with a pitcher of beer.

"Down here," Tetris instructed the young man. "The ladies are drinkin' iced tea."

"I'm not," Liam said, pushing his frosted mug toward the wizard.

"Ah ha ha," Tetris roared, drawing the attention of the few who were close. He poured the man some beer before filling his own frosted mug to the rim, spilling a good portion in the process. He then lifted his mug to the young bloke. "To ladies night out."

Liam met his mug with a slosh before downing a good portion. "Yes," he repeated quietly while looking at Ember. "To ladies night out."

Ember looked away, trying to hide her embarrassment.

Jade wrapped her arm around his shoulders. "So, I hear you're a doctor," she nearly purred.

He lifted her hand from his shoulder and placed it back onto her lap with a pat. "A surgeon, actually. I specialize in head traumas."

Jade pouted like a child who had been refused a favorite candy bar. When Liam leaned closer to her sister, she outwardly sighed.

I smiled at her, knowing how she must feel. I had felt that same way around my old friend Jamie. She seemed to have an angle with the men that I seemed to lack—not that I was ever interested. I pushed everyone away who dared to get close.

I thought of Drew. It seemed I was still pushing people away.

"Then stop," said Skye in a voice only meant for my ears.

I turned to look at her. "I wish I could. I just don't

know how."

"Drew is a good man for you Elle. Don't let him go."

"I can't even talk to him. How will I get to explain?"

"Reach out to him with your heart. He'll feel you."

I let out a short laugh. "I can't even open my heart enough to hear your thoughts. How can I possibly reach him?"

She squeezed my hand. "You let go and allow yourself to feel him, completely—no conditions, no expectations, no fear."

I nodded my head. "Easier said than done, eh?"

"It will get easier."

We finished eating our salads and headed toward the theater. The air felt heavier than usual. I noticed Skye and Tetris were a bit more on edge. Jade and Ember didn't seem to notice. Liam had his arm draped lazily over Ember's shoulders.

Eve and Sunjia had been engaged in conversation since lunch and were still at it, neither of them appearing to notice a difference in the air.

I looked around, but saw nothing. The feeling, however, was like that of the coffee shop the day those Shadows came in to talk to Jamie and me. The hum of it shook like a well-worn memory in my chest.

"What is it?" I asked Skye.

"You feel it too?"

"Yes."

"Shadows," said Tetris. "Ye ladies stay close now. They won't bother comin' near me."

He flicked his hands as if warding off a horde of flies and then softly chuckled.

The feeling from the Shadows dissipated. "What did you do?" I asked him.

"Gave 'em a taste of somethin' less enticing."

I realized now why Khalen was so comforted knowing the old wizard would be accompanying us during this outing. Tetris was a bit odd, but even I felt more comfortable knowing he was near—especially now.

After purchasing our tickets, we proceeded to the V.I.P. lounge and ordered our drinks and snacks. Skye highly recommended their Malbec wine, so I followed suit and ordered a glass for now and another to be brought to me in another hour after the movie started.

The young man who brought us our drinks and snacks lingered by me far too long for my comfort. I also noticed that my glass was filled nearly to the brim whereas the others had only been filled half full.

His dark eyes rested on me as he smiled like a cat cornering its prey. "Can I bring you anything else?"

I looked around at the others. Tetris glared at the young man. Skye smiled but was not entirely thrilled with his advances. Jade, of course, matched his smile with one of her own.

"I would love a box of Milk Duds," she purred.

His eyes shifted to her. "Of course." Again, he looked at me. "Anything for you?" he asked.

I smiled. "No, thank you."

When he left, Skye leaned into me. "That was thick."

"Disgustingly so," I replied.

"I think he's cute," said Jade.

Ember nudged her arm. "You think anything male is cute."

Jade shrugged, but did nothing to hide her smile.

The man returned with Jade's Milk Duds. She handed him a $5 bill and said, "Keep the change."

He nodded. "Thank you." Tucked into the bill was a

piece of paper that I was sure had her name and number on it. He offered me one last look, as if to say, "Last chance, darlin'," before turning and walking away.

"So," I said to Skye. "How do you see a movie when you're blind?" I knew her well enough to know she would not be offended by the question.

She chuckled. "I don't. I see movement and hear the action. My mind fills in the details."

"That's got to be weird."

"Not much different than reading a book, really."

I shrugged. There was logic in that statement. The reason reading was so enjoyable was that it enabled your mind to create the details. In an odd way, reading made the story your own and pulled you into the action.

"I could see your books making it into film," said Skye.

"Hmm," I replied. "Robert Landon meets The Mummy. Yeah, I can see that happening."

Skye rolled her eyes. "More like Dr. Temperance Brennan meets Indiana Jones," she giggled.

"There's a match made in heaven—like fire and oil. It starts with a blaze and fizzles to nothing."

Eve leaned forward. "Are we still talking about your stories becoming a movie, or about something else?"

I sat back and thought about that statement for a moment. I never did answer. The lights grew dim and the movie screen resized. In a sense, I was grateful for the timing, not wanting to really answer that bizarre yet revealing question.

Drew was like oil to my fire and it frightened me. I was drawn to him as a moth is to light—even when the light meant death. To love Drew, I would have to allow a part of me to die. I wasn't willing to do that. But, on the other hand, I didn't want to lose him either.

Skye reached over and patted my hand as if understanding my dilemma. She had been reading my thoughts. Strangely enough, I trusted her with them.

I T WAS A PERFECT MOVIE for the day; light, funny, and hugely entertaining—a nice break from the dismal reality of war and danger.

After we left, we ventured through the shops nearby, but none of us bought anything. Tetris kept a close watch on our surroundings, keeping his senses sharp like a soldier in charge of the Queen. I guess, in a sense, Skye was like a Queen. She was the mate of the regional leader—not a position to take lightly.

Two hours later, we decided to have dinner at The Green House, an organic restaurant that had recently opened.

Jade immediately migrated to the bar where a handsome man in a cowboy hat enjoyed his beer. Ember shook her head, noting her sister's forwardness.

Liam wrapped his arm around Ember's shoulders and pulled her close. "Leave them be," he said.

Skye eyed Jade and the cowboy with an appraising glance and then jabbed Tetris in the ribs. "He's a Spirian," she whispered.

"Aye," he responded. "But not a Shadow."

"Jade should know."

"She knows," said Ember. "We've been around your kind so long, it's difficult not to."

"Do you think it's wise to allow them to mingle?" said Skye.

"She is not our concern," Tetris replied. "That man is not from this region. If they do get involved, there is nothing we can do about it."

"Khalen will not like the laws being broken in his region," said Skye.

"Tell him," said Tetris.

The hostess showed us to a table in front of a cozy fireplace. We motioned for Jade to join us, but she just shook her head. She was obviously more interested in the cowboy.

Skye frowned. "Khalen has more important things to worry about."

"She knows the risks," said Ember.

We ordered our drinks as well as some calamari for an appetizer.

"I worry about Tria," said Sunjia. "She has been acting out lately and Aidan is at a loss with her."

Skye nodded. "Yes, Khalen and I worry for her as well."

"Why?" I asked. "It's normal for young women to act out some of the time."

"It's more than that. There is a darkness in her heart," said Sunjia. "She is manipulative, disrespectful, and careless with her gifts, despite Case's training."

"She is at a difficult age," said Eve. "Always outdone by her older brother."

"What can we do to help her?" I asked, not really knowing much about raising kids let alone a difficult daughter.

"She must make a choice," said Skye. "Either she lives by our clan's rules, or she must find another clan to join."

"Does that happen a lot?"

"Yes," said Skye. "It is common."

"Too common these days," said Tetris. "I remember a time when the clan was yer family, yer lifeline. Now it is viewed as a prison amongst the young. They are so eager to make their way alone in life, and worse yet, they are not patient to learn from the elders before they leave."

"Sounds pretty normal to me," I said with a chuckle.

"Not for Spirians," Tetris added. "Clan life is critical—loyalty more so."

"What happens if she decides to leave the clan?" I asked.

Sunjia shuddered. "Khalen will sever her ties with us. Her thoughts will be silent to me as ours would be to her."

"She can still visit, right?"

Sunjia's eyes grew dark and deep as a pond on a moonless night. "Not if she joins the Shadows."

"She wouldn't," I said, truly believing it.

"If she has too much of her father in her, she might," said Sunjia. "I fear she does."

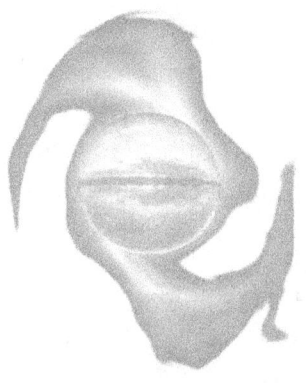

Chapter 13

~ I a n ~

THE ENERGY IN CAMP WAS thick with Shadows. They
stunk like mold in a damp shed and cooled the
surrounding air with an eerie emptiness.

Khalen was on edge and ordered the clan to be alert.
The attack was coming—everyone could feel it.

Aidan ran toward me and Jazen. We had been
constructing the new frame for the front of my cabin.

"I need you two to stay with the women," he said.

"I will fight," I retorted.

"Ye have no gifts, Ian. It is too dangerous for ye."

I tossed down the hammer and faced my brother.
"I will not hide like a child underground, brother. I will
fight, gifts or no."

"As will I," said Jazen, tossing his hammer aside.

Aidan looked from him back to me. "I will not lose
my brother to stupidity," he said.

Khalen approached. With a touch of his hand, I felt

the sting of my gifts returning. "I will not leave you two unprotected. Know this. If you use your gifts against each other again, or against another clan member, the repercussions will not be short of intolerable." He looked at me and then at Jazen. "Understood?"

"Yes, sir," I replied.

Jazen nodded. "Thank you, sir."

"The attack will come fast and hard," said Khalen. "Don't allow yourselves to be distracted. The Shadows' goal is to weaken us and take our women. Stay focused."

"Take care, brother," said Aidan, before turning to leave with Khalen.

"Always the big brother," Jazen said with a snide grin.

"I take it ye have one too?"

Jazen laughed. "Too damn many. But they taught me to fight and watched my back."

"Are they all mated now?"

"Everyone but me."

A pang of sympathy sang in my heart to that chord. He was the future leader of his father's remaining territories, but that role could not be filled unless he was mated. "I'm sure there are many fine women in New Zealand."

"None as fine as Erika," he said. "She's a true catch, that one. And, she carries the blood of Shanuk."

I never saw her that way. I saw her as the woman my heart yearned for—strong, adventurous, and full of life. Never did I consider her blood—until now.

"If ye want to win her over," I offered, "ye cannot stronghold her."

"Christ, old man, can you not see that's exactly what she wants?"

I frowned.

"A strong woman needs a strong man, don't you see?"

I never saw that side of her. She always responded well to my tender side. Then again, she seemed drawn to Jazen's domineering demeanor just as strongly. Women were so confusing.

Aidan was the strong one. I was fun loving—the proverbial lover versus fighter. I love a good fight now and then, but when it comes to women, I want to offer nothing but pleasure.

Jazen started to laugh, obviously finding my thoughts amusing. "Find yourself a nice docile flower of a gal, mate, and leave Erika to me."

That got my hackles up. "She will make that decision, mate, not you."

Again, he laughed. "You're a good man, Ian, but daft as a bloody pole." With that, he walked away.

I wasn't daft.

THE ATTACK CAME SWIFTLY, JUST as Khalen predicted it would. Our camp was so thick with Shadows that I felt we were fighting them in the pitch of night instead of in the bright summer afternoon.

Using my gift of illusion, I projected my image elsewhere, giving me a solid advantage over my enemies. I had also been strengthening my telekinetic skills and used them now with deadly accuracy.

Jazen fought with elegant precision that rivaled the skills that Case and Arcadie often displayed.

The elders of the clan made quick work of the young Shadows that challenged them. Mastery in the old ones was well known amongst all Spirians and few were bold or stupid enough to ever challenge them.

Unlike older people in the human population, Spirian

elders are strong, wise, and respected. They are our teachers and guardians of the customs and traditions that enable our kind to survive. There is no need to protect and care for them.

Shanuk once told us to fight evil with purity of heart. A wave does not break rock with sheer force without the ability to equally yield to the stone's strength. Shadows were strong, and forcefully direct. Thanks to Drew, I had learned to use that strength against my opponent. I yielded to each attack, allowing the enemy's force to drive him forward and down to the ground with minimal effort.

After a time, it became more of a dance, similar to a hurricane kissing the earth.

Jazen fell to the ground with three Shadows looming above him. Without much thought, I came to his aide. For a split second, I allowed my thoughts to stray and felt the fear and pain when a blade pierced my gut. The rest was a blur. I continued to fight as if my body acted on its own accord. My spirit was detached. Darkness finally consumed me.

~ K h a l e n ~

THE BATTLE WAS FOUGHT AND both sides lost. Shanuk was correct when he said there were no victors in war. Through the dust and smoke, I saw Tanen emerge like a dark lord of the underworld.

"Where is the healer?" he asked.

"Beyond your reach, Shadow."

I heard Seth's thoughts as he telepathically told his sister to stop. Carefully, I kept my own thoughts closed. Unfortunately, Seth had opened his to the many listeners who stood among us. Tanen turned his attention to Tria, running across the torn and battered camp toward a young man in his ranks.

The leader's expression changed from a direct challenge to obvious triumph. "We will meet again, young Khalen, son of Damon," he added with a smile.

With an overly dramatic wave of his arm, he and his band vanished, along with Tria.

Seth looked as if his heart had been torn from his chest. "Kill her, Khalen. Kill her now!" he screamed.

"What did she tell him?"

"Everything. They're going after Skye."

Seth grabbed my arm and then immediately released it under the weight of my intent. "Khalen, Tria will betray us. You must end her life."

"It's too late," I said. "She's under their protection." I turned to Aidan. "Can you reach your mate?"

He shook his head.

"Nor can I," said Case. "Tetris, too, is unreachable."

Arcadie's mate ran toward him from her shelter. Erika followed in her wake. When they reached him, he held them close.

"Where's Ian?" Erika said, almost in a panic.

Aidan led the way in a near blind panic. He found his brother lying in a pool of blood with Jazen hovering over him.

"I can't stop the bleeding," he said. His hands shook as he pressed his shirt into the wound in Ian's belly.

Ian was unconscious and rightly so. The sword had pierced through him, possibly rupturing his appendix and lower intestines.

I lifted his wilted body and carried him to the surgery, a small building we had erected some time ago but rarely used. It was the best place for him now.

"Case, gather the supplies and bring them to the surgery. Aidan, you must come as well. We will need your blood."

Aidan followed me to the structure nestled between my yurt and the underground supply storage where the women and children had hidden.

"What about our mates?" he asked softly.

His expression reflected the pain that dulled my eyes. "Arcadie, Caleb and the others will search for them. I have sent them images of where they were before the battle."

"They have to be under an illusion. That's why we cannot contact them."

I nodded. "Yes, I know."

"How will the others find them?" He opened the door to the surgery.

I carried his brother to one of five beds and gently lowered him down. "I trust they will."

His attention returned to his brother. "How bad is he?"

I met his sullen eyes, weary from battle and helplessness. "Bad. If we don't find Skye soon, he may not make it, Aidan."

Jazen stepped inside, seemingly hesitant to approach us. Blood seeped out of his side but he didn't appear to notice. "Will he be all right?"

Both Aidan and I caught the large man before he slumped to the ground.

Aidan grunted. "Christ, he's heavy."

We lifted him onto a table.

Erika and Kitta came in with pans of hot water and clean cloths. Like Eve, Kitta had the gift of acceleration. Boiling water in a matter of seconds was not an issue.

Right now, it was a great gift to have. I just wished it worked as well on healing wounds. Strangely enough, it didn't.

"Put them there," I said, pointing to the stainless steel table in the center of the room.

Erika eyed the two men lying unconscious. When she saw the wound in Jazen's side, she stifled a gasp, pressing her fist to her mouth.

"What happened?" asked Kitta.

"They were both injured," I replied.

"What can we do?" asked Erika, straightening her shoulders and displaying the strength that honored her bloodline.

"We need to clean them up so that I can examine the wounds." Ian's pulse was weakening. "Aidan, get on the table here next to Ian."

Case rushed in with an armful of supplies.

"Get Aidan set up," I said, taking an IV set from the pile. "Ian needs blood now."

I pointed to the cauterization tool in the pile. "Erika, get that plugged in."

She tossed the bloody rags she held into a pile on the floor and did what was asked with fluid calmness. I knew what she must be feeling right now. I, too, felt consumed with fear and worry over my mate, whom I couldn't contact.

I set up the IV and began transfusing Aidan's blood over to Ian. I then began the arduous task of finding and stanching the bleeding vessels to stop his loss of blood.

"Hand me that tool."

Erika pressed the handle of the cauterization iron into my hand.

"Hold this," I told her, releasing the clamp. "Stay very

still."

I could feel her body tremble, but her hand remained stone steady. The smell of burnt flesh rose in the air. It was the kind of smell that made your eyes water and your gut turn with disgust, but she held her post with the diligence of a trained nurse.

I smiled. "You make a good assistant."

Tears welled in her eyes. "Just save them, Khalen—please."

My brow was damp with perspiration as I repaired the last of the bleeding organs. "There," I said. "I think that's the last of them."

Now it was time to attend to Jazen. He had not lost as much blood as Ian but his spleen was pierced and had to be repaired. We were not exactly set up for such an operation, so the results would be sketchy at best.

Caleb contacted me telepathically. *I've contacted my brother and alerted him about the attack.*

There was an awkward silence. *He's going after Elle, I finally answered.*

Yes.

I'm guessing he's blind with fury and armed with nothing more than adrenaline?

He has a small band of men with him, but they are not prepared to face the kind of battle we were up against.

I tied the last stitch, securing Jazen's wound. The rubber gloves I removed snapped off my hands. I tossed them onto the pile of soiled cloths. *Contact him. Tell him to return here immediately.*

"What the hell is happening?" I asked Case.

He shook his head. "The Shadows are retaliating, as they typically do every ten years or so. Only this time, there is a confidence about them."

"Raphael mentioned that the fallen angels aid their intent. It appears the wall between our dimensions has been torn beyond repair."

"We are up against an arduous battle."

I walked toward him and sank down on a chair, my clothes soaked in blood. I watched as Case clamped the tube stretched between Aidan and his brother.

"Check their pulses," I instructed, too exhausted to stand at this point.

"They are both weak, but steady," he reported. He started a bag of fluids for each of them before coming to sit beside me. The women began cleaning the space of blood and debris, probably needing to keep busy.

"What do you intend to do about Tria?" asked Case.

Kitta and Erika looked toward me wearily, no doubt interested in my answer.

"Right now, she is under their protection. I have severed her connection with us, but that is all I can do for now."

"And when this battle is over?"

I met his eyes. He knew the answer already. "I will take her life."

"She knew the consequences of her decision," said Case.

"She is under the illusion that they will protect her from me." I met his dark, obsidian eyes. "She is young and innocent—and my brother's daughter."

"The duties of a leader are rarely glorified," he said. "And often disputed."

"That doesn't help."

He stood and patted my hand. "It wasn't meant to." With that, he walked out of the room.

Arcadie returned with his band of men. Caleb carried Tetris, limp and unconscious.

"What happened?" I asked. The images I had gleaned from their minds were scattered and confusing.

"We found the car in a ditch off Highway 3. The old wizard was energetically bound. If we hadn't reached him in time, he would have been drained."

"What kind of force could bind a man in such a way?" I asked.

"The dark angels," said Case.

"Bring him to the surgery," I told Caleb. "Any status from your brother?"

"No." He laid the old man down onto a fourth table. He was cold and had a grayish tone to his skin.

"I don't know if I can bring him back," I said, feeling about as useless as a paddle in a sinking boat. "Raphael," I said quietly. "I could really use your help."

A blue haze shimmered in the air as the Archangel appeared in the room, his expression sullen and worn.

"The battle continues," he reported.

"It does." I gestured to the wizard on the table. "His life force has been compromised. Can you help him?"

Raphael stood next to the old man. Bright light radiated around them both.

"Can this battle be won?" I asked.

"Battles are never won, young Khalen, only fought."

"Did we cause this?"

"The wall between our dimensions has been thinning over the decades. It was only a matter of time before it was breached. The true question now is what can be done to restore the balance."

Aidan stepped up. "Our women are missing. Do you know where they were taken?"

"Gabriel has been tracking them. They are under a shield off the coast. Cassiel is trying to neutralize the dark ones' influence. There are many of them aiding the Shadows."

"If I create an illusion of stillness, will the dark ones know you are there?" asked Aidan.

Raphael shrugged and smiled. "This is all new to us young man. We haven't seen this much activity since the rising of Mohandas Karamchand Gandhi."

On the table where Tetris lay, the wizard shuddered and coughed. His eyes flew open as he flung his arms wildly.

"Easy, old man," I said, placing a steadying hand on his shoulder. "You're safe now."

"No," Tetris muttered. "The women. They've taken the women."

"We know," I assured him. "We'll find them."

"There were too many of them," he said. "I tried to hold them off, which should have been easy, but there was a dark one with them—very strong."

Raphael seemed to grow an additional three feet, making his already formidable size even more so. "What was his name?"

"Az something," said Tetris, rubbing his eyes.

"Azazel?" Raphael offered.

Tetris nodded. "Yes, that was it."

"God help us all," Raphael murmured.

"Who is this Azazel?" I asked.

"The original evil," said the Angel. "He was one of us, he and his followers—very powerful. His power developed an ego that eventually ate his heart. Now the only thing he's interested in is gaining more power."

"Can we stop him?" I asked.

Raphael shook his head. "No. But we can drive him away."

"How?"

"Remove the darkness that feeds him. Sometimes a fire is so powerful that even an ocean can't cool its flame. Azazel is such a force. He feeds on negative emotions and he can assume any shape, much like us. His followers are his strength. Remove them, and he will leave."

"Tanen," Tetris blurted. "His name was spoken."

"Yes," Arcadie chimed in. "He is the base of this attack, I'm sure of it."

"Two dark powers banded together," said Case. "If Tanen wins this war, the Shadows will rule for many years to come."

"They will target the humans," said Raphael. "As you have witnessed with Eve, the strong ones will survive the transition."

Arcadie stepped forward. "Are you saying the Shadows intend to transition humans to Spirians?"

"Yes. Once they overpower you, they will change the laws. The barrier between dimensions has been torn, leaving many possibilities open. The humans will transition or perish."

I looked around at the ruins of the camp. Children clung to their mothers and to each other. Gabrihen, my oldest son, provided comfort to his siblings. He would make a fine leader in the future, I was sure.

"We will treat this fallen one like any other Shadow. His power must not convince us of defeat. There is too much at stake. And I, for one, am not going to see it fall."

"That's the spirit," said Raphael, his smile as bright as the sun. "I will stay here with the injured and help protect the clan. Save your women."

"I'm coming with," said Tetris. "My part in this has now become personal."

Gabrihen touched my arm. "May I come, father?"

My son, pushing ten years, wanted to fight. His golden eyes reflecting my spirit, stared up at me. "No, son. I need you here to protect our family."

His shoulders straightened but he said nothing before turning and walking away.

"Gabrihen," I called to him.

He turned.

"Stay strong, son. I'm counting on you."

He nodded and returned to his siblings.

"He looks up to you," said Tetris.

"Aye," I said. "He does."

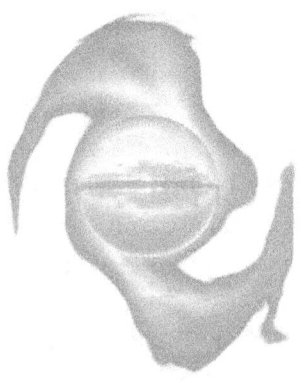

Chapter 14

~ S k y e ~

I **AWOKE IN THE DARK.** The sound of water splashing against hollow metal underlay a myriad of voices above us.

"Where are we?" Eve asked, her voice groggy.

My body ached and felt heavy and warm. "On a ship," I said.

"My head aches," said Elle.

I placed my hands on either side of her skull. "I think we were drugged," Looking over at Sunjia, I noticed she was still and the energy that surrounded her body barely flickered. Tetris was not in the room with us. Ember left with Liam in her car, so I was pretty sure they were safe.

"Where's Tetris?" I asked

Eve looked around. "I don't see him."

I crawled over to Sunjia and placed my hands on her. She had not responded well to the drug. I conjured the healing blue mist and waited for the hum in my hands to subside. Still, her energy faded.

"Come on, Sunjia." Her kidneys were weak and her liver was failing. Again I placed my hands on her but my gift was compromised. Perhaps it was the drug?

"Is she all right?" asked Eve.

"No. She is very weak and my gifts are not as strong."

"I can't read your thoughts," said Eve. "Nor my mate's."

"No, I cannot reach Khalen, either. We must be under some kind of shield."

"What does that mean?" Elle asked, panic mounting in her voice.

"I don't know yet, Elle. Try to stay calm."

"It's so dark in here."

I placed my hand over hers. "We are safe. If they wanted to harm us, we would not be alive right now. Please, you must stay calm."

A rusted door above us announced its movement with a loud screech followed by a heavy thud as it fell open. Light streamed around the silhouettes of four men as they descended the stairs.

"Which of you is the healer?" asked the tallest of the men. He looked to be an elder, only more ragged like an aged human rather than a refined Spirian male. I couldn't see the details of his face, but his energy told me more than I wanted or needed to know. He was a Shadow and a powerful one at that.

"I am," I said.

A bright beam shone as if he were smiling. "Taezza Wallace, she who brings dreams," he drawled.

I felt the blood rush from my face; my stomach twisted in kind as if it had absorbed the shock of hearing that name. "Do I know you?"

"Oh, aye, you do, my dear. We met many years past

when you were only two days old. Imagine my surprise when they told me you were dead."

"They?"

"Your parents. They paid dearly for that deception," he added almost distantly.

My first instinct was to crush his windpipe with a thought, but then I remembered that it would only serve to feed his miserable dark soul. My gifts were no match for his own.

"Do it," he seethed. "Inflict me with unbearable pain."

With his finger, he drew a line over his arm. The smell of blood followed. I fought the urge to seal the wound.

"Heal it," he ordered.

When I ignored him, he grabbed a fistful of Eve's hair. She cried out as his massive hand encircled her throat.

"Heal it, or she dies."

I immediately healed his wound.

His laugh reverberated off the steel walls surrounding the small space that smelled of diesel fuel and mold.

He tossed Eve down to the hard cement floor as if she were no more than a wad of paper. She hit hard, gasping as her knees took the brunt of the fall.

Next the old man's eyes focused on Elle. I felt the hum as she built her shield.

"No," I told her.

The old man waved his hand, reversing Elle's shield and slamming her against the far wall. He followed with a painful energetic blow to her stomach, knocking the wind from her lungs. She held her belly and struggled to breathe.

"Do try again dear." He chuckled and looked directly at me, his eyes glowing like phosphorous hematite. "Come with me."

"No," Eve cried, grabbing my arm. He zapped it, causing her to pull back. The scent of burnt flesh dominated the air. Eve lay unconscious.

"Let them go," I said, "and I will come with you."

He laughed. "Take her," he ordered his men.

I felt the pain of their grip as they hauled me up from the ground. "I'll be all right," I said, pushing back the fear from my voice. Shadows frightened me, but I had been up against them before and triumphed. They couldn't take what wasn't offered. I had to remember that.

There was no way to overpower this man. He would, no doubt, try to intimidate me into cooperating. If I were going to survive this trial, I would have to keep my wits about me and stay true to my beliefs.

The men's tight grip on my arms caused my hands to tingle. My feet barely touched the floor as they hauled me up the stairs and down a dimly lit corridor.

I was tossed into a dark room like a rag doll. I fell to the ground and banged into what felt like a hard piece of furniture. I tried to get up.

"Stay there," the man roared, backing his statement with a sharp pang of energy.

It felt like hot pokers against my body. I curled into a ball and breathed through the pain, pushing my fear deep inside.

"You're much tougher than I thought," he mused. "Then again, you are the granddaughter of the great Shanuk." He said the name with bitter vengeance.

"You sound jealous," I said, my jaw painfully clenched as his energy continued to bite through my flesh. The comment didn't help. The pain intensified.

"Brave, but not very bright," he said. He backed his energy off a bit, leaving a slight tingle to keep my attention.

Another man entered the room. I recognized him as Victor, the ousted leader of the southern states. "You promised I could have her, Tanen," he reminded the old man.

The man called Tanen turned his steely eyes toward him. "In due time, Victor. For now, she is mine."

"I want her alive."

Victor fell back against the wall, his eyes glazed with pain. "My back," he groaned.

"Ah, you remember," Tanen purred. "I could have left you in that pathetic situation, Victor. Remember who it is you're talking to." He released his hold on the former leader and smiled as Victor slithered to the ground.

"You may leave now."

Two thugs lifted Victor to his feet and practically tossed him out of the room.

Tanen returned his attention back to me. "You've shown me how you can heal, young Taezza, now show me how you inflict harm."

I didn't correct him on my name. He knew me by my birth name. I didn't want him to know the name Shanuk had given me. He had kept it a secret for many years for a reason.

When I didn't respond, the expected blast of energy pierced through my center like hot blades.

"Slice my arm with a thought and the pain will stop."

My own pain intensified. I curled into a ball and thought about something else. I imagined Khalen's arms wrapped around me, holding me tight against him. His smell was familiar and comforting.

My head slammed against the wall. My body was numb. Darkness soon followed.

When I awoke, Elle sat beside me, shivering. She brushed the hair from my face. Eve and Sunjia were there as well.

"Thank God you're all right," said Eve. "We feared the worse."

I sat up and immediately removed the pounding throbs in my head. My tired and battered body was next. "Are you all right?" I asked them.

"Other than freezing to death," Elle chattered, "we're doing fine."

I was back in the small metal room. It was very cold. "Have you tried contacting the Angels?"

She nodded. "We are under some kind of shield."

"The men will find us," I said, trying to keep my teeth from chattering.

The metal door slammed open. Several men came down and hauled us all to our feet. We were taken to another room that was empty but bright with sunlight. It was nice to be able to see shapes again.

I felt a waver in the space around us as if the shield was being tested.

"The Angels are here," Elle whispered.

A deep roar echoed from the doorway. "Highly unlikely, my dear. Your Angels have no power here. You are alone."

The women and I knew differently. We could feel the Angels' energy.

Tanen approached me with the intent of a cat cornering its prey. "Now, young Taezza, shall we continue where we left off?"

He reached over and grabbed Elle.

"Inflict me with injury, or I will break her bones, starting with this one." He held Elle's right arm, positioning her elbow against his knee. She released a sharp cry as he applied pressure.

"I assure you, I will do it slowly." He added more pressure. The sound of ligaments tearing was quickly drowned with Elle's screaming.

I caused the skin in his arm to part, leaving a bleeding gap on his upper arm. He laughed.

"Now, heal it!"

I did as he asked and then healed Elle's elbow.

He motioned for one of his blokes to step forward. The big man obeyed, completely oblivious to what would be asked next.

"Rupture his kidney," Tanen demanded.

The man's eyes widened.

I shook my head. "My gifts are used to help people, not cause them harm."

Tanen grabbed Elle's arm again. She cried, having remembered the pain he had so easily inflicted before.

I focused my intent on Tanen. He immediately shielded me. I knew better than to test that shield, having pitted my fury against my mate a time or two. It never ended well for me. If I continued obeying Tanen's cruel wishes, it would weaken me and he knew it. Once I was in that weakened state, he could control my mind—end of game.

Elle released another sharp cry.

With a thought that felt draining and thick as tar in my veins, I ruptured the big thug's kidney. I felt sick inside and repulsed by my actions.

The man fell to the floor, unconscious.

Tanen laughed. "Excellent!"

Without being told, I healed the tortured man. So long as the man remained unconscious, Tanen wouldn't know—or at least, that's what I thought.

Tanen waved his arm, sending me flying toward the back wall of the room. I slammed into the wall, knocking the air from my lungs.

"You are under my command, healer. You will be wise to do only what I tell you to do."

His power over me weakened my spirit. I felt it drain of hope and will as he pierced me with numbing energy. Still, I refused to cry out.

The surrounding energy wobbled again. It seemed odd that the old man didn't notice.

He grabbed Elle's throat and started to squeeze. Her eyes glistened as she struggled with each breath.

"Vow your loyalty to me, healer, or your friends will die one at a time, slowly and most painfully, I assure you."

The anger I felt toward him weakened me further. It was the Shadows' way to invoke negative emotions. Soon, those dark feelings overpowered any good that dared to shine. I had to stay positive and strong.

His grip on Elle's neck tightened. "Break her legs," he demanded.

"No!" I said. "I will not!"

His foot slammed down on Elle's lower leg, snapping her left knee. Her scream filled the space like shards of glass.

I immediately removed her pain and healed her leg. I then retaliated quickly, attacking the old man. He fell to the floor, gripping his ribs as they snapped one by one. The power that flowed through me was fueled with hate and anger. I continued breaking his bones until he lay disfigured on the floor, unconscious from the pain I had caused. When my eyes met his thugs, they scrambled out of the room. I downed the big one with a thought of shattered femurs. He fell in a heap with a loud cry.

I started focusing on the others when Eve touched my arm. I slapped her away as if she were an annoying fly.

"Skye!" she yelled. "Stop! This is not who you are."

A deep, roaring laugh sliced through the madness stealing my reason. The old man rose from the floor, whole and strong. "Now you are mine," he seethed.

"No!" said Elle. "She's not." She pressed herself against me, edging me back against the wall. Sunjia and Eve stood by me. I could feel the power of their shield and the sting of Tanen's eyes.

"Come to me," he demanded.

My legs moved on their own volition as if my soul had been severed. Apathy was all I felt.

Eve gripped my arm in an attempt to hold me back. She cried as Tanen blasted the women's protective shield, tossing them back against the wall. They fell to the floor, silent. I absorbed their pain.

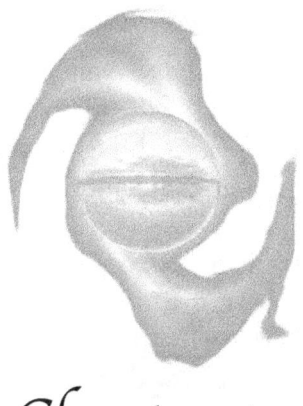

Chapter 15

-Khalen-

I FELT SOMETHING SLIP FROM ME. Like a glacier losing a chunk of its stabilizing base, my soul wavered, threatening to topple. I held tight to Case for balance.

"What is it?" he asked, looking to Arcadie.

Arcadie's expression tightened, his face grew pale. "Cassiel, we need a break in their shield," he growled. "Quickly!"

Archangel Cassiel appeared before us, his size formidable and his light brilliant as the sun. Like his ethereal brother, Raphael, he was young in appearance, yet his strength was incontestable.

"Gabriel and the others are near." He sent us all a mental picture of where the large ship rested in the waters nearly three miles off the Washington coast—a good twenty miles from where we now stood near my cabin at Ocean Shores.

"Aidan, ready the boat."

I looked over at the large Angel. "Can you break the shield in time?"

He nodded. "Keep your thoughts pure, young Khalen. Do not allow anger, hate, and your need for vengeance to open your soul to them."

I nodded back. I understood the concept; putting it into practice, however, was an entirely different beast to face. "How many are on board?"

"We counted thirty-two," said Cassiel. "Tanen and Victor are your worst danger. The others are young and easy to defeat."

"Victor?" Arcadie questioned. "I took care of that old bloke in Brazil."

"He serves Azazel now, which makes him nearly immortal, as is Tanen."

"Immortal Shadows," I muttered. "Bloody perfect."

"Nearly immortal," Cassiel repeated. "To destroy them, you must first drive Azazel away and then take them down together. It won't be easy, but it's not impossible."

I heard the roar of the cabin cruiser come to life. Aidan backed it out of the boathouse and pulled it alongside the dock.

"Let's go," I said, leading the way.

We clambered into the large boat and Aidan sped away toward the unsuspecting vessel.

I tapped his shoulder. "Can you create an illusion to hide our presence?" I asked him.

He nodded. I felt the area around us waver and settle. My body was calm but my temper raged in my head.

"Easy lad," Arcadie said, urging me to sit beside him.

"Something's happened to Skye."

His lips grew firm across his coarse stubbled face. He looked surprisingly strong given the past days' events.

There was no question that he was the strongest Spirian among us. Case was a close second.

"Her soul is compromised," Arcadie explained. "That is why you felt her slipping away from you."

"No!" I shouted.

Arcadie placed his large hand on my shoulder. "Keep your head right, Khalen. This anger you harbor will destroy you both."

"Can we save her?"

I felt the presence of Shanuk but could not see his form.

"She must save herself," I heard him say. "The choice must be hers lest she weaken under the pressure."

"I don't understand," I replied.

"If you pull her out, she will always be susceptible to the Shadows' influence. Allow her to make this choice herself, and she will become stronger for it."

"And if she makes the wrong choice?" I asked.

"If you know your mate at all, Khalen, that question should never enter your mind."

With that, the old man's presence vanished like a subtle spring breeze.

Arcadie smiled. "Always good to hear his voice," he mused.

I looked at him, almost angered by the placid expression he displayed. My mate was in danger, and this fool smiled as if there was not a care in the world.

"This attitude of yours will be the end of you," Arcadie finally said.

"If it were Kitta in Skye's predicament, I doubt you would be smiling now."

His age-old eyes, blue as the Mediterranean Sea, studied me deeply. "Dig deep into your soul, Khalen, and tell me what you see."

I sat back, not really knowing what to do. How does one search his own soul? Emotions were all that surfaced. Dark, putrid emotions that were best left buried.

"Yes," Arcadie said. "That is how the Shadows will conquer you. They will raise those emotions you have stored for so long. They will use them to eat what is good in your heart."

I frowned. Hearing that truth only served to fuel my anger to a fiery roar.

I felt Case's eyes upon me. "If you feel the need to fight, son, do it with us. Get it out of your system now, before it's too late."

My anger faded. Fighting the two men I had grown to love and respect was neither my intention, nor my desire. "I don't know how to let it go."

Case laughed. "You just did. The moment I asked you to fight us, it shrank back like a snake in the face of a sandstorm."

"Because it is not you I want to fight," I seethed. "It is those damn Shadows who constantly threaten all that I love. I want to wipe them from the face of this planet."

Case laughed. "You may as well remove the salt from the ocean while you're at it, dear boy."

He was mocking me. They both were. I wanted to stand and pace the deck, but Aidan's breakneck speed would no doubt launch me into the water if I tried. Once again they peaked my anger.

"Your anger will not save her or the others," Arcadie said. "Do what you must to drown it, but do it quickly."

"Eve is in there," I said to Case. "Do you feel nothing for her?"

"Eve is strong, as are the others. I know they will be

all right."

"And if you're wrong?"

"Then I'm wrong," said Case. His eyes, however, showed no doubt.

"Part of what you're feeling is Skye slipping away. Hold on to her, Khalen. Do not allow her to sever your link. Stay strong for her and remember the love she instills in you. Think about your family and how happy they make you. Hold on to that."

I envisioned Skye in my arms, lying in bed, her soft skin against mine. Her scent was pure like fresh rain. I closed my eyes and imagined the taste of her lips.

"Excellent," Case said. "Those feelings are what will bring her back, son. They are the daggers that will pierce the will of your enemies."

Aidan slowed the engines as we approached a dark shadow in the distance. Through the thick fog, it looked like a demon ship. I could feel the hum of its shield.

Aidan could too. He killed the engines. Only the sound of the water lapping against the sides of the hull broke the eerie silence.

Cassiel's presence was strong, as were the other Angels. "Expand your illusion to include us," he instructed Aidan.

The illusion wavered as it absorbed the Angels. The Shadow's shield quickly dispersed. Aidan started the engines and slowly drove toward the ship.

- S k y e -

DARKNESS SURROUNDED ME LIKE a cave of cold black space. I heard Tanen's commands and obeyed them, not really conscious of what I was doing. All I could hear was his rough voice and roaring laughter.

Inside, I huddled like a child, knees drawn in tight to my chest, a single candle in my mind flickering against the coldness threatening to extinguish it completely.

Another command broke through my thoughts.

Make your choice, a voice echoed in my head. It was Shanuk. *Remember who you are, Skye.*

Help me, I replied. *Please, I feel like I'm fading away.*

It's because you have given up, he said. *You have chosen to give this Shadow power over you.*

No, I inwardly cried. *If I don't comply, he will hurt the ones I love.*

And if you turn, will that not hurt them more?

I don't want to turn.

Then make your choice! he roared. *Do it now, before it's too late.*

How?

His presence faded. I imagined how Khalen would feel if my soul had turned. It would destroy him, I was sure. Another command pierced through my thoughts like red-hot pokers. The child in me shrank back.

I thought about my children, their smiles and charming wit. I imagined Khalen holding me in his strong arms, loving me with his eyes and feeling his touch.

Tanen's command came again, this time bouncing off the loving bubble of thoughts that filled my mind. I thought of Eve and her innocent joy that always found its way into everything she baked or grew. I thought of Elle and the happiness that beamed around her every time Avel had come near. She was so happy then. Since his death, that happiness only reappeared when Drew was close. He was good for her.

Again, I thought of Khalen, cuddling in his arms

as if none of this horror was happening. I wanted—no, needed—to find my way back to him and our children.

Tanen roared with anger. I felt the piercing of his blow, shaking me to my bones. The pain was nearly unbearable.

Skye!

Khalen, I thought. *Help me!*

Where are you?

I sent him an image of where Eve and the others were located and then collapsed under Tanen's energetic blows.

~Khalen~

WE MADE QUICK WORK OF the blokes on deck. Victor was nowhere to be found and the image that Skye had sent me was faded and vague. I relied on my instincts to pull me through the various decks.

Skye was not responding to me anymore. I felt a coldness in my center where there was once warmth. Pushing back the worry that weakened my senses, I connected back to the image that she had sent me.

"I cannot hear Eve," said Case. "But I feel her. She is near."

A large metal door on the floor drew my attention. With a thought, I flew the heavy door open. Aidan pushed past me and flew down the stairs toward his mate, who lay unconscious on the floor next to Eve and Elle.

Their pulses were weak and their breathing was shallow. Elle had taken the brunt of the attack. Her ribs were nearly shattered. Moving her now would prove fatal. I had to find Skye. Again I called out to her. No response.

"Leave them here," I said. "We must find Skye."

Aidan and Case looked down at their still mates with

hesitation.

"We can't help them now," I seethed.

Tetris froze and then suddenly turned to deflect an attack.

"How?" a gruff voice boomed. The dark angel appeared, taking the form of a tall, dark man with a hooded cape. He looked around him and shuddered. "No!" he roared. "Impossible!"

Gabriel came into the room, filling it with light. "Improbable, Azazel, but not impossible."

Azazel shielded his eyes from the light before suddenly disappearing.

Gabriel sent me an image of where Skye was. "Hurry," he said. "She needs you. I'll stay here."

"Where's Victor?" Arcadie asked.

"He'll find you," said the Angel. "Go now!"

We ran up the stairs and out of the room. Driven by fear and rage, my feet pounded the deck as they carried me to the location that Gabriel had provided. Pure instinct mixed with adrenaline was a poor recipe for rational thinking.

The room at the end of a long corridor glowed, drawing my attention. I ran toward it, slamming the door open with a thought, startling the old man on the other side.

I slammed him against the wall. He countered with an energetic blow that nearly tripled Case's harshest reprimand. I fell to the floor and struggled to breathe. Skye was curled up against the far wall. I crawled toward her.

Another blow crushed my ribs. I countered with an attack that brought Tanen to his knees.

"Her spirit is gone," he said, his voice laced with pain.

"You've nothing left to fight for, Khalen."

She wasn't gone. I knew it. I cast another blow toward him. He deflected it, but it was clumsy and cost him energy.

Case, Arcadie and Aidan ran into the room with Tetris close behind. Together they kept the old man from attacking me further.

"Skye," I said, gently tapping her face. "Come on, love. I'm here now."

Her eyes fluttered open. "Khalen?"

"Yes, love, I'm here." I held her tight, ignoring the pain in my ribs.

She felt stiff in my arms, not right. I pulled away and studied her face. Her eyes were focused on Tanen. They widened with terror, then glowed silver.

Tanen screamed and then collapsed to the floor unconscious. Coldness enveloped us as Azazel entered the room.

"She is mine, young Khalen. Give her up gracefully."

"No!" I roared.

"Yes," he seethed. "I feel your anger." He closed his eyes and looked up as if welcoming a cooling rain. He breathed in deep.

"No, Khalen," Case said. "You're making him stronger."

"Come to me," Azazel ordered Skye.

On shaky legs, she tried to stand. I tried to stop her, but she looked right through me as if I were not even there.

"Skye!"

The pain in my ribs paralyzed me as I watched her walk toward the dark angel. "No!"

Let her make the choice, Shanuk reminded me. With a faint touch of his ethereal hand, my pain subsided.

Azazel looked down at Tanen lying crumpled on the floor. "Heal him," he said.

Skye looked down at Tanen.

I love you, she thought to me. I felt my ribs heal and the pain leave. *Stay in control—for me.*

"Heal him," Azazel roared. "Now!"

Skye looked up at him with such compassion that Azazel had to look away.

"I'm not afraid of you," she said. Her eyes glowed so bright that they lit the room.

"Another time," Azazel said and then left as quickly as he had come.

Tanen stirred. "My Lord," he said. "Take me with you."

Skye placed her hands on him to remove the pain and heal his wounds. When he gripped her hand and pulled her down to him, she didn't resist.

"Why?" he asked.

"It is not my place to judge you, Tanen, nor is it my place to inflict harm—on anyone. I apologize for the pain I caused you."

His grip tightened on her hand. She winced, causing my protective instincts to kick in. I cast him a painful blow.

"Release her, Tanen."

His eyes darted between me and the other men with me. There was no chance of victory for him and he knew it. Reluctantly, he released Skye's hand.

"I had you," he said. "I owned you."

"No," she replied. "You only thought you did."

"Impossible!" he roared. "He will come back for me."

Gabriel manifested before us. "I wouldn't count on it. He is gone and will most likely be so for quite some time."

Tanen's eyes grew dim.

An electric charge filled the air, quickly deflected by Gabriel. Victor stood at the door, eyes filled with hate and anger.

"You should have finished me off when you had the chance, Arcadie."

Tanen raised his hand. "It's over, Victor. We have lost."

Victor walked into the room to stand beside him. "What do you mean? It can't be over. Aza—"

"Is gone," said Tanen. "Can you not feel the lack of his presence?"

Victor looked like a child lost in a storm of emotions he couldn't decipher. He dropped to his knees.

Together we could end both of their lives and we would be justified in doing it. Something about that felt wrong, though, and disadvantageous.

Arcadie and Case must have felt the same. Neither of them made a move to destroy the Shadows. Without a word, I lifted my mate into my arms, and carried her from the room. The others followed in silence.

"I can walk," she whispered.

"Right now, I just want to hold you."

She buried her head against my chest and quietly sobbed.

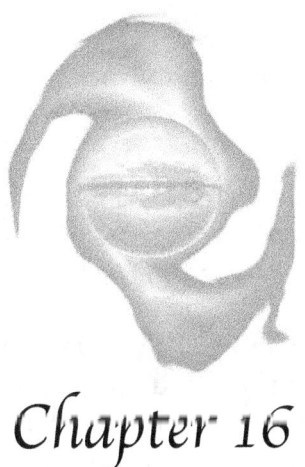

Chapter 16

-Elle-

BY THE TIME WE GOT BACK to the shore, Skye was exhausted from the ordeal and from healing the lot of us. A resounding explosion pierced the night as the ominous ship exploded. No one knew why or even seemed to care, for that matter.

We didn't talk much during the long ride home. We were lost in our own thoughts.

Skye snuggled close to Khalen as he drove. Aidan and Sunjia held hands, and Eve rested her head on Case's shoulder. Arcadie was staring out the window, and Tetris had his eyes closed as if he were meditating.

I sat in the far back of the Escalade, alone and thinking of Connor. I prayed he was all right. Khalen had mentioned the attack. There were some casualties, he said, but didn't reveal the details to me. I was sure the others had read his thoughts.

Images of Drew came to mind, making me smile.

In my mind, I pictured him working with Connor as he measured wood and reconstructed the damage caused by the battle. An empty sadness quickly replaced that image. Drew would not be there.

I closed my eyes and tried to imagine Avel. I wondered what he looked like as my true husband over three-hundred years ago. He said he was tall with dark hair and hazel eyes. I remembered those eyes. I missed him and started to wonder if I would ever see him again.

You think too much, a voice echoed in my head. I smiled, knowing that voice to be Raphael.

Not much else to do right now, I silently answered.

Rest, he said. *There is much to do here when you return.*

"**Elle, wake up." I felt** someone jostle me. "We're home."

My eyes fluttered open. Skye leaned over me.

"I'll get her," said the deeper voice of Khalen.

He easily lifted me from the seat and carried me toward their yurt.

"I'm awake," I muttered, groggily. "I want to see Connor."

As expected, he didn't respond. When Khalen had an idea about something, not even a freight train could deter him. I decided to give in to my exhaustion and quickly fell back into a deep sleep.

I **was floating now, like a** feather in the breeze, fluttering with no direction. It was a dream, of course, albeit a very real dream. The wind brushed against me, yet I felt no arms or legs. I was a cloud, perhaps?

Then, as if a new dream had started, I found myself

standing on the top of a mountain with snow all around me. It was so silent up here. The mountain peak rose above the cloud bank. I looked around me and saw nothing but white, yet I wasn't cold—not at all.

I didn't much like the snow, or the cold, for that matter. This was different, though, almost surreal. It was surreal, I reminded myself. I was dreaming.

"Are you?" a strange yet oddly familiar voice said.

"Either that or I'm dead," I responded to no one in particular. I looked around but didn't see anyone. When I turned back, a luminous figure stood before me.

It took a while, but the image sharpened into a largely handsome man with dark hair and eyes the color of fresh hay.

He smiled. "You think I'm handsome?"

Great, I thought. Even my dreams can read my thoughts. "Do I know you?"

He stepped toward me and slowly lowered his lips to mine. I closed my eyes and allowed the delicious familiarity to seep into my soul.

"Avel," I sighed. "Have I finally come home to you?"

He tried to step back, but I held him to me as if letting him go would end the dream.

"No," he answered. "Not yet."

"Why am I here?"

He pried my hands from his hips. "You need to let me go, Elle."

"Never!" I cried. "I will never let you go. I can't." My breath grew ragged and my lungs felt compressed with a heaviness that threatened to crush me.

He touched my face and his eyes seemed to glow. "Listen to me. There is another man who loves you. I want you to take him and love him as you once loved me."

"I still do love you," I pleaded.

"Then let me go."

"No!"

He shook me slightly. "Show me you love me by loving him. Give him your heart."

"No!" I repeated. "I can't."

"Then you force me to remove my memory from you." His hand came up to my forehead.

I stepped back. "Please, no. I don't want to forget you—ever."

"If you cannot love another in my stead, you leave me no choice." He stepped toward me.

"Okay," I whispered. "I will love another as I still love you."

"Say it again," he demanded, "with feeling."

I looked into his languid eyes. His image blurred behind my tears. "I will love another as I still love you."

"Again!"

"I will love another as I still love you."

"Be it so," he said, smiling. "As above, so below." He gently kissed my forehead.

Darkness prevailed, accompanied by a heaviness and warmth.

I awoke to the delicious smell of coffee and cinnamon streusel. I sat up and looked into a face that seemed to have aged many years.

"Skye, you look awful," I said.

She scoffed. "You should talk."

I ran my hand through my tangled mess of hair. "How long have I been sleeping?"

"Two days." She pressed a hot cup of liquid into my hands. "Drink this."

The scent was salty with a hint of something gamey.

"What is it?"

"Elk bone broth. It will help you gain your strength."

I sipped the liquid slowly, anticipating a flavor I would find less than appealing. Surprisingly, the broth tasted good.

Skye laughed. "You act surprised."

"I have to admit, elk bone broth does not sound the least bit appealing." I eyed the streusel.

"Finish the broth first, and then you may have the streusel," she said with a smile. She then turned to the door. "Someone here is eager to see you."

My son peeked around the doorway and then ran into the room to my side. He had grown since I last saw him, even though it had only been a few days. He seemed taller and lankier than before.

I wrapped my arms around him, breathing in his familiar scent. He had been working with cedar wood. Pieces of it still clung to his dark wavy hair. "It's so good to hold you again," I whispered against his head.

"I missed you, mummy," he mumbled into my chest. "Are you all right?"

"Yes," I laughed. "I'm fine. I was just tired is all."

"I'm helping to rebuild the camp," he said. "Drew is here, showing me how."

"Drew is here?" I looked to Skye for confirmation. She smiled and then looked away. I focused again on Connor. "Why don't you go back outside, Connor. I'll be along shortly."

"Okay." With that, he gave me one more hug before running out of the room, leaving a trail of dust and debris in his wake.

I looked at the mess and shook my head. "I'll clean that up."

"No need," said Skye. "It's bound to get worse over the next few days with all the activity. I'll take care of it later."

I started to get out of bed. "I want to talk with Drew." She gently pushed me back down. "You're still a bit weak, my friend. Get some food in you first and then get cleaned up. You don't want to see him looking like this." There was sadness in her voice.

"What are you not telling me, Skye?"

She just shook her head and walked away. "I'll get you some clean towels and clothes to wear."

By the time I got outside, the afternoon sun was setting. I still felt a bit wobbly on my legs, but I drove them onward toward the team of people constructing new dwellings. My own humble cabin had been crushed and burned. Few of my belongings remained in the rubble.

Drew pounded an anchor on two boards that Connor held together. I smiled.

Drew looked up and his face visibly paled. "Elle?"

"Drew. It's good to see you again."

"Connor," he said. "Take this segment to Aidan, okay?"

"Okay." Connor gripped the small window frame and ran off.

"How have you been?" Drew asked.

"Good." I looked down. "I missed you."

He smiled, but there was something hesitant about it. "I have found a new clan."

My heart threatened to break. I breathed deep and blurted what I had been wanting to say for many weeks now. "I want you to stay."

A woman approached. She was tall with dark shiny hair and brilliant golden eyes, another Native American. Her bronzed skin shone in the sun, attractively accented by the clothes she wore; a yellow shirt and faded blue jeans. She held a glass of lemonade in her hands.

"I thought you might be thirsty," she said, pressing the glass in Drew's hand. I noticed the pendant that hung around her neck. It was Drew's promise crystal. I thought he had left it behind. Another thought sank in my gut. They were to be mated.

My breath caught in my throat and my legs wavered.

"Are you all right?" the young woman said.

Drew caught me and helped me sit on a nearby stump. "Elle, this is Tamarla, my mate to be. Tamarla, this is Conner's mother, Elle."

I held out a shaky hand. "It's nice to meet you," I lied. It must have been evident, because she looked between Drew and me with speculation.

"I'll let you two talk," she said before turning and walking away.

"Elle," he said, squatting before me. "I didn't want to tell you like this."

He reached out to touch me, but I shrank away. "No," I said. "It's better this way." I had to choke out the words.

"I'm sorry I left." His eyes, those deep amethyst eyes, looked into my soul as if there was hope. It was false hope, though.

"I'm sorry I pushed you away."

"Avel is lucky to have your heart," he said.

You have it too, I wanted to say, but held my tongue. He had given his heart to another. My feelings no longer mattered.

With teary eyes, I looked up at him. There was so much I wanted to say, but the words clung in my throat like hooked thorns. Nothing came out.

"Perhaps you should go back to rest some more," he

said, standing. "It was nice to see you again."

I watched, still unable to speak, as he walked away. I stood and wandered into the woods, mindless and numb. I was too late. Drew had found another.

I SAT IN THE DARK ON the large boulder in the meadow that Skye had shown me. My thoughts swam in my head, cruel reminders of how stupid I had been. My chest was raw with pain and my heart ached with every beat.

This overwhelming emptiness felt familiar. The pain called to me like an old friend. Thoughts of piercing a dagger through my heart raced in my mind. I wanted the pain to end. I wanted to be with Avel.

But now I knew. Ending my life would only sentence me to eternity without hope of ever seeing him again. I had promised him to live this life and raise our son to remember him.

Avel had said that another man loved me. Was he talking about Drew? Did Avel know that Drew had given his heart to another? If so, why was it so important for me to make that promise to him to love another in his stead?

Hoof beats echoed in the distance as Belle cantered into the meadow. Skye slid off her back before she came to a stop.

"Everyone is worried about you," she said, huffing from her recent exertion. She climbed onto the boulder to sit beside me.

Without saying anything, she wrapped her arm around me and pulled me close.

The torrent of tears that I had been trying to suppress flowed like rain from my eyes. My entire body trembled.

"I was ready to give my heart to him, Skye," I wailed.

"Why does the loss of love have to hurt so much?"

She squeezed me and pulled me in tighter to her. "I don't know," she said quietly. "It just does."

I told her about my dream, though I doubted she heard any of it through my uncontrollable sobs.

Maiyun came running into the meadow, tongue hanging out of her mouth, and eyes glistening with mischief. She leapt onto the boulder and sidled up to me, offering her own kind of comfort.

"Did you tell Drew how you felt?"

I shook my head. "It wouldn't matter. He loves another now."

"Did he tell you that?"

I looked up at her, confused. "Skye, he's promised to mate another woman. His love for her goes without saying."

"Hmm," she responded. "Are you hungry?"

"Not really."

She grabbed my hand and hauled me up with her. "Well, come and eat anyway, because I'm starved and have been waiting for you."

We rode back to camp in silence. Skye was good about letting me stew in my own thoughts. It was the thing I especially appreciated about her.

I felt many eyes upon me as we meandered our way through camp toward the main fire. Two plates of food sat waiting along with two glasses of red wine. My stomach growled as the scent of stew tickled my sense of smell.

Khalen cleared a spot beside him for Skye. His eyes were riveted on me as I sat across from them.

"What?" I finally asked him. The man could be so annoying at times.

"My mate told me what you did for her back on the

ship. Thank you."

A lump formed in my throat. "You're welcome," I said, stirring the food around on my plate. It smelled good but I honestly didn't feel like eating. I put the plate down and picked up the glass of wine. Borolo, my favorite. It slid down easily—almost too easily.

Khalen reached over and refilled my glass, his eyes still set on mine.

Tamarla came to join us, looking at Khalen as if he had summoned her.

I suddenly lost my taste for the wine as well. I set the glass down. "Congratulations," I said, not really meaning it.

She smiled and sat beside me. "Masking your feelings is fairly absurd in the presence of Spirians, wouldn't you say?"

"I really wouldn't know," I responded. There was a hint of sadness in my voice. "Reading everyone's mind is obviously not one of my gifts."

Did she have to be so damn beautiful? It was no wonder Drew had chosen her so quickly.

"What makes you think he chose me?" she asked.

Khalen and Skye took up their plates and moved to sit beside Case and the others. Now it was just me and this woman.

"You wear his pendant. That tells me he chose you."

She shook her head and her smile broadened. "You know so little of our customs," she chided.

Her luminous eyes glowed against the firelight, nearly matching its color.

"Do you love him?" I asked, wanting to take it back the moment the words left my mouth.

"There is much to love about that man," she said, not

really answering my question.

I took another long pull from my wine, grateful it could still affect me. I was not a full-blown Spirian and my mere human qualities still outranked my gift of an Angel's touch. It was more of a curse at this point, but who really cared?

"Do you love him?" she asked.

Again, my words clung to my throat, reminding me of a sticky weed in the fall. "Why does it matter?"

"Do you love him?" she asked again.

I took a gulp of wine this time. My head started to spin a bit—good.

"You should tell him," she said.

"There is nothing to say."

The young woman caressed her glass like a lover, her eyes trained on the fire. "It was not Drew's decision to mate me," she said. "My father gave him an ultimatum. He could stay with the clan if he agreed to take a mate."

"Why would he do that?"

"Drew is a man of worth and strong status. My father would have ties to that status if one of his clan members joined with Drew."

"That's ridiculous!"

She laughed. "Spirian ties are important, Elle. They ensure the success of our race. There was a time when we were becoming extinct. Now that our numbers grow strong again, it is imperative that our bloodlines ensure our survival."

"You're a beautiful woman, Tamarla. I'm sure you could have any man of your choice."

"The men of our clan are all mated. I would have to join with a man from another clan, thus leaving my father. If Drew agreed to live with our clan and take me as a mate, I would be able to stay near my father. His mate died many years ago and he is alone. I choose not to leave him."

"That's terrible," I said, feeling a strong sense of compassion for her. "Drew is a good man," I said. "I know he will take care of you."

She sighed. "A union is a lifetime commitment. There is no turning back once it is set. Drew loves another. He compromises that by joining with me."

"It is still his choice."

Music played in the background, a lively beat that reverberated through my bones. Seth came running toward us, his eyes bright in the firelight. His strong resemblance to Khalen became more evident as he grew into his lanky frame. They shared the same strong jawline and thick muscles. Seth, however, was much more sweet natured than his overbearing uncle.

"Dance with me?" he said, holding out his hand.

I looked over at Tamarla. "Thank you for talking to me," I said, leaving to take Seth up on his offer.

He spun me around in the dance circle, expertly guiding me around other couples. He was growing into a fine man, I thought.

"Thank you," he said, smiling, having obviously read my thoughts. "It's about time you noticed."

I shook my head, cursing my open mind and transparent emotions that could be read so easily.

The music slowed. Seth wrapped his strong arms around me. "One more dance?" he said, swaying our bodies to the rhythmic beat.

"Okay," I said shakily. It felt odd being held by him. My body responded, yet he felt more like a sibling than a man I should be attracted to. He was a good dancer, commanding, confident and agile.

Before the song ended, someone tapped his shoulder. "May I?" asked Drew.

Seth frowned before reluctantly stepping aside.

"We'll dance again," I told him.

He responded with a beaming smile.

"He still loves you," said Drew, taking me into his arms as if I belonged there.

"Perhaps," I responded.

"Tamarla tells me that she and you had a talk."

"Yes, She's a beautiful woman, Drew. You chose well."

"Did I?"

I resisted the urge to lay my head against his shoulder. The desire to meet his eyes, however, was not so easily ignored. "I'm happy for you."

"Really?"

I cleared my throat. "Yes. It's nice to see you happy."

"You seemed disturbed to find my crystal around Tamarla's neck this afternoon." He spun me around until we reached the center of the circle, discouraging me from breaking away, I was certain.

"I was a little surprised that's all."

"Tell me something," he said, his voice as silky as a dark truffle. "Do you love me?"

I looked away. He stopped, tenderly held my chin, and tilted my head up to meet his eyes. I glanced away, not ready to face him on that matter yet.

"Look at me, Elle."

I closed my eyes, took a long deep breath and then met those dark windows to his soul. They were the deep color of purple with shining flecks of gold—mesmerizing.

"Do you love me?"

"It doesn't matter. Your heart is promised to another."

"Answer my question!"

His sharp tone startled me. I wanted to escape but his arm wrapped firmly around my waist.

"Yes," I said. "I do love you."

We started dancing again. He acted as if he had never even heard me. When the song ended, he kissed the back of my hand, leaving as quickly as he had come.

I stood there, dumbfounded. Was that all he needed to hear? Did he need confirmation for how much his engagement hurt me?

My gut wrenched. Before I could run back into the healing sanctuary of the woods, Skye came to collect me.

"You think too much," she said. "Come join us at the fire."

"I don't much feel like it tonight," I said.

Her grip around my hand tightened. "Tough!"

"Now you sound like your mate."

She smiled. "Who do you think asked me to get you?"

I rolled my eyes. "The man is set on torturing me."

"I don't think so," said Skye. "You're still standing."

Tamarla had left and Drew was not around either. They probably retired to their tent to laugh about me.

"I thought you knew my brother better than that," said a voice from behind. It was Caleb, the older brother. He and his mate were drinking brandy. Dania wore a brightly colored blouse that seemed to flow with the slightest breeze. She was a stunning woman who enjoyed tending the children. Many of them called her teacher.

"We had an odd interaction a few moments ago, that's all." I don't know why I bothered to explain myself when my mind was obviously an open book for all to read and exploit. It was frustrating, really.

Khalen came over and grabbed my arm. "Come sit,"

he said, gesturing to a spot next to Skye. She smiled up at me.

"Actually, I was hoping to retire for the night. I have some writ—"

"It will wait," he said, urging me down to the log bench. "You spend too much time alone. I want to hear more about what happened on the ship."

"I'm sure Skye revealed everything already."

"I don't remember much of it," she said.

I gave them the Reader's Digest version, seeing I didn't have much of a knack for telling stories, even when they were true.

As I talked, I watched my son interact with Gabrihen. Despite their five-year difference, they were oddly compatible now and Gabrihen was developing a strong protective instinct for him. A discussion seemed to be getting quite heated between Gabrihen and another boy, however, and I paused to listen.

The others, too, noticed the commotion. The boy reached for my son and Gabrihen zapped him with a surprisingly strong concentration of energy. The boy fell back. He wasn't moving.

"Natel?" Dania cried. She stood and ran toward them with her mate close behind.

Skye and Khalen followed.

Skye placed her hands on the boy and frowned. Both she and Khalen looked at their son.

"He was going to hurt Connor," he said.

"Can you help him? Dania cried.

"He'll be all right," Skye assured her.

Khalen rose to talk to Gabrihen. The boy's eyes widened and then he vanished, much to Khalen's surprise.

"Oh boy," said Tetris. "This is not good."

"Where is he?" Khalen asked. "I cannot feel him."

"It appears your son is a wizard," said Tetris. "And, judging by his impressive display of power, a very gifted one."

"Find him," Khalen roared. "Bring him to me."

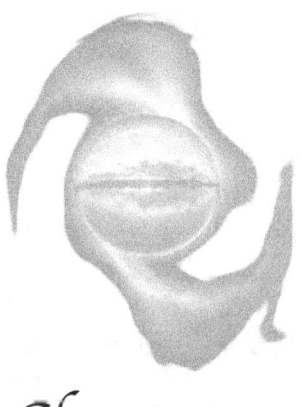

Chapter 17

~ I a n ~

A COMMOTION STARTLED ME OUT OF a much needed deep sleep. I nearly rolled out of my cot as Khalen rushed in with Caleb's boy in his arms.

Thanks to all the healing Skye had given me, I was alive. I was still weak, but able to move around. Not having a better place to rest, I chose to sleep here in the surgery until my cabin could be restored.

My brother followed the procession with his mate close behind.

"What happened?" I asked, squinting against the bright lights piercing my brain.

"Gabrihen zapped Natel with an energy blast that knocked him unconscious."

I stood, fighting the nausea that typically followed a headache from hell.

"Damn it," Khalen roared. "I need a bag of fluids!"

"They're gone," said Aidan. "We depleted them after

the battle."

Khalen looked around and spotted Sunjia. "Get me some broth, quickly."

She ran from the room.

"Khalen, he'll be all right," Skye assured him. He just needs time to rest."

Khalen checked the boy's vitals again, visibly relaxing.

Tetris came in with Gabrihen draped in his arms. "He needs help."

Gabrihen's limbs were limp and twisted at odd angles.

"He didn't transition completely," Tetris explained. "Dematerializing can be tricky."

"Where was he?" asked Khalen.

"Near the lake. I followed his energy trail."

Skye's hands shook as she assessed the damages. "Oh, Gabrihen, why did you do this?"

Khalen, too, assessed the boy, his jaw tight with concern and anger.

"Come," I told him. "Skye can handle this."

I led him outside, fighting the dizzying weakness that threatened to buckle my knees.

"My God," Khalen mumbled. "My son nearly took Natel's life."

"He has your temper," I mused, then immediately wanted to take it back when Khalen's eyes met mine.

He spied Elle talking to her son and made a beeline for them.

"Easy, lad," I said, catching up to him. "The boy is only four."

When Khalen approached, Elle stood between him and her son.

"I want to talk to him," he growled.

"Not until you calm down," she countered. "He's

shaken up as it is."

Case and Arcadie stood beside her.

"How is Natel?" Case asked.

"Physically fine," Khalen said. "Mentally, I'm not sure."

Arcadie placed his hand on Khalen's shoulder. "This is not your fault, Khalen."

Khalen sank down on a log and buried his face in his hands. "It's too soon for his gifts to be this strong. Why didn't I see it coming?"

"You were his age when you discovered your gifts," he reminded me.

Connor tapped Khalen's arm. The weary leader glanced down at him, his face drawn and worn by the recent onslaught of events. "Connor," he said, acknowledging the young boy.

"Is Gabri in trouble?"

"No," Khalen replied. "He's not in trouble." He closed his eyes, struggling to calm his anger. "Can you tell me what happened?"

"Natel said I was a halfling, and that my father was human. He said I could never have kids of my own."

Again Khalen closed his eyes and breathed deeply. "And then what?"

"I said he would be cursed for saying such things. Then he tried to grab me and Gabri stopped him."

"Why did you say he would be cursed?" asked Elle. "That is an odd thing to say."

"I wanted his bones to be crushed into pieces," said Connor.

"No!" Elle cried. "You must never imagine such things."

Connor sniffled. "I didn't know it would come true.

Tria said it would, and told Gabrihen, too, that he could help make it happen, but we never believed her. She told people many things like that."

Khalen growled. "Connor," he said, his voice low and controlled. "You must never use your gifts to do harm. Do you understand me?"

The small boy nodded. "I didn't really want it to happen."

"But it did, and it cannot be undone."

Tears welled in the young boy's eyes. When he finally calmed down in his mother's arms, he looked back at Khalen. "What is a halfling?"

"Nothing you need to worry about now," said Khalen.

Skye approached with Caleb and Dania.

"How are they?" asked Khalen.

"Good," Skye sighed. "They just need some rest."

He grabbed her hand and pulled her down beside him. "You look ready to collapse."

"Why did this happen?" she asked.

Khalen filled her in on the details with mental images.

"So soon?" she asked.

"My gifts surfaced at his age," Khalen said, "and they were just as lethal."

Tetris joined the group with another plate of food and a bottle of dark brew. "I'd be honored to train the lad for you, Khalen."

"He's too young," Skye cried.

"He's dangerous," Case retorted. "It's best if he leaves camp and goes with Tetris back to England."

"That's so far," said Skye.

"It's only for a year or two," Khalen assured her. "He'll be back."

"I'll fly you up to see him," I offered.

"Often?" she asked.

I laughed. "As often as you like."

Arcadie poured everyone a glass of wine and then raised his glass. "To raising the young," he said. "What a delightful challenge it is."

"I often wondered why you only had two children," I said, smiling.

"Exactly, dear boy."

Khalen growled. With two girls and two boys, he had his hands full already. It made me think about my own family if I ever had one.

I glanced over at Erika, standing by the overly possessive Jazen. She smiled at me. We hadn't spent much time together—Jazen made sure of that. I was planning to put a chink in that armor of his very soon.

MY STRENGTH RETURNED BY MORNING and I was ready to join the clan in reconstructing the camp. I had spent the night at my brother's cabin, delighting in the sounds of his and Sunjia's children as they playfully padded through the house, laughing and giggling.

A note was left for me on the dresser. There wasn't much left of my clothes except two pairs of jeans and a few shirts. What the fire hadn't destroyed, the battle took care of. Aidan loaned me some of his clothes until I could replenish my own.

The note that was left informed me of the community breakfast this morning. Judging by the constant hum of conversation nearby, I gathered it was not too late to join everyone. I threw on some clothes, combed my fingers through my hair and meandered outside.

The scent of buttermilk pancakes, sausage, and

scrambled eggs called my attention. Maple syrup, warmed by the fire, glistened in a cast-iron cauldron. It was Dania's contribution, I was sure. She made the best maple syrup I ever had. My mouth started to water as I collected a plate and utensils.

Khalen came by to refill two mugs of coffee. "How are you feeling?"

"Better," I said, piling my plate with cakes, meat and eggs.

"Your appetite seems to have returned," he said, smiling.

"Aye, it has. I plan on workin' with the clan today. I need my strength."

He poured goat milk into the coffee and added a touch of maple syrup. "Don't overdo it, Ian. Your body suffered a serious trauma."

"Yes, doctor," I bantered back. "How are Gabrihen and Natel?"

Khalen gestured to the two boys sitting quietly together eating breakfast. "Obstinate as ever," he said. "I plan on talking with them after breakfast."

I knew what that meant. Firsthand experience reminded me just how unpleasant repercussions could be. Thanks to the battle, mine and Jazen's daunting sentence was cut short. "I think I'll eat quickly and start working."

Khalen laughed. "You don't want to be a part of the talk?"

I shook my head. "No thanks, my friend." I shuddered and took my place next to my brother and his mate.

Conversations about the battle were still fresh on everyone's tongue. I could tell Skye was feeling uncomfortable and moved to sit beside her.

"What bothers ye, lass?" I nudged her side to get her

to smile.

Erika discreetly watched me from the other side of the fire, but I definitely noticed. Occasionally, I met her eyes and smiled. Jazen noticed and quickly chastised her for teasing. A low growl rumbled in my chest.

Skye laughed. "So are you going to take that woman or not?"

"She looks taken already," I said.

Skye frowned with disappointment. Strange how that made my belly knot.

"It isn't like you to give up so easily," she prodded.

"How am I to take her when her bodyguard is at her side at every wakin' moment?"

"You walk up and tell her you need to speak privately with her."

I cocked a brow at her. "We both know how that will end."

"Jazen is under the same oath as you, Ian. He has no more say in this matter than you do. Erika belongs to you; she just needs to know you feel it too."

Now it was my turn to frown. "Did she say so to you?"

Skye laughed. "No, she doesn't have to. Women know women, Ian. She is strong and needs a man who is stronger. You just need to show her that side."

Aidan is the strong one, I thought. I was always the fun-loving one who made people laugh.

"There is a strength in you," she said. "You just need to let it come out."

With that, she stood and carried her plate to the soaking bins before wandering out to the pastures. I chuckled softly. "Damn, she did it again."

Khalen heard my curse and sidled up next to me. "She's good at deflecting the conversation away from her, eh?"

"Aye, she is. Somethin' eats at her though."

Khalen sipped his coffee. "The incident on the ship disturbs her," he said. "Her Shadow side nearly took over her soul. The memory of it still lingers."

"You of all people understand that pain," I said, remembering the awful moment when he was forced to take my sister's life. She was an evil, manipulative female, but Khalen had loved her just the same. A part of him died that day.

"I do," he responded, his eyes distant on the flames in the fire pit. "This is something she must work out on her own. It pains me to see her suffer so much, but the process is necessary."

I chuckled. "Ironic, is it not? She can heal any injury except the trauma haunting her soul."

"That too will heal with time." The sadness in his voice was eerily familiar. He worried about his mate, how could he not? Once a Spirian used his or her gifts to inflict harm on another soul, that Shadow door lingered partially open and tantalizing, often beyond restraint.

"She is strong," I offered. "She will recover and be tempered for it."

He placed his large hand on my shoulder as he stood. "I pray you're right," he said before turning and walking away.

I glanced over to where Erika and Jazen had been standing. They were gone. I looked around camp but did not see them. How could they have disappeared so quickly?

Aidan was conversing with Arcadie when I walked up. "Have you seen Erika?" I asked.

Aidan sighed. "I heard they were going to town and

then were planning to spend some time at Khalen's beach house."

I looked over at Arcadie, trying to gauge a reaction. There was none.

"They have not joined yet. Do ye not think it improper for them to be—together like that?"

Arcadie shrugged. "She's an adult, Ian. She makes her own choices now."

They would not join without ceremony, I thought. Arcadie would never allow it. Erika wouldn't allow it, would she?

I pulled my phone out and began texting her. *What are you thinking?* I typed.

It took several minutes before she responded. *We are just talking, Ian, nothing more.*

Staying with him at the beach house? I replied.

What are you talking about? We are just spending the day together.

I slipped my phone back into my pocket. Clearly confused, I sent a thought to Khalen.

Did you give Jazen and Erika permission to use your beach house?

They did not ask, he responded.

Aidan and Arcadie were still talking by the fire. I interrupted them again. "Are you sure you heard them correctly about spending time at the beach house?"

"I heard Jazen's thoughts, that's all." He studied me for a moment. "What's going on, Ian?"

"Something's not right."

Khalen walked toward us with keys in hand. "I'm heading to The Wellness Center to get some supplies." He looked between me and my brother before setting his gaze on me. "What's going on, Ian?"

"Something's wrong with Jazen," I said. "He intends to take Erika to your beach house, yet she knows nothing about it."

Arcadie looked at Khalen. "Did you know of this?"

Khalen shook his head. "Not until now."

"It is not like him to make such plans without asking," Arcadie said.

Jazen was an arrogant arse at times, but he was not an inconsiderate one.

"I'll alert Erika," said Arcadie.

"Is it wise to alarm her?" I asked. "If she acts with caution, Jazen will know something is wrong."

We all thought for a moment, shuffling uncomfortably, when Kitta joined our circle.

"Is Erika in trouble?" she asked.

Arcadie filled her in telepathically.

Kitta gasped. "We must warn her."

"I don't think that's a good idea," I repeated.

"Surely he won't hurt her," she stated. "We've known his family for years.

"I don't think it's him—entirely."

Khalen's brows pressed together. "What do you mean?"

I matched his expression, not really comfortable with what I was about to say. "I've worked with him, fought him, and battled beside him. In an odd sense, I know him."

"Know him?" Aidan drawled out.

I could only imagine what he was thinking. Typically when someone said they knew someone, there were sexual connotations attached. "Not like a lover," I clarified. "More like a—"

"Brother?" said Arcadie.

"Yes."

"So, if Jazen is not Jazen," said Case, "then who is he?"

Khalen looked at Arcadie. "Can you tap his thoughts?"

Arcadie shook his head. "He's not from my clan."

"My connection to him is not strong enough to span the distance," said Khalen.

"My daughter is not concerned," Arcadie admitted. "If something is amiss, she is not aware."

I pulled the Jeep's keys from my pocket. "I'm heading to the beach house," I said.

"Wait," said Khalen. "What's your plan?"

"I'll mask my presence in an illusion and observe. If something goes amiss, I'll intervene."

Aidan raised a brow with question. "And if Erika decides to give into Jazen's wishes, will you stand down?"

My gut churned at the thought. "She wouldn't do that," I growled.

"She wouldn't," Arcadie affirmed. "My daughter is many things, but careless with her affections, she is not."

"Do you think she's in danger?" asked Kitta.

We all just looked at her, not really knowing how to answer.

"I'll come with you," said Arcadie, placing a reassuring hand on his mate.

"Me too," said Aidan.

"No," I responded. "I can handle this, brother." It was an odd response, coming from me, and it earned a harsh look from the others.

"We are stronger together," Aidan reminded me. The doubt etched in his eyes made me feel small. I would always be his younger brother.

For years he had taken care of me, kept me safe in all situations. When we tangled in bars and clubs, he always had my back. That security allowed me to be careless and loose in my ways. I knew I was always safe with him. My own strength had never developed. Now I needed to stand on my own, to know my own power.

"I will go alone," I said.

"Take Arcadie with you," Khalen suggested, but the tone in his voice was more of a command.

I nodded, appreciating his support on this matter. He could have easily assigned Aidan to me as well and he knew it. Something in Khalen's eyes, however, showed marked concern.

"Keep your thoughts open to me," he said, gripping me with those unyielding gold eyes.

When Aidan started to say something, Khalen raised his hand to silence his words. "Go," he said, holding my brother back.

Telepathically, I assured Aidan I would be all right and sent him feelings of gratitude for all the times he stood beside me.

His response was pure confusion with a dose of concern.

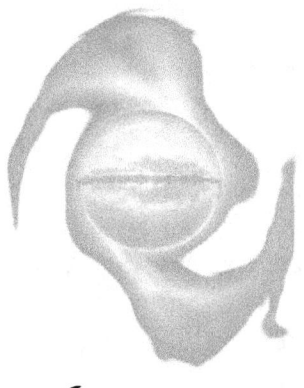

Chapter 18

ARCADIE AND I REACHED THE beach house in two hours. Having read his daughter's thoughts, he announced that they were still in Port Orchard eating an early dinner. There was no mention of going to the beach house afterward. If that was still Jazen's plan, he hadn't shared it with Erika yet.

We decided to eat as well and chose a high-end steak house on the water. It was within walking distance to the beach house and concealed my Jeep nicely.

The hostess sat us near a window and brought us two glasses of whiskey before taking our order. Arcadie studied me as if trying to gauge my motives.

"You think I've lost it," I commented, sipping my drink.

"Have you?"

I smiled. "It's easy to do when your daughter's concerned."

He raised his glass. "Touché."

"What kind of a Spirian can overtake a person like

Jazen?" I wondered out loud.

"An illusionist perhaps?"

"I know of none who can take over another's body."

"A wizard might."

I contacted Tetris, asking if he knew any wizard who possessed such talents. His reply was a definite no. According to him, a wizard with such capabilities would be highly unusual and would not escape the notice of other wizards.

I relayed the information to Arcadie without words. His response was a grunt as he sipped his drink.

Our food came, giving us both a chance to contemplate our thoughts as we ate.

"How are things going between you and my daughter?" he asked, testing my mood on the matter. It was understandable, really. He was here to support me. It seemed only right that he knew where my emotions stood.

"I love her, but she seems to have made her choice."

"So you've given up?"

"I cannot force her hand in my direction. You of all people should know that."

"Should I now?" he said, his brow quirked with an understanding I couldn't possibly comprehend.

"Meaning?"

"Some women must be shown what they want. You have not shown that you want her."

I sliced into my meat as if it were my enemy. My jaw tightened. "I believe I have."

"You've done the best you could. I understand."

I stabbed the piece of meat and stuffed it into my mouth with as much grace as a starving Neanderthal. I then choked it down, half chewed, almost grateful for the pain as it slid slowly down my throat.

"What would ye have me do?" I finally asked.

He laughed. "That, my boy, is something you must discover yourself."

"You talk in riddles, old man." I knew the jest was disrespectful toward a man of his stature, but my emotions were raw and he bloody knew it.

"Keep your head, young Ian. Right now, it is all you have."

I wanted to growl in response, but held my tongue. He was right. My emotions were off the chart and all I wanted was to battle someone to a bloody end. Sick thought, but an honest one. My gifts were strong, but nowhere near the strength of Arcadie's. Jazen, too, out-powered me. Aidan was right. I was a fool to go in this alone.

Well, fool or no, I thought, I'm doing it. I held my glass up to the waitress, prompting her for another.

Arcadie switched to wine. He sipped it now as his blue eyes studied me. The man could read me like a book and here I sat feeling like a Thomas the Train story—I think I can, I think I can.

"I have faith in you, Ian. Have faith in yourself."

I pushed my near-finished meal away and sipped my drink.

Arcadie's expression changed. Reading his thoughts, I knew that Erika had just been told about the beach house. Her response was not what Jazen expected.

"She's concerned," said Arcadie. "Jazen refused to take her home."

"Tell her it will be all right," I told him. "Tell her we are here but not to alert Jazen."

"No," he said. "Jazen will intercept. He will be listening."

"Can he do that?"

"Aye, he can."

"What's the plan?"

He cocked a brow like an old professor looking to catch a cheater on a test. "This is your gig, Ian, not mine. I'm merely along for the ride."

"We return to the beach house. I'll mask our presence and we wait."

"We still don't know who we're dealing with," said Arcadie.

"We can't do anything about that now."

We paid the bill, walked to the beach house and waited. My illusion was strong enough to mask our presence. The hum of my power radiated around us as we sat in silence.

"I'll take care of Jazen," I said. "You make sure Erika is safe."

Again, he looked at me with question. It was an odd choice of pairing, I know, given our various strengths. I was no match for Jazen let alone the entity that consumed him.

"If you need help," he said, "ask for it."

I nodded.

Jazen pulled up in Khalen's Escalade and the engine faded to silence. I heard the second car door slam and then the jangling of keys.

"I still don't know why you are bringing me here," said Erika, as they walked through the door. "I told my father I would return this evening."

"Contact him and let him know you've changed your mind. Tell him where you are, if you must."

She did, making sure to keep concern from her thoughts. She knew that Jazen was monitoring the communication.

Arcadie replied with a simple acknowledgment, though it was fuzzy from the illusion.

That fact did not escape Jazen's notice. He, too, contacted Arcadie and waited for a reply. If Arcadie did, Jazen would know and our plan would be foiled.

Jazen grabbed Erika and held her with an energetic hum. "Show yourselves," he said.

Erika gasped. "Jazen, you're hurting me."

He turned her around and kissed her hard on the lips. She struggled to get away but his hold on her was too strong.

My illusion shattered against the rage of adrenaline coursing my veins. Arcadie and I stood exposed.

"Let her go," I warned Jazen. My voice was deep and demanding to the point where even Erika looked surprised.

As soon as his attention was on me, his hold on Erika lessened. I immediately zapped him into an illusion.

"Get her out of here," I told Arcadie.

"I'm not leaving you," he said.

I had never battled someone trapped in my illusion. It was considered impossible. Right now, I didn't care. I pierced Jazen with an energetic blow, knocking him off his feet. The look of surprise on his face matched my own.

He countered with a blow to my midsection. Since it was my illusion, I dissipated the blow as if it were fog. This was my domain and whatever I thought would be revealed in vivid color.

Jazen screamed as I issued another attack. The entity that consumed him separated. Jazen collapsed.

Keeping one person in this complex illusion was difficult enough. Keeping Jazen and the Shadow I now recognized as Tanen, was near to impossible. I released

Jazen and retained Tanen. In theory the task sounds simple enough but, it is highly taxing. My illusion wavered.

"I thought you were destroyed in the explosion," I said, hoping to distract Tanen from my weakening illusion.

He laughed. "I have an alliance with the dark one, Azazel. I cannot be destroyed."

Now would be a good time to leave, I told Arcadie.

Tanen roared again with laughter. "It's too late for that."

With a wave of his hand, he obliterated my illusion. The force of the breach slammed me back against the wall, knocking the air from my lungs.

Arcadie engaged with Tanen. Jazen lay unconscious. Erika tried to pull him from the battle, but he was far too heavy.

I placed her into an illusion along with Jazen. It was a simple protection and one that Tanen could easily breach, but it was better than nothing.

I cast a blow to Tanen. He countered with something that rivaled the force of a speeding Mac truck. He then slammed through my illusion and grabbed Erika's throat.

"I could snap her like a twig," he said, his hand tightening around her neck. She struggled to breathe as he lifted her off her feet.

Arcadie was about to end the fool's life, but in turn, the act would cost him his own. Tanen was too powerful.

"No!" I shouted. "He's mine."

Tanen laughed. With a thought, I turned Erika's throat into red hot iron. Tanen dropped her with howl of pain. Before he could counter, I surrounded him with venomous snakes to keep him busy.

He laughed, ignoring the illusion until one of the snakes bit him. Again he raged with pain. The hum in the room was deafening. I created more illusions, overwhelming him with all the distractions my demented imagination could summon.

Trying to push his way through them was draining. I could see it in his fading eyes. He called out to his new master Azazel, but there was no reply.

A feeling of calm swept through me as I allowed my mind to venture into the depths of illusion. Like a dream, I conjured creatures from other dimensions, mesmerized by the image of dragons devouring the evil before me. Fire enveloped him, drowning the horrible screams escaping his lips.

With my last bit of energy, I swept him up in a cloud of flame and watched as he vanished in ash and smoke.

I RECOVERED IN MY BROTHER'S CABIN some time later. I don't remember the journey home, or anything after the battle. Part of me wondered if the whole thing had been nothing but a horrible dream.

"You're awake," came a familiar voice in the doorway. Erika looked radiant. She held a cup of steaming liquid in her hand.

"Skye told me to bring you this. Elle prepared it and said it would help you recover."

I wrinkled my nose. I had tasted that woman's vile brews before. "What is it?"

She smelled it and tried to hide her reaction. "Nothing I can identify."

I took the cup from her hands. The concoction smelled like dirt with a hint of seaweed. "Ugh," I said, placing the cup on the end table.

"How are you feeling?"

I sat up, allowing the covers to slide down my torso. Someone had stripped my clothes off before placing me in the bed.

Erika's face blushed, a color that deepened as I smiled in response.

"Well," she said, looking away. "I should let you wake up and get dressed."

I grabbed her arm as she started to stand. "Dun't go." Trying to ease her discomfort, I pulled the covers up to my chest. "How long have I been sleepin'?"

"Two days."

She tried pulling her arm from my hand but my grip only tightened.

"Tell me what happened," I said, moving my hands to hers. They were cold and slightly damp. She was nervous but didn't try to pull away.

"How did you know about Jazen?" she asked. "My father said you knew something was wrong."

I shrugged. "I just knew, that's all. He was behavin' oddly and my gut responded."

She laughed nervously. "That's quite the instinct you have."

My eyes narrowed. "Why are ye so nervous, lass?"

She immediately stiffened. "I'm not."

I pulled her hand to my lips and brushed soft kisses over the back of her fingers. "Really?"

"Stop it, Ian. You're playing with me." She tried pulling her hand away. I wouldn't allow it.

"I'm not playing," I said, with more seriousness in my voice than even I thought possible.

"You shouldn't do that," she said.

"Why?"

This time, she did pull away. "Because Jazen has asked

me to join him."

My heart beat so loudly, I was sure it would soon make an appearance outside of my chest. "And what was yer answer?" I asked coldly.

She looked down. "I said yes."

"When did he ask ye?"

She stood and walked toward the window. "Last night."

"Does my opinion matter?"

She turned and looked at me, her blue eyes a cobalt flame against an icy exterior. "You will always be my friend, Ian."

"Yer friend," I muttered. "We are more than that," I said, "and ye know it."

"Are we?"

I stood and reached for my clothes. She quickly turned away.

"What are you doing, Ian?"

"I'm stoppin' ye from makin' a mistake."

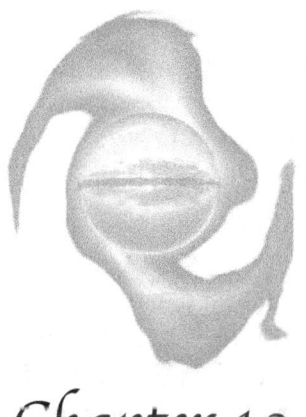

Chapter 19

-Elle-

THE PAST THREE DAYS WERE torturous as I watched Drew and Connor work together. Drew's mate-to-be was not around and I assumed she had returned to her clan. Drew would no doubt join her after the camp was restored.

I did my best to avoid him, though his presence was like a chocolate cake that I couldn't have. Long walks in the woods helped a bit, but my avoidance of everyone created tension during meals.

I sipped my coffee and stared out at the camp, watching as everyone chipped in. I was not exactly doing my part and felt the guilt of it. Putting my cup in the sink, I made my way out of Skye and Khalen's yurt and walked toward a group of people erecting a frame where Drew's old cabin had been.

"Welcome to your new home," said Caleb, orchestrating the construction.

"No," I said, shaking my head. "This is Drew's old home. I couldn't stay here."

"Well, you are," he said coldly.

"I liked my old cabin."

"That was a guest cabin," he said. "You are no longer a guest."

The frame resembled the same layout that Drew's cabin had before the fire destroyed it. My heart sank.

"I can't stay here," I said quietly. "Please."

"Take it up with Khalen," he said.

That wasn't helpful. Convincing Khalen to change his mind was like trying to stop a storm. "I'm taking it up with you," I said. "I cannot and will not stay here."

"What's the problem?" Khalen said from behind. The way he could move without a sound was unnerving.

Caleb smiled. "Why don't you tell him, sweetheart?"

I glared at him before meeting Khalen's cold stare. "I cannot live here," I said, resting my hands on my hips.

He glanced down at me and his lips grew firm. "But you will," he replied, his tone even and firm.

"This is Drew's old home. I don't want to stay here."

"You have no feelings for the man. Why does it matter?"

Pitting myself against the arrogant, unyielding leader was not a good strategy. I decided to take the female route and feign despair. Slowly, I removed my hands from my hips, glanced down at the ground and bit my lower lip. "I do have feelings for him, Khalen, and knowing he will never return here again weighs heavy on my heart."

"Does it now?" he said, stepping back to study me. I could hear laughter in his voice. It took everything I had to keep my anger in check.

"Yes, I made a mistake. I really don't need this house

to remind me of it every day."

"So, given another chance, you would do things differently?"

Knowing my answer would be safe, I met his golden eyes. "I would."

He laughed before turning and walking away.

"Does this mean I can live elsewhere?" I called after him.

He turned around long enough to answer with a hearty, unchallengeable, "No!"

"I despise that man," I growled under my breath.

Caleb laughed as well.

"I'm glad I provide you all with so much merriment," I said, turning and walking away.

This entire camp was heartless, I decided. Unfortunately, living without them was not a choice I wanted to make. Shadows officially scared me now and I did not want to make myself vulnerable by stepping out on my own. The book tour that my agent, James, wanted me to embark on was beginning to sound intriguing. I could ask Tetris to be my escort and get away from here.

A smile crept over me. That would definitely raise a few eyebrows. I silently giggled. Drew's union was coming up fast. I didn't want to be around for it and this book tour would be the perfect excuse to miss it.

THAT NIGHT, WE ALL SHARED dinner outside, which was becoming quite common during the dry summer months. The season seemed to have come late this year, but I certainly wasn't complaining.

After arranging the dates with James, I was ready to announce my untimely tour. Khalen would choke on it,

I was certain. Well, my schedule was set and there was absolutely nothing he could do about it.

New hope put a bounce in my step that everyone noticed as I made my way to the food. I could feel Khalen's eyes pierce through my head but I had learned from Skye to block my thoughts. I silently sent her a thank you.

With a plate full of food and a glass of red wine in my hand, I joined the group by the fire. Even the presence of Drew didn't disrupt my mood. He would be mated soon and was no longer my concern. Although that thought saddened me a bit, knowing I would not have to witness it was a huge relief. I might even find a new clan to live with in Europe during my tour. Wouldn't that be perfect?

"You look like a cat with a fresh kill," said Skye as I sat down beside her. "What's up?"

"I'm going on a book tour in Europe next week," I announced. I then looked over at Tetris. "Since you were planning to return to England soon, I was hoping you would escort me."

Tetris looked at Khalen and then slowly shook his head. "I cannot, lass, I'm sorry. I am to begin young Gabrihen's training shortly after Drew's union."

My heart sank. I didn't have the foresight to come up with a contingency plan. Now what?

"Can someone else escort me?" I looked over at Skye.

"I'm helping with the union," she said.

I looked around for Liam, the young doctor who was sweet on Ember.

"Liam took Ember to his parents' place in Oregon," said Khalen.

How did he read my mind? I was purposely keeping him out.

He smiled.

My hopes were starting to shrivel. "Well, I'm taking Connor with me, so technically I will not be unescorted."

"He is not an adult male," Khalen said.

My hopes brightened as I spotted Seth sitting next to his mother. "Seth, will you escort me?"

His smile brightened and then faded as he looked over to Khalen. "I can't," he said. "Sorry."

"Why?" I asked.

Seth looked over at Khalen. "I must be there for Drew's union."

"Err," I growled. "Is Drew's union the only focus of this camp?"

"Not for you," said Drew, setting his empty plate aside and reaching for a glass of wine.

"Yes," I huffed. "Well, my plans are nothing if I cannot find an escort."

"I'll be happy to do so after the ceremony," he said.

I wanted to wipe that damn smile off his face but restrained that urge. "That would hardly be appropriate," I seethed. "I'm sure your new mate would object."

"She wouldn't dare," he replied.

"It's settled, then," said Khalen, slapping Drew's back. "You will leave for the book tour in three weeks."

"No," I argued. "I'm scheduled to leave next week."

"Not without an escort," said Khalen.

"This isn't fair," I retorted.

"Such is life," he replied, verbally dismantling my plans.

"I want to hurt him," I whispered to Skye.

"You're welcome to try," she said, scooting away from her mate. He grabbed her waist and pulled her up close beside him.

We both knew it was useless to try. Khalen could

destroy me with a single thought, though I knew he wouldn't. He had promised Avel to keep me safe. Khalen wanted to torture me instead, I was certain.

I picked up my plate and stared down at the food. I just wasn't hungry. I stood and carried the plate to Maiyun.

Drew came over and took the plate from my hands. "You need to eat," he said.

"I'm not hungry."

"Eat anyway," he demanded. "Come, let's talk," he added, leading me away from the others.

"Where's Tamarla?" I asked.

"Home," he replied rather tersely.

"Shouldn't she be here with you?"

"No," he said, setting down the two glasses of wine in his hand. With a thought, he moved a log over for us to share. "Here, sit."

He placed my plate in my hands. All I could do was push the food aside with my fork.

"Would you like me to feed you?" he asked.

My eyes widened. "I most certainly would not!"

"Then you best feed yourself." There was no question in his tone, and he was just arrogant enough to try to force me. Not wanting to cause a scene, I managed to nudge some of Eve's shepherd's pie into my mouth. It was delicious.

He wrapped his arm around me. "That's my girl," he said.

"I'm not your girl," I reminded him. "And your arm around my shoulders is inappropriate."

He reached down and handed me my glass of wine.

"Thank you," I said, taking a sip.

"You're welcome."

His arm returned to my shoulders. I glanced over at it.

"Inappropriate," I reminded him.

"I will determine what is and what isn't appropriate."

"What would Tamarla think if she were here?"

"She isn't, and I'm sure she would say nothing of my actions if she were."

That was an odd statement, I thought. "Funny," I said. "She didn't seem like the overly obedient type."

He huffed. "She's not."

"What do you like about her?" I asked, taking another bite of the layered stew.

"She's beautiful."

I nodded with agreement.

"She's witty and honest."

Again I nodded.

"She treats me with respect."

I stopped chewing, suddenly regretting my question.

"She has a beautiful voice," he continued. "And she knows—"

"Okay," I said, holding up my hand. "I get it. You love pretty much everything about her." I set my plate down.

He picked it up again. "Eat, Elle."

"You are not my charge," I reminded him.

He looked over at Khalen. "The command comes from him," he said.

"And if I refuse?"

"He has given me permission to force you."

"You wouldn't dare!"

He raised an eyebrow as if questioning my assumption, and I quickly took another bite before polishing off my wine.

"You asked me what I liked about her, not what I loved."

"I don't want to know what you love about her." I

handed him my empty glass of wine. "Would you mind?"

Khalen came over with a bottle in hand. He refilled my glass and then set the bottle beside Drew with a smile.

"Thank you," he said to the leader.

"No problem," Khalen replied, giving me the look that nearly shouted with victory.

So much for my hopeful reprieve from Drew with his possessive arm around my shoulders.

"Are you sure?"

"About what?" I said, finishing my meal and setting down the empty plate.

"You don't want to know what I love about her?"

"No, I don't."

Finally, silence—beautiful, peaceful silence.

"Okay," he finally said.

More silence. His arm tightened around me, making me feel uncomfortable.

"We should probably rejoin the others," I said. "I'm feeling kind of cold."

Using his impressive telekinetic skills, he formed a pile of dry branches and then poof, created a fire.

"That was cool," I said, reveling in the heat.

"Nothing," he said.

I looked at him questioningly.

"There is nothing I love about her."

I huffed. "Then why are you joining with her?"

"I'm not," he said, staring into the flames.

"Oh," I replied, feeling at a loss for something more intelligent to say. "I'm sorry," soon followed.

"Really?"

I chuckled. "No, not really." Another thought passed through my mind. "So if you're not getting hitched, you'll be free to escort me to Europe."

"In three weeks," he said.

"Why? The whole reason we were waiting was because everyone else thinks you're getting married."

"Not married," he corrected. "United. There's a difference, Elle."

"Whatever. You're not, so that makes you free to escort me."

He pulled something out of his pocket. When he opened his hand, I saw the pendant that had last hung around Tamarla's delicate neck. My stomach sank.

"I want to have you as my mate, Elle. You said that you loved me. I assume you are ready to give me your heart."

I opened my mouth to protest, but nothing came out.

"If I'm wrong," he said, "close my hand and I will not ask you again."

This is your chance, I told myself. You screwed up once, don't do it again. My hand slowly moved toward his. Part of me wanted to close his fingers and never look at that pendant again. Another part of me knew that he was the one I wanted. With shaking fingers, I took the pendant from his hand.

"Your entire heart," he said. "Promise now, Elle."

"My entire heart," I said. Though the voice was not my own, the words were. This was what Avel wanted. It was what he needed, I thought.

"I don't care what Avel wants," said Drew, his voice edged with warning. "I want to know what you want."

I picked up the pendant and handed it to him. "I want you to place this around my neck and never let me go," I croaked out. My throat felt tight, nearly choking my air. "No matter what, never let me go."

He took the chain and slipped it over my head. "You have my word, love." His lips pressed against mine so tenderly that I started to sob.

"The union everyone is planning is ours. You will be there."

"Yes," I sobbed. "I want to be there." I held him tighter than I thought was possible. The past few days had been hell.

He held me for a while, his warm breath feathering over the top of my head.

A ruckus stirred at the main fire. Ian and Jazen were face to face. Arcadie and Khalen jumped between them.

"Oh, oh," Drew said. Taking my hand, he led me back to the main fire.

~ I a n ~

"IAN, STOP," ERIKA YELLED. "PLEASE, you're not right in the head."

"What is this about, Ian," Arcadie asked. His strong, unyielding hand gripped my arm.

Kitta looked curious. By all rights, she should have been terrified. "Ian?" she inquired.

"I want Erika to be my mate," I shouted, as if wanting the entire camp to know.

"She's already agreed to be mine," said Jazen.

I looked at Erika. "Is this truly what you want?"

"Yes," she said. "It is." Her thoughts said otherwise.

My mind snapped. I broke away from Arcadie and reached for Erika. I claimed her lips with a possession I had never displayed before. She didn't pull away. Instead, she melted like chocolate in my arms.

Continuing to hold her, I looked to Jazen, still bound by the promise we had made to Khalen not to fight one another.

"I formally challenge you for her hand, Jazen. Do you accept?"

Jazen looked over at Erika, still in a stupor after our kiss. "I do," he replied.

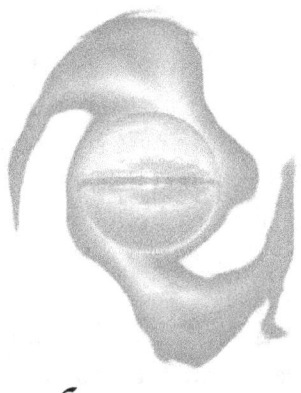

Chapter 20

AIDAN STORMED TOWARD ME WITH a chiseled expression. "What are ye doin'?"

I removed my shirt and entered the circle that Khalen had defined. "I'm claimin' what is mine," I said.

"He can kill ye," said Aidan. "In case ye haven't noticed, yer still weak with exhaustion."

I smiled. "Killin' is against the rules," I reminded him. "Besides, I'm well rested now and fueled with anger."

Aidan threw up his hands. "Watch yer left side. Keep yer guard, mind yer hook," he said.

"Yes, coach," I jibed. He and I had fought since we were old enough to walk. At times, it was how we vented our anger. I was no stranger to brawling and he knew it.

Khalen entered the circle. "No gifts will be used. The first man whose knee touches the ground loses. Stay in the ring or forfeit the fight. Understood?"

I nodded, and so did Jazen.

Khalen left the ring. "Begin."

Jazen and I circled one another. He, too, was no

stranger to fighting. He stood a good three inches above me and carried at least thirty pounds of extra brawn. I had lost weight during the past three days and it showed.

He threw the first punch, which I easily dodged. I countered with a blow to his gut. It barely registered a grunt. For the first time since I challenged him, I felt the mistake of my actions.

"She enjoyed the kiss," I said, trying to knock him off guard. His reply was a solid blow to my temple. I staggered back, struggling to remain in the ring.

At the last minute, I skirted around him lest he push me out of the ring all together. I landed a good blow to his jaw, sending him back. I followed with a punch to his ribs and an elbow to his face, splitting his lip.

He came back faking a low punch and rising with a solid hit to my nose. It snapped like a dry twig. Blood oozed down my face. God, I loved a good fight.

"She said she loves me," he seethed, blood spewing from his torn lip.

New anger fueled my failing energy. I punched him again in the mouth. "She won't say it again," I assured him. "She kissed me back, and there was hunger in it."

His fist found my chin, ringing my ears. I stumbled back, my knees threatening to buckle beneath me. I roared, urging them to work.

My eyes blurred after enduring several blows. My legs had since grown numb.

Jazen pulled back his fist. "She's mine, Ian," he said, aiming one last final blow.

I ducked sideways and met his face with my fist. Following through, I sent him flying out of the ring.

"Not anymore," I stammered before my legs collapsed and I yielded to darkness.

"He's not moving," I heard Erika say. My eyes were still very swollen and I couldn't coax them to open. In fact, my entire body felt numb. I tried moving my finger to no avail.

I tried reaching her with my mind but she didn't respond. Voices echoed around me before quickly fading.

"If he doesn't recover, I'm making you mine," said Jazen. That did it. My eyes flew open and my fists tightened. "Over m' dead body," I growled.

"Easy," said Skye. "I'm not done with you yet."

"Leave him," said Jazen. "The bloke deserves to suffer a bit."

"Stop it!" said Erika. "It was a clean fight."

"Are ye askin' for a rematch?" I said, sounding a bit drunk.

"I am," he responded.

"There will be no rematch," said Khalen. "The fight was fought and won."

"I still have the final choice," said Erika.

I grabbed her hand and pulled her down to meet me, despite Skye's groan. "No, you don't."

"Can you two please give this a rest? If I don't set your nose properly, Khalen will have to re-break it."

"I'll do it," said Jazen.

Skye turned to him and glared. "Erika, please, step outside."

"Gladly," she said. "This place reeks of testosterone."

I growled as the bone ground against its severed counterpart.

"Got it," said Skye.

I glared at her, knowing she had deliberately neglected to remove my pain.

She smiled sweetly in return and the pain vanished. "Be nice," she warned.

"Yer mate has a mean streak in her," I said to Khalen.

"Then you best mind your mouth," he warned. "It has gotten you into enough trouble already."

"There," said Skye. "You're both back together."

Aidan helped me stand from the dirt. "Come on," he said. "Let's get ye cleaned up."

A FTER HAVING THE NIGHT TO recover, I began looking for Erika. Skye said she was out by the lake. Her thoughts were closed to me.

"Hey," I said as I approached her from behind.

She turned to face me before returning her gaze to the lake.

"Are ye angry, lass?"

"What gives you that idea?"

I pursed my lips. "Cold shoulder, terse response, avoidance, ang—"

"Yes," she snapped. "I'm angry."

"Care to talk about it, love?"

She brushed my hand from her shoulder. "No."

I spun her around to face me. "Look me in the eyes and tell me you'd rather mate with Jazen."

She looked away but said nothing.

"In my eyes," I warned her.

I could feel her soften against me as her eyes met mine.

"Do you want to join with Jazen?" I asked, my voice softer now.

When she tried to look away, my grip tightened.

"No," she whispered.

"Tell me what you want," I said, confused by her admission.

"I want to know that you love me," she said. "Or do you want me only because you know you can't have me?"

My lips crushed down upon hers, demanding and possessive as they were before my challenge. The battle between me and that Shadow, Tanen had changed me somehow. I felt strong and more in control than I had ever been. For the first time in my life, I knew what I wanted and had the courage to go after it. I wanted this woman.

"I love ye, lass. Can ye not see that?"

"Say it again," she said, her lips slightly swollen.

"I love ye, Erika, and I want ye to be my mate."

She smiled. "Thank you," she said.

"Christ, woman. Dun't tell me that was all ye needed to hear."

"You could have saved yourself a fight," she said, rising on her toes to kiss me.

"Ye could 'ave told me, lass."

"It's not the same," she said. "You should have known."

I growled, lifting her into my arms. "We'll have to work on our communication skills," I said, pressing my lips to hers.

Jazen was working up a sweat pounding nails into boards when Erika and I entered the camp. His eyes were dull and sad when he looked up at us.

"The boards are crooked," I said.

He tossed them aside. "Doesn't matter. They're for your bloody cabin."

"Mother's calling me," said Erika. "I need to go."

We both watched as she scampered toward the guest lodge.

"You best treat her right," said Jazen.

"I always have," I assured him, holding the next set of boards together.

"You trust my aim?" he asked.

"I do," I replied.

We worked together in silence for a moment before he spoke again.

"Thank you," he said.

"For?"

"Saving me from Tanen."

"You would have done the same," I said.

"Would I?"

I smiled. "I'm sure of it."

"Don't be," he said. "I'm not sure I would have."

That unsettling statement sent me adrift. I lowered the next set of boards.

"I'm not the man you think I am," he said. "I'm an opportunist. I wanted Erika for her status. Uniting with her would make me strong. I'm the future leader of the largest clan in New Zealand, Ian. I need a strong mate."

"Ye'll find one," I assured him.

"Not with her blood."

"You are strong enough without it," I assured him.

He chuckled. "Not according to my father. The chance of this union made him proud of me for the first time in my life."

"Ye join for love, lad, not for status."

"Not when you're a leader," he said. "Khalen knows the truth of that one."

"Khalen loves Skye," I said.

"Yes, of course he does. She's the granddaughter of the great Shanuk. What's there not to love?"

"He didn't know that until just recently. She didn't

even know that."

Jazen tossed the hammer down. "Doesn't matter," he said, walking away.

"Jazen," I called to him.

He turned.

"I want you to be her templar."

He smiled sadly before turning to leave.

It was an honor to be chosen as a woman's templar. I understood his reaction, though. If the table were turned, I would already be plotting his demise.

I laughed inwardly. He wouldn't be, would he?

A strange car came barreling down the driveway toward camp. It came to a sudden stop right in front of Khalen and Case.

I ran toward them and was soon standing beside Aidan and Arcadie. Jazen also stood guard.

Ember flung the door open and rushed toward Khalen. "You have to stop her," she cried.

Khalen probed her scattered thoughts and quickly became irate. "Who?"

"Jade," she nearly screamed.

"Ember, calm down. I can't make any sense of your thoughts."

Liam stepped out of the car, shaking his head. "She's been hysterical since we found out."

Skye and Eve came running toward us.

Ember ran to them, crying. "You have to help her," she cried.

Khalen noticed the clan gathering, all curious about the commotion. "Inside," he said, walking toward his yurt.

The rest of us followed.

Eve and Skye set upon the task of making tea and cookies while Khalen stoked the fire. He patiently waited for Ember to calm down before asking questions. Liam did his best to ease her mind, but quickly gave up when she insisted on pacing.

"It's craziness," she said, waving her hands for emphasis. "She wants to be a Spirian like Eve. I told her she's mad, but she wouldn't listen."

"Jade wants to be a Spirian?" asked Eve.

"Yes. That cowboy she met at the restaurant has filled her head with rubbish."

"What cowboy?" asked Khalen, clearly confused.

"You have to stop them," said Ember.

"Jade met a man from Texas," Skye explained. "She left with him. I tried to tell you but you were busy at the time."

"And he was a Spirian?" asked Khalen.

"Yes," Eve and Skye said simultaneously.

"Where's Tetris?" asked Khalen.

"He's coming," said Case, after summoning him with a thought.

Tetris knocked and then entered the already crowded yurt. Gabrihen stood by his side.

Khalen encouraged his boy to join him on the couch. The boy did so enthusiastically.

"Did Jade leave your company with another Spirian?" Khalen asked Tetris.

"Aye, she did," he answered.

"Did you recognize him?"

Tetris shook his head. "He was no Shadow, I assure you."

Khalen nodded.

"Where is she now?" he asked Ember.

"Somewhere in Texas," she replied.

"That doesn't help, Ember."

"Please Khalen, you need to stop them."

"I cannot stop them if I cannot find them," he replied. What's his name?"

"Gus," she said. "No, Mel."

"I think it was Bud," said Liam.

Khalen rolled his eyes.

"Bud," Ember shouted. "Yes, it was Bud."

Bud was not a Spirian name, so it must have been short for something. What was a Spirian doing up here from Texas?

"What else did she tell you?" asked Khalen.

Skye and Eve brought over some tea and cookies before sitting beside Ember and offering her comfort. I, for one, was hungry and snagged the first cookie—peanut butter with oatmeal.

"She wanted to unite with him. I told her how dangerous that was, but she kept saying how Eve survived and so could she."

"When?" asked Khalen.

"She told me this morning," Ember stated, clearly confused.

"No!" Khalen snapped. "When is their union?"

"Oh," said Ember, searching her memory that was obviously as scattered as her thoughts. "Um—soon, very soon."

Again Khalen rolled his eyes. Skye rubbed his arm, reminding him to be patient.

"So," he said, "I'm supposed to find a Spirian named Bud in Texas that is scheduled to unite—soon?"

"Yes!" Ember exclaimed. "But you need to hurry."

Skye must have sensed her mate's building fury because she ushered Ember out of the yurt.

Khalen looked over at Liam, who was busy piling a

plate full of cookies. "Tell me what you know," he drawled, knowing the man knew nothing of importance.

Liam shrugged. "Not much more than what you've been told," he said, pouring a cup of tea.

Eve placed her hand on his. "Liam, please. If you can think of anything that can help, let us know. Jade is in serious danger."

Liam sat back, racking his thoughts. "I didn't talk to Jade, but I thought I overheard her say something about Austin. She also mentioned the twentieth."

"The twentieth of what?" asked Khalen.

Liam shook his head.

"Christ," Khalen snarled. "There must be a dozen clans in Austin."

"Let's start contacting them," said Case.

"It doesn't make sense for them to return to his clan," I said.

All eyes focused on me.

"He knows he's breaking the Spirian laws," I explained. "He won't return unless Jade survives and becomes a Spirian."

"With no birthrights?" asked Case. "She would be questioned and then killed along with her mate. The laws cannot be broken."

"True," I said. "I'm not convinced they're thinking along the same lines, though."

"Still," said Khalen, "we need to find them."

Skye entered the yurt. "His name is Buchanis," she blurted out.

"How do you get Bud out of that?" I questioned.

"Buchanis," Khalen muttered. "Never heard of him."

"Nor I," said Case.

"I can ask the Council," said Arcadie.

"No time," said Khalen. "The twentieth is less than a week away."

"How do we know she meant this month?" I questioned.

"Because Jade has no patience and could not stand to wait another month," said Khalen.

No one argued with that one.

"Ask the Council," said Khalen. "Either way, this Bud character will have to answer for his actions." He looked over at Liam. "Take Ember to the beach house. I'll call you if anything turns up."

Liam nodded.

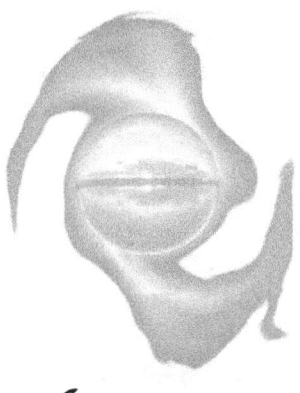

Chapter 21

SOMETIME DURING THE NIGHT, KAILI screamed; the quieter twin of Skye and Khalen's oldest daughters. I heard Skye and Khalen scramble down the hall toward her room. Soon after, Skye came into my room.

"Ian," she whispered. "Ian, wake up."

I rolled over. "What is it, lass?"

"Something is wrong with Belle."

I whipped off the covers, threw on some clothes and followed her out of the room.

It was dark and the night was silent—eerily so. Guided only by partial moonlight, we made our way to the barn.

"I feel her pain," said Kaili. "Here." She pointed to her belly.

"Okay, baby," said Skye. "We're going to help her, okay?"

Kaili nodded. Her gift of communicating with animals was growing stronger. She had shown signs of it last year but her comprehension had been sketchy at best. No one doubted her now.

Belle was lying under her shed, groaning and straining for every breath.

"Oh God!" Skye exclaimed, running to the mare's side. Her hands desperately scanned the mare for injury but found nothing.

"Ian," she cried. "Can you help her?"

"Get my bag from the barn," I told Kaili. She ran back to the large dark building.

Khalen knelt down, feeling the mare's breath. "It's cold and damp," he said.

I shook my head and telepathically contacted my brother. I think she's colicing, I said to him.

"I can't help her," cried Skye. "I'm trying but I can't."

"Ease her pain," I told her. "You can do that."

I looked at Khalen and silently told him to scan the mare's intestines. Look for a kink, I told him.

Belle's breathing was labored and weak.

"I see something," said Khalen. He touched my arm and sent me an image of what he saw.

"Her gut is twisted," I said.

Kaili came running back with my bag in hand. I removed my stethoscope and listened to the mare's heart. It was slow and irregular.

"She's going into circulatory arrest," I said. "Khalen, see if you can untwist her gut."

Aidan brought over a bucket of vegetable oil and a long stomach tube.

"Okay," said Khalen, "She's clear."

"We need to get her to stand," I said.

Khalen hefted her up telekinetically, a feat that was difficult to master. Having tried the skill myself, I knew it was similar to threading a needle when you had no feeling in your fingers and limited vision.

The mare groaned. Her eyes were cloudy and her breathing continued to labor.

"Continue to ease her pain," I told Skye. "We need to lubricate her intestines."

Aidan handed me the tube. He was trained on small animal care. Large animals were more my specialty. I slowly fed the tube up through the mare's nostrils and down into her stomach. She was weak enough not to offer a fight.

I emptied the bucket of oil into the tube before pulling it out of her stomach.

"Now what?" asked Skye.

"We wait."

Khalen telekinetically urged the blockage in her gut to move. The oil provided a helpful push. Before long, Belle's vitals improved and the blockage was expelled.

Skye hugged her daughter. "Thank you," she cried.

"Will she be all right, mummy?"

I nodded to Skye.

"Yes, sweetheart, Belle's going to be fine now."

"My belly doesn't hurt anymore," said Kaili.

Khalen swept the young girl into his arms. "You did well, little one."

Kaili rested her head against his shoulder and wrapped her tiny arms over her father's wide chest, barely reaching across it. At eleven years old, she was small for her age, reminding me of a delicate flower. Her twin sister, Shaiya, was slightly taller, yet hadn't shown signs of any gifts yet other than a vague promise of healing like her mum.

"Get some rest," I told them. "I'll keep an eye on her for a while."

Skye gave the mare a hug and then allowed her mate to guide her back to their yurt. *Thank you*, she silently said to me. The simple thought was filled with so much gratitude that it filled my center with warmth that could only come from sincere love.

No problem, I answered.

"You're quite the hero this week," said Aidan, rolling the hose up and placing it back into the bucket.

I didn't feel much like a hero. My feet were wet and my body was covered in oil.

Aidan laughed. "I'm proud of you, brother," he said, slapping my shoulder.

I watched as he carried the bucket back to the barn. I then realized I was standing in the paddock with a mare that had once tried to kill me. She looked at me as if to say, "I'm really not in the mood."

I scratched behind her ear. "I hear ye," I said.

MORNING CAME FAR TOO EARLY. I was still in the barn lying on top of the hay pile when I awakened to the acrid scent of mold. I heard someone rustle about the place. Glancing over the barrier that separated the aisle and feed room, I saw Skye sorting through her grooming brushes.

"Mornin'."

She jumped. "Oh, Ian, you scared me."

"Mmm," I moaned, pulling myself free of the hay pile. "Have you been feedin' this to Belle?"

"No," she said. That is what is left over when I clean her stall. I was planning to add it to the compost pile. Why?"

I sifted through the pile. "It's full of mold."

"Mold?"

She walked over to the bales of hay in the far corner of

the barn and began smelling them. "This seems all right."

I pulled out a center flake and carried it out to the light. "Hmm. No, this stuff is no good, lass. Ye best toss it to the goats."

Her forehead wrinkled with confusion and concern. "What's wrong with it?"

I showed her the patches of white on the tender alfalfa flowers. She couldn't see them, of course. She sniffed the area.

"I can't smell anything but alfalfa," she said.

I banged the flake against the railing a few times. "Here, lass, now smell."

She wrinkled her nose and pulled back. "Lord, that's awful."

I followed her gaze to the towering bales of hay. "We need to check them all," I said.

"That's a shame. We just received that load two weeks ago."

"This might be what caused Belle to colic last night."

She placed her hand over her mouth. "I nearly killed her."

"Easy, lass, ye couldn't 'ave known."

"I could have killed her, Ian."

I pulled her into my arms and offered what I hoped was an assuring hug. "Ye didn't, and she's fine now."

When she let me go, I handed her a bucket. "Fill this halfway with hot water," I told her.

When she returned, I added bran, steel cut oats and wheat mash to the water until it started to thicken. "Give it a bit to soften," I told her. "Then give it to Belle. It's easy on her stomach and will help move things through her system."

"Thank you," she quietly said.

I smiled at her. She had been in such a funk this past week, and it broke my heart to see such deep despair in those liquid eyes. Even Khalen couldn't make her smile.

Both Case and Arcadie said it would take time for her to recover from the ordeal on the ship. She was becoming more reclusive these days and something had to be done.

I watched as Skye brought the mare in to eat the mash. Skye picked up a curry brush and circled it down the mare's sticky coat. Belle was still covered in mud.

"How are the union plans comin' along?" I asked, needing to break the silence.

"Good. I understand you and Erika will be having your ceremony as well?"

"Aye."

"She's good for you, Ian."

"That she is, lass."

"Any news on Jade?"

"No," I sadly reported.

"There's only a few days left," she said.

"Aye."

Silence fell between us. I picked up a stiff brush and began flicking the mud free from Belle's coat.

"Tell me what happened on the ship," I finally said.

She dropped the curry into the bucket and picked up a stiff-bristled brush. "Not much to tell you, really. Tanen manipulated me to use my gifts to cause harm, and I complied."

"Complied?"

"Yes. I did as he instructed."

More silence followed. I wished Shanuk were here. He would know what to say. I had no idea.

Arcadie quietly entered the barn escaping Skye's notice. He silently warned me not to alarm her. I nodded, continuing to brush Belle's coat.

"I'm sure ye had good reason," I prompted, wanting her to continue.

"Not really," she said. "I simply gave in to his demands."

I smirked. "That doesn't sound like ye, lass. Ye dun't give in to anyone's demands, not even Khalen's."

A smile drifted over her and then quickly dissolved into despondence. "Tanen destroyed my will," she said. "Made me not care anymore." Tears started to well in her eyes. "I don't know if I can get it back."

I dropped the brush into the bucket and walked up to her. "Ye still care, lass. I saw it in ye last night when this little beauty was sick. I felt it as you healed my wounds."

"On the surface, yes," she said. "In here,"—she pointed to her chest—"I feel nothing."

Arcadie stepped in. "He left you with a hole there," he offered.

Skye jumped. "Arcadie. I didn't know you were here."

"We need to address this, Skye," he said.

She shrank back, something I never saw her do before. Tanen had really done a number on her. The thought of it made my blood boil.

Arcadie silently ordered me to keep it together.

I took a deep breath and picked up another brush, needing something to do.

Skye checked the bucket of mash. "She didn't finish it."

"Leave it for her during the day," I said. "She'll take what she needs."

Arcadie turned Skye to face him. "My dear. I want you to tell me what Tanen did to gain your compliance."

She shook her head as if pushing back the nightmare. "I don't remember."

"You do," he said, almost angrily.

Skye shuttered beneath the power in his voice.

Khalen hurried around the corner, obviously sensing his mate's discomfort and alarm.

Arcadie raised his hand, stopping him.

Skye's hands shook and she dropped the brush. Sinking down, she fell upon the soft mats and pulled her knees up to her chest.

"Tell me, Skye." Arcadie's voice was cruelly demanding. It made my stomach twist with discomfort.

Skye trembled. Arcadie kept Khalen at bay.

"What did Tanen do to gain your compliance?" he asked again.

"He tortured Elle," she cried. "He hurt Eve and Sunjia."

Arcadie frowned. I read his thoughts. None of the women showed signs of being tortured.

"Then what happened?"

"I took their pain. I wrapped it up and aimed it toward Tanen. His kidneys exploded. After that, I felt dead inside."

Arcadie knelt beside her. "How did you take their pain, Skye?"

"I made it my own," she sobbed.

"God," he sighed. "No wonder you're so messed up."

She looked up at the old man with glazed eyes. "It felt good to hurt him," she admitted. "I wanted to do it again and again. I couldn't turn it off."

"Yes," he whispered. "That is exactly what he wanted."

"I don't feel right anymore," she said. "Nothing feels right."

"We're going to fix that, Skye."

"How?"

Khalen, too, looked curious.

With a wave of Arcadie's hand, Skye fell limp.

"Get her to your room," he told Khalen. "Have Case meet me there." He looked over at me. "Take care of Belle, Ian and then join us."

I did as he asked, quickly cleaned up, and then left to join the others. Only Khalen, Arcadie, Case, Aidan and myself were allowed in the room. The women were asked to stay outside.

Arcadie stood over Skye. "Khalen, listen carefully. You need to take her life."

"No!" he shouted. "I won't!"

"No one else can do it. Her soul is split. Half of her is dead already."

"Her spirit is strong, Khalen," said Case. "You can bring her back, whole and complete."

"You don't know that," he seethed. "She just needs time to heal, that's all."

"She grows worse with each passing day," said Arcadie. "Have you looked into her eyes? They're fading, Khalen."

Khalen trembled as he took her hand.

"She took on the others' trauma. She's suffering. You can help her."

"I cannot take her life."

"She's already dying," Arcadie said. "Form a circle," he told everyone. "Lock hands and don't let go. She'll need a focal point to come back."

I locked hands with Case and Arcadie. The hum of their power flowed through me like raw current, causing my arms to tingle and ache.

Khalen hesitantly released Skye's hand before joining the circle.

"The power will be intense," Arcadie warned. "You will feel the need to let go, but don't do it. It is her only link back."

"Have you done this before?" asked Khalen.

"Yes," he said. "But that time we did not have someone with your power. You must keep your focus. Can you do it?"

Khalen nodded.

"Keep your mind open to me," he said. "Let my thoughts guide you and Skye. Understand?"

"Yes," he said, glancing over at Case. If he were uneasy, he did a fine job at concealing it.

The hum in the room increased. Jolts of energy flowed through me. My limbs were on fire, my nerves felt raw. God, the pain was almost too much.

"Now, Khalen. Release her now."

He sobbed as Skye's spirit pulled away.

"Now bring her back, Khalen. Do it now. Call her back to you."

"I can't feel her."

"Reach out," Arcadie growled. "You're losing her, Khalen. Be quick about it."

The intensity quickened and I struggled to endure the pain. Case and Arcadie must have sensed it too. Their hands tightened around mine.

Shanuk's presence filled the room. The pain intensified. My legs quivered beneath me.

"Reach out, Khalen," Shanuk said. "Find that which is familiar."

Khalen groaned. His pain became our own.

Shanuk increased the power. "That's it, Khalen. Now bring her back. Call her to you. Bring her into yourself."

"Guide her spirit back to her body," said Arcadie. "Do it slowly."

"I feel her," Khalen sobbed. "She's coming back."

The hum in the room slowly diminished to a tolerable level.

When Arcadie and Case broke the circle, Khalen rushed over to Skye. She lay still on the bed, her face pale and drawn.

"She's cold," said Khalen, drawing the covers around her.

"Lie with her," said Arcadie. "It will take some time for her to recover."

He motioned for the rest of us to leave. I followed Case out, struggling to control my numb legs.

He looked at Aidan and me. "You boys impressed me in there. The energy equaled that of a Council meeting during an argument."

I sagged down on the couch with the others. Eve hurried to bring us some tea and biscuits laden with cheese.

"How did it go?" she asked hesitantly.

"A bit rough at first," said Case. "But it ended nicely."

"Will Skye be all right?" asked Elle.

"Time will tell," said Arcadie. "Hopefully, when she came back, she left the darkness behind."

"Why wouldn't she?" asked Elle, taking a seat by Arcadie.

"If she had identified herself with it, she may have brought it back."

"She wouldn't have done that," said Elle. "She hated that darkness."

"It will be nice having her back again," said Sunjia.

"Aye, it will," I agreed, still shaking from the ordeal.

Arcadie tapped me with his knuckles. "You did great in there," he said.

Aidan, too, was shaking as he pulled Sunjia tight

against him. I wished Erika were there to hold me like that.

As if on cue, she bounced in. Arcadie smiled as Erika sidled up next to me.

"God, Ian, you're shaking."

I reached over and pulled her onto my lap. "Better hold me till it stops," I growled in her ear.

She giggled, snuggling up against me. It felt good and right holding her in my arms.

"Jazen almost has your cabin finished," she said. "Drew is helping him with the roof today. After that, it will be ready for furniture.

"That's great news," I said, enjoying the scent of her hair.

Arcadie smiled, reveling in our interaction. "It's good to see you smile again, young lady."

"I'm happy, father."

"Yes, it shows."

She wiggled off my lap. "I told the men I would bring them something to eat and drink."

Eve said, "There are more biscuits in the oven, and iced tea in the fridge."

"I'll help," said Elle.

I didn't much like the idea of my future mate serving a rival suitor, but it seemed to make her happy.

"Nothing to worry about, Ian," Arcadie chuckled. "That woman's heart is yours completely."

"Yes it is," I admitted.

Aidan smiled. "How does it feel to be a near-mated man?"

I smiled. "Damn good, actually."

He laughed. "Good to hear it. Me little brother has finally grown up."

Arcadie stood and left the yurt without a word. Case watched him go as if knowing the reason.

"The Council calls him," he explained.

Moments later, he returned. "They've located Buchanis' clan. He and Jade are not there."

Case glanced toward the hall leading to Skye and Khalen's room. "Let's take care of it," he said.

"This is Khalen's territory, Case. We cannot interfere."

"He's busy."

"He needs to be informed."

Case sighed. "The man is taxed, brother. This is a petty infringement that any leader can handle."

Arcadie nodded.

"Ian, call the airport and have them ready my jet."

"Aye," I said, pulling the phone from my pocket.

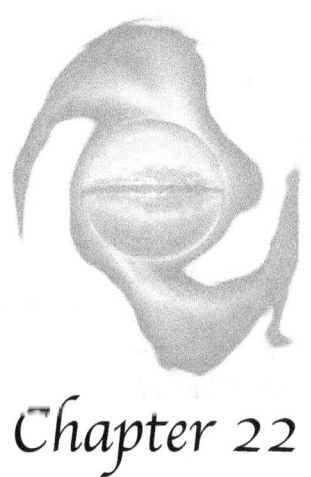

Chapter 22

-Arcadie-

WE ARRIVED IN AUSTIN BY LATE afternoon. The leader of the small Clammat clan waited for us in a large black limo.

He stepped out of the car as we approached. His large frame doubled my brother and me in width, but his height didn't quite measure up to my chin. He wore a pale beige suit and a crisp cowboy hat to match. His dark leathered skin reflected hours of hard labor in the sun.

I extended my greeting. "Cameron," I said, shaking his beefy hand.

"Arcadie." He glanced over at my brother, offering a greeting. "And Case."

Silence grew between us. The man was obviously nervous. He reeked of stale milk and vinegar. "What brings you to visit?" he finally asked.

"Your son," I said. "Do you know where he is?"

Cameron shook his head. "Uh, no. He left for college

several months ago. I haven't heard from him."

"College?" Case inquired.

Cameron gestured that we get in the car. "Please, we can talk on the way."

Before the driver pulled away, I killed the engine. "We talk here," I said. "Where was he attending college?"

"The University of Washington. He's studying to be a doctor." The big man chuckled with pride. "Speaking of doctors, how's young Khalen?"

"Busy," Case replied rather tersely.

The man shuffled in his seat, rattled by Case's tone. "Uh, he governs that region now, does he not?"

"He does," said Case.

Again the man chuckled. "You two are rather high on the chain, you might say, to be seein' the likes of me."

Silence ensued. Neither Case nor I wanted to be here, and it showed. I stared out the window.

"Uh, has my son done something wrong?"

I stared the man down. "Word has it that he's taken on a human and intends to join with her soon."

His reaction was perfectly rehearsed, but his mind was clear. "I'm sure it's just a rumor," he laughed. His brow glistened with sweat.

"Don't waste our time," I said, leaving no room for doubt in my tone. "You know where he is, Cameron."

"No, I don't," he stammered.

Case was growing impatient with the man. I silently cautioned him to stand down.

"We heard about his plans," he said nervously. "But he never said where he was."

"You are his father," Case growled. "Are you not?

The man nodded.

"Tap into his mind and find him!"

"I—I can't."

My eyes narrowed. The bugger was telling the truth. Case sensed it as well. The connection between the man and his son had been severed.

"When did you lose connection with him?" I asked.

"A week ago."

"Why?" asked Case.

The large man shook his head. "I—I don't know," he stammered.

"And you didn't bother to find out?" Case roared.

Cameron shrank back into his seat. The leather creaked in protest under his weight. He reached over and attempted to pour himself a drink. Most of it spilled over his hand, staining his sleeve.

"This is a waste of time," I said. "Where is Tate, your district leader?"

"Tate?"

"I grow tired of your incompetence," I said. My energy started to peak and the big man felt its hum. His driver exited from the car, no doubt uncomfortable with the charge.

Cameron loosened his collar as sweat began dripping from his flaccid chin. With shaky hands, he pulled the phone from his breast pocket and began dialing a number.

"Sir," he said. "Yes, I know you are busy—"

Shouting rang through from the other end of the line.

"Case and Arcadie are here."

The phone went silent.

"They wish to speak with you."

"What about?" I heard Tate say.

Cameron handed me the phone.

"Hello, Tate," I said calmly.

"Arcadie. What an honor it is to have you in my

district."

"I wouldn't be here if there wasn't an issue," I assured him.

"An issue? What kind of issue?"

This place reeked of Shadows, and Case felt it too. My instincts became sharp and alert.

"Something's going on, Tate. Tell me what it is."

There was a pause on the line. "Meet me at Galalaoe's in fifteen minutes," he said. The phone went dead.

"Galalaoe's? Do you know where it is?"

Cameron nodded.

"Get us there."

He motioned for his driver to get back into the car. The engine refused to turn over. I quickly remedied the problem and we were on our way.

Texas was a desolate place compared to the Northwest. The heat was intolerable in summer. Unnatural cool air wafted in through the vents as the driver pulled onto the highway.

The Spirians of this region did not see much of our family line. We tended to keep to the northern states. Apparently, our names were well known and respected. I sometimes forgot that we were considered the most powerful line in Spirian history, thanks to our father Shanuk. He earned the title after challenging the elder, Terishicot, a well-respected leader who later praised Shanuk for his strength and wisdom.

I rarely wasted my time with such trivial matters as law infringements. If Jade were not related to Khalen's clan, we would most likely allow Tate to see to the matter. Unfortunately, Jade's life was in danger and time was running out.

The small coffee shop stood out amongst a strip of

trinket shops that offered everything from tobacco to second-hand clothing. The limo pulled up to the front and the driver killed the engine.

Cameron made no effort to leave the car until I gave him a look. With a groan, he pried himself out of the cushy seat with the driver's assistance.

As we entered the small shop, our presence earned the attention of everyone in the room. With a thought, Case made quick work of clearing out the patrons.

"You have such a way with people," I said, smiling.

"Odd place to meet, don't you think?"

I nodded. "Indeed."

Tate entered moments later, his face pale with concern. He didn't bother to shake our hands before taking a seat beside us.

"Tell us what you know," I said.

"The Shadows have some kind of an alliance," he whispered, his eyes darting around the room as if the walls were rigged with poisonous darts waiting to find their mark. "Many of our women and young men have been taken. My resources are dwindling."

The man looked haggard.

Suddenly, this trivial matter was growing in scale. "Yes," I said. "We have had a few run-ins as well."

"Do you think Buchanis was overtaken?" asked Case.

Tate looked genuinely confused. "Buchanis?" He looked to Cameron. "Your son?"

Cameron nodded.

"What about him?" asked Tate.

"He's taken a human female," I explained. "A friend of ours. He intends to make her his mate."

"A human?" he said.

"Yes."

His eyes focused on Cameron. "You mentioned nothing of this to me."

Cameron squirmed in his chair. "I didn't want to bother you, sir."

Tate's green eyes darkened with disgust and shame. "This will be addressed later," he said in a terse tone, and then readdressed Case's assumption. "Where is he?"

"His communication with Cameron was severed a week ago."

Tate growled. "This is the work of the Shadows."

"Tanen?" I asked.

Tate frowned and shook his head. "No, I believe the Chinese leader, Tao, is behind this."

"Tao?" Arcadie questioned with a laugh. "Highly unlikely, Tate. The man is closely tied to Jebu's region in Russia. They have no alliance in the States."

Tate raised his hands. "I'm telling you what I know."

"How certain are you?" asked Case.

"I saw him myself."

Case and I looked at each other. Tanen had been able to assume Jazen's shape and be very convincing about it. Could the same hold true for Tao?

"Ian said he had destroyed Tanen."

"Yes," said Arcadie. "Just like we thought he had blown up with the ship."

"Could Azazel be heading this up this?" asked Case.

"Possibly," I said.

"Who is Azazel?"

"A fallen Archangel," I explained.

Tate laughed. "Archangels? In this dimension? That's unheard of."

"The barrier between our realms has been torn," I explained. "We are just beginning to see the results of it."

"What can we do?"

"Balance will be restored, it always is. We ride it out as best we can."

"What about my son?" asked Cameron.

"I'm afraid he must be found and destroyed."

"I'll see that it's done," said Tate.

Cameron's mouth dropped open. "No. You can't!"

The three of us ignored him.

"Gather your clans," I said. "Keep a close watch on your young. Azazel works on the emotions. Once he opens the door with enough negativity, the soul is his to claim. Warn them."

"Understood," said Tate. "Do you need a ride back to the airport?"

"I can take them," said Cameron.

Tate pierced him with a warning. "Go back to your clan and gather your things. I will meet with you in an hour. Have everyone ready to move."

"Uh—yes sir."

"I will have my son take you back to the airport."

"Time is of the essence," I told him. "Buchanis is planning to join with Jade on the twentieth."

"I'll find him."

We shook hands. "Thank you."

He nodded. "My father was from your region, Arcadie. He had great respect for you."

"I remember him. His name was Jeb, mated to a distant cousin of mine named Ebby."

"Yes," Tate smiled, obviously pleased with my ability to remember his parents. "He's passed on now. Mother has taken another mate."

"I'm sorry," I said. "He was a good man."

Tate smiled. "I'll keep you informed."

Case handed him a piece of paper with his number on it.

"It was an honor to meet you both."

W**E RETURNED HOME JUST AS** the evening meal was at a close. Eve, bless her heart, had saved us each a large portion, which she now brought out with a bottle of Pinot Grigio.

The meal was a perfect cap to a difficult day. Grilled tilapia on a bed of dark greens and colorful veggies accompanied a chunk of hot rye bread.

Eve, Aidan, and Sunjia came to join us.

"How is Skye?" I asked.

"Still out of it," said Aidan. "Khalen has not left her side."

"I'll check on them after dinner," I said.

"I'm sure Khalen would appreciate that. Any word on Jade and her man, Bud?"

"Tate, the district leader, is looking into it."

"The weaker clans were hit hard," said Case.

"In what way?" asked Aidan.

"The Shadows are getting into the heads of the young. Women and children are missing."

Aidan frowned. His mate began fidgeting.

I sipped my wine and studied the two of them for a moment. "You worry for Tria." I stated.

"Aye," said Aidan.

Sunjia bit her lower lip.

"What are you not saying, Sunjia?" I questioned.

Case had picked up on her discomfort as well. He was good at probing one's thoughts without any notice.

"My daughter has unique gifts," she said.

"Are they cause for concern?" asked Case.

She twisted her hands together. I felt the turmoil within her. Whatever she had stored in her mind had been hidden from Aidan as well. He did not display the same discomfort as his mate.

The sudden shock in his expression indicated he had tapped a piece of her that hadn't presented itself until now. His face visibly paled.

"You kept this from me?" he growled.

"I told you something had to be done about her," she explained, trying her best to be respectful.

Aidan's temper was flaring. His mind was a torrent of indecipherable thoughts.

"We need to speak with Khalen," he said. "The sooner the better."

"Tell them," he ordered his mate. "Tell them everything."

Her lower lip quivered. She closed her eyes and took a deep breath. I could smell her fear, as acrid as the ocean during a red tide. There were repercussions for holding such information, not only from her mate but from Khalen.

"Tria is an assimilator. She can mimic another being to near perfection."

There was more. I waited for her to take another breath.

"She also absorbs their gifts—all of them."

"Bloody perfect," Case muttered. "If she's working with Azazel, we have a serious problem on our hands."

"She's the link," I blurted. "She's what binds the dark angel to this Earth and gives him form."

Case's eyes brightened. "Kill her, and Azazel returns to his ethereal cave?"

"In theory," I said. "We must speak with the Angels to know for sure."

We finished our meals before I left to talk with Khalen.

We found him huddled against his mate, tenderly touching her forehead.

I knocked on the door.

Without turning to see who it was, he spoke. "Come in, Arcadie." His voice was drained of emotion.

"How is she?" I asked, entering the room. I had convinced the others that it was best if I saw Khalen alone. Case agreed. He could monitor the conversation from outside anyway.

"She breathes, her heart beats, but she does not respond."

I knew in my mind that she may never respond. It was rare for a person to return from such an ordeal, especially when so much time had passed from the time her spirit left to the time it had returned. It really was her only chance, though, that I knew. In a short month's time, she would have driven herself completely insane, a condition that could not have been reversed.

In my heart, however, I sensed her spirit. She was here and she would return. Skye was stronger than most. She had depth to her and a purity that no Shadow could mar, no matter how cruel the punishment.

I placed my hand over her forehead. "It was a rough transition," I told him. "Give her some time."

He hadn't touched the food sitting on the end table. Not even the wine had been sipped. "You should eat," I told him.

"Not until she returns," he said.

"That could be a long time, Khalen. What good would

it serve if you were too weak to welcome her back?"

He eyed the food and sat up. I gave him a few moments to gather his wits. He sipped the wine and nibbled at the salad.

"What news do you bring me?" He said.

I quickly filled him in on all that had happened using images and thought. It was a far more elegant way to communicate than with words.

A heavy sigh escaped him. "Tria. I should have known."

"Those gifts are rare among Spirians, Khalen. Even rarer in females. How could you have known?"

"Seth was adamant with me about killing her before the Shadows took her away. I should have given him more notice."

"He said nothing to you about her gifts?"

"I never gave him a chance," he said. "I dismissed him as I always do."

His jaw tightened. "Why did Sunjia keep that from me?"

"And Aidan," I added.

Khalen growled. "God, he must be furious."

"Beyond reason," I said.

He shook his head and sighed heavily. "So much to deal with," he said. "I don't know how you and Case have done this for so many years."

I laughed. "We appoint many competent leaders such as yourself, so that we don't have to."

"I need more sons," he said.

"Like Gabrihen?" I jibed, knowing the young was the source of Khalen's many worries.

He grunted. "Ah, good point."

He picked at his salad before setting it back on the nightstand. "I'm worthless without this woman," he said, glancing down at his mate.

"Right now, your clan needs a strong leader. You must find a way, Khalen."

"Tell me we did the right thing," he said.

"You know we did. She would have declined into a dismal hell, and I think you know it. If she had gone too far, we would not have been able to bring her back."

"Do you suppose Shanuk watches over her tonight?"

"I'm sure of it."

Khalen sipped his wine. "What am I going to do about Sunjia?" he sighed.

"A woman who can hide information from a clan leader is a danger, Khalen."

"As we have discovered," he said. "But she is the mate of my brother."

"Talk to him. Ask him what he wants."

"Perhaps I should let him calm down first?"

I laughed. "Probably a good idea."

"I will summon Seth. I'm sure he has much to share."

I stood to leave. "I will keep you informed of Jade's situation."

"Thank you. I appreciate what you and Case have done."

"I know you do, young Khalen. Think nothing of it."

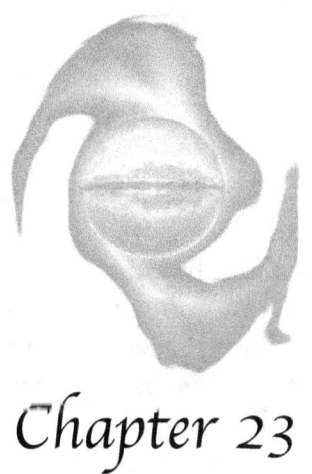

Chapter 23

-Khalen-

SETH APPROACHED MY ROOM LOOKING sullen and worried.

"Come in," I told him.

"This is about my mother, isn't it?" he boldly asked.

I gestured to a chair in the corner. "Grab that chair," I said.

"I told her to tell you," he stammered. "She was scared, Khalen; please don't be angry with her."

"I'm not angry, Seth, but I am concerned. Keeping information like this from a leader is near to impossible, let alone immoral. Your mother has some powerful gifts that could threaten our clan, as does your sister."

Seth lowered his head. "I should have told you," he said quietly, as if the words were not meant for my ears.

"Why didn't you?"

"I didn't want to get my mother into trouble. When Tria started doing bad things, I knew something had to be done. Mother tried to talk to her and explain how such gifts could be harmful. Tria wouldn't listen. She kept messing with the minds of the other children, telling them what they were all capable of doing—bad things."

A low growl rose deep from my chest. "You, too, have the ability to block minds. Do you not?"

He nodded. "I can also make people do things they don't want to do, but I haven't done that, I swear it. I used to manipulate my sister, but I haven't done it since we joined this clan. It's an evil gift," he added with disgust.

"Only if used inappropriately," I told him. "With proper training, your gifts can become quite useful, Seth, not evil."

"What will happen to my mother and sister?"

"I'm not sure yet."

"Tria has turned, Khalen, I'm sure of it. She's been seeing that boy from the Shadow clan for some time. She said they were planning to unite."

"They may have already. I cannot sense her."

"She may be blocking you."

I shook my head. "Now that I have been made aware of such a gift, I'm able to absorb it and counter it as if it were my own. It is the right of a leader. This is why the older leaders are so strong in their abilities."

"So, I can no longer block my mind from you?"

"No, you cannot."

He sighed with relief.

"I have summoned your mother and Aidan. Would you like to stay or go?"

He looked down, his thoughts open. In a sense, he wanted to bolt from the room and never have to face his mother again. On the other hand, he wanted to man up and stand by her side. He was a young man and one who matured rather slowly. In time and with training, he would become a very powerful asset to the clan, I was sure.

Aidan stood at the doorway, his hand gripped tightly around Sunjia's arm.

"Grab two chairs, Aidan, and come in."

Aidan shoved his mate into the room. Seth stood and offered her his chair. She nodded at him and took a seat across from me, her eyes focused on the ground.

I was tapping her intent when Aidan entered the room with two chairs. The woman was torn in so many directions that her thoughts resembled a wet newspaper that had been trampled repeatedly.

Aidan's eyes met mine, filled with pain, worry and anger.

I silently assured him that things were well between us. He was loyal and I knew that if he had been told about Tria, he would have informed me without hesitation.

"Sunjia," I said, keeping my tone even and calm. "Do you understand the weight of your actions?"

She nodded.

"Address me with your eyes," I told her. "I am not a Shadow and I expect you to respect that fact." The words came out more harshly than I had intended. I took a deep breath and a brief moment to calm my temper.

Her dark eyes met mine. There was an emptiness in them that made me feel hollow. "She is my daughter, Khalen. I thought I could turn her around. I had never considered how far she had slid, or how dark her heart had become."

Her words were clear and honest. My eyes softened on her, encouraging her to continue.

"I didn't mean to block you out. I had done it so often with Traeger that the gift had become subconscious. I did not intentionally deceive you." She looked over at Aidan. "Or my mate."

Aidan's lips grew firm. He was struggling to hold his anger. I could only imagine how he must feel. If Skye had done the same to me, I would find it difficult to forgive her. I glanced down at her now as she continued to sleep, her mind somewhere I could not be.

Back to Sunjia. Her intentions were pure and she was telling the truth. If Traeger would have known she was keeping things from him, her life would be over without a second thought. Aidan, in his own position, had that right. If he chose to end their union this moment, I would not blame him for it.

"But you deceived us both," I reminded her. "How am I to overlook that?"

Her back straightened. "I don't expect you to. I understand the repercussions of my actions and will not ask for your forgiveness. Before you make your decision, however, I will tell you that I can help you find Tria."

This got my attention. "How?"

"I, too, have the ability to assume gifts from those I infiltrate. The act of infiltration is an infringement, I know, but in Tria's case, I had no choice. I knew what she was planning to do, and if she succeeded, she would be impossible to find. But before she left, I infiltrated her mind, assumed her gifts, and created a connection that cannot be severed or masked. Not even she knows what I have done."

The woman was full of surprises, I thought. "Impressive."

"After I help you find her, I shall accept any punishment you see fit." Her eyes were cold now, and impenetrable.

I looked over at Aidan. "What are your intentions on

this matter?"

"Deception is unforgivable," he said. "If we allow it to go unpunished, we open the floodgates to similar infractions."

"The punishment for such an act is death," I reminded him.

His jaw tightened and I felt the strain on his chest. He was hurting.

"It is," he agreed.

Sunjia's lip started trembling as tears welled in her eyes.

Seth looked stunned, his eyes flashing between me and the man he loved as a father.

"I could strip her gifts," I offered.

Any Spirian knew that a life without your gifts was a sentence akin to a living hell.

"I would prefer death," she said.

Aidan stood, knocking his chair to the floor. "Damn it, woman! Why have ye done this to me?"

She jumped back. "Is that what you think?" she said, matching his tone, "that I did this to you?"

Aidan's anger rose to a new level. I stood between him and his mate.

"You're not thinking straight," I warned him. "Calm yourself."

"Your trust in me has been shattered," she said. "I see that. Despite what you think, know this; I did not intentionally hurt you. What happened is unfortunate. It now borders on disastrous. I cannot right it or change your opinion of me. Do what you must, but I know the truth of it. I am not a Shadow and my actions were purely to protect my child. That feeble attempt has failed and nothing can be done about it."

"I warn ye to watch yer tone, woman," Aidan growled. He was still amped and the hum in the room rose to painful levels.

She opened her mouth to speak but the words were choked by the weight of Aidan's anger.

"Aidan, back off," I said, forming a shield against him. "Now is not the time to take action on this matter."

Seth rushed to his mother's side. She gasped for air.

Aidan turned to leave the room but before he crossed the threshold, a small voice stopped his momentum.

"Aidan," Skye said, her voice small and weak.

Immediately, the brain-pressing tension in the room fell to a light tingle.

"Skye," I said, taking her hand. "Oh God, thank you," I cried, kissing her face. "Thank you."

She smiled up at me and then frowned at Aidan. "What angers you so?"

"It does not concern you," he said, his voice tight with emotion.

"You are my templar, are you not? And Sunjia is my friend." She tried to sit up and winced against the pain behind her eyes.

I helped her sit and handed her a glass of water. "Here, love. Drink this. It will help."

She took a few sips before handing the glass back to me.

Having read my thoughts, Arcadie and Case rushed into the room, followed by an overly enthusiastic Eve. She nearly pushed me aside to reach Skye.

Sometime during the commotion, Aidan slipped out of the room. He was in a fragile state, I knew, but I didn't want to leave my mate.

"Go," she told me, squeezing my hand. "He needs you

now."

"So do you," I told her.

She smiled and pointed to her chest. "I have you here and always will." God, it was nice to see that smile again, genuine and filled with light. "Go," she said again, releasing my hand.

"Stay here," I told Seth and Sunjia as I left the room.

I left my yurt just as Aidan was driving away. With a thought, I killed the engine.

Leave me be," he warned in thought.

We need to talk, I responded as I approached the car. As expected, he wasn't there. I sensed the illusion.

"Aidan," I said. "You cannot run from this, my friend."

His illusion faded. "I almost killed her," he said.

I opened the door. "Come, let's walk."

He stepped out of the car and walked beside me toward my thinking log. I remember taking this same walk with Case after Skye and I had a dangerous confrontation. On a deep level, I knew what Aidan was feeling.

I gave him this time to reflect upon those feelings, just as Case had done with me many years ago. When we reached the log, we sat in silence, staring out at the ducks meandering on the water.

I loved this spot from the moment I found it. My father smoothed the log we sat on now for many days before setting it up here under the willow tree. We had many conversations here. Even Shanuk liked it and had spent many hours in quiet contemplation on this log.

"What should I do?" Aidan said, breaking the silence.

"That is a decision that you must make."

"I'm asking you, as a leader—as my brother."

"Unions are complicated at times. The ending of them even more so," I told him.

"So you think I should end it and send her on her way to the Father?"

"I didn't say that, Aidan."

"If it were Skye, what would you do?"

"Lean her over my lap and tan her hide to where she couldn't sit comfortably for many days."

Aidan's eyes widened. He cleared his throat, obviously taken aback by my bold statement. "Well, as intriguin' as that solution sounds, I hardly think Skye would allow such a thing."

My face grew serious. "She wouldn't be given a choice."

"Right," he said, nodding his head. His expression changed to a complex twist between confusion and hope. "Are you saying I sh—"

"I'm telling you what I would do," I clarified.

"Skye would be mortified," he said.

A smile swept over my face. "Exactly."

Silence followed for a few minutes before he spoke again.

"I'm not sure I can trust Sunjia again," he said. "Things have become complicated between us."

"Things are as complicated as we choose to make them," I said.

He quirked a smile. "Blimey, ye sound more and more like dear old Shanuk every day, brother."

I laughed. "Now, if I can only tap his endless wisdom," I said.

"I think ye have, brother. I think ye have."

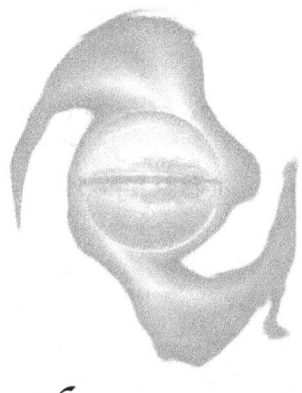

Chapter 24

-Elle-

THE CAMP WAS BUSY WITH activity. My good friend
Skye was back to her old, loving self and we had
taken many long walks together. Belle followed along as if
she had been taking lessons from Maiyun.

It was a sunny day. We ventured down to the meadow
and sat down on the large boulder.

"Are you scared?" she asked.

"Of what?"

"Your union."

I laughed. "Should I be?"

She grew a bit uncomfortable—an unusual attribute
for her to display.

"What?" I said. "Is there something I should know?"

She said nothing.

"Skye?"

"It's nothing," she giggled.

"For Pete's sake. If it was nothing, you wouldn't have

brought it up."

"Spirians are different from humans, Elle."

"Ha, yeah," I laughed. "No kidding."

"When you unite, you will become Spirian."

"That's the theory," I said.

Her face grew serious. "The Angels said you were closer to being Spirian than human now, but . . ."

I waited, but she didn't continue. "But what, Skye?"

She shrugged. "What if you aren't?"

"Why would you say that?"

"You can't read our thoughts and your gifts have all but faded. You still get drunk if you drink too fast, and—"

I held my hand up. "All right, all right. I get your drift. But Angels don't lie."

"They can be wrong, can't they? I mean, they even admitted that this was a rare occurrence."

"Okay, now I'm scared."

She placed her hand over mine. "I'm just thinking things through, that's all."

"So what happens if they are wrong?"

"The act of joining with a Spirian male could be dangerous."

"How dangerous?" I asked.

Her face showed no signs of humor. "You could die."

"And you tell me this now?"

She shrugged. "I didn't think it through until now."

"I finally find the courage to love another man and you spring this on me? Really?" I started to stand but she pulled me back down.

"I'm sorry. I shouldn't have said anything."

"Yeah," I snorted. "It's much better to let me march to my deathbed—literally."

She rolled her eyes. "I'm not saying you will die, I'm

just saying there's a chance."

I looked at her, completely absent of words. Was she kidding me? "I won't die," I told her. "I'm not that lucky."

"Believe me," she chortled, "dying has nothing to do with luck."

I had forgotten how closely she had come to death last week and I had heard it wasn't the first time. I wasn't sure what to say.

"Hey," she jibed. "Don't get all serious on me."

"What's it like to join with a Spirian?" I asked.

"Magical," she said, her eyes sparkling with some distant memory. "Nothing like anything you have ever experienced with human men."

I laughed. "Nothing to go on much there. I've only had one man and he was a spirit."

"Hmm," she said. "I don't know how they compare."

"Well, I'll find out soon enough." I traced my fingers over the tattoo-like scar on the underside of her left wrist. "Do you think I'll be left with something like this?"

"All women are after they are joined. Why?"

"Did it hurt?"

"Like hell," she said. "But only for a moment."

I shook my head. "I'm really not happy I talked with you today."

She frowned. "Why?"

I scoffed.

IT RAINED THAT EVENING. The mood in the camp was bleak and disturbing. Everyone stayed in their cabins and yurts. I still shared space with Skye and Khalen. They had invited Drew over for dinner.

I helped Skye prepare a simple dish of what she called

hobo stew. It was a hodgepodge of lamb and veggies served over brown rice.

Khalen sat with the children next to the fire. They were playing a game that enabled the children to strengthen their basic skills of telepathy and telekinesis. The odds were slightly skewed to Khalen's favor, but he didn't abuse his power.

The oldest son, Gabrihen, watched his father with respect and pure awe. It was interesting to see him try to mimic Khalen and then deflate when his power fell short. Khalen encouraged the boy to keep trying, praising him for the slightest improvement.

"He's a good father," I said.

Skye smiled. "Yes, and a wonderful mate."

She poured me a glass of wine before carrying another to Khalen. They joined in a long, lingering kiss after clinking their glasses together in a silent toast. I remembered doing the same thing with Avel and my stomach churned.

A knock sounded on the door. Khalen opened it with a slight wave of his hand. He made it look so easy.

"Drew, come in. We were just settling in with some wine. Can we pour you a glass?"

He looked at all of us but his enthusiasm for wine was lacking. "Uh, sure."

I smiled. "We have a bottle of cognac open if you prefer."

His eyes brightened. "That sounds perfect."

I poured him a glass and handed it to him. Before taking a sip, he tapped my cup with his and stepped closer to me.

He lifted the pendant I wore over my heart and kissed it. "To our union," he whispered. Slowly, gently, he pressed his lips to mine.

Although showing such open affection was common for the members of this camp, it was still quite foreign to me. I felt the blood heat my face and tried to step back. His arm slipped around my waist and pulled me closer, his grip unyielding. His kiss deepened. My glass dropped from my hand. He stopped it before it crashed to the floor.

Apparently his telekinetic gifts were nearly as polished as Khalen's. Only a few drops of wine hit the wooden floor. Maiyun was kind enough to clean them for me.

The kids giggled, causing my face to flush even deeper. A stern look from Khalen calmed them immediately.

We came to join Skye and Khalen in the living room by the fire. Drew possessively pulled me down beside him on the loveseat while the children rushed off to the playroom.

Khalen had a knowing smile on his face that made me want to slap him. When the vision of that satisfying act entered my mind, he gave me a warning glare.

"Thank you for rescuing me," Drew said to Khalen. "I love my brother and his family, but if I have to stay one more day in that house, I believe I'll go insane."

Khalen laughed. "Yes, Caleb and his gang can be quite loud. I figured you could use some peace."

"Your kids are so quiet. I don't know how you two manage it."

Skye set her glass down. "If you had Khalen for a father, would you want to keep him on edge?"

Her mate gave her a look that could stop a tiger from charging.

I laughed. "You can be a bit alarming," I told him.

Drew joined in. "Alarming? Is that what you call it?"

"There is nothing wrong with earning respect," Khalen said.

There was definitely no lack in that department.

"Arcadie and Case have respect and they don't frighten me nearly as much as you do at times," I said.

Khalen raised his brow. Drew nearly choked on his next sip.

"You didn't grow up under their charge," said Khalen.

"Well, Erika did and she doesn't seem the least bit afraid of her father."

"Have you ever heard her tell him no, or raise her voice toward him?" he asked.

"He's never given her reason to," I said.

Skye sipped her wine and in a way that was typical of her, she ended the subject with a simple truth that rattled the emotions. "Remember your training with Case?"

"Right," I said. End of conversation. I remembered it very well. The man was a formidable teacher, whose censure when my control got out of hand made Khalen look gentle and forgiving by comparison.

Khalen laughed. "Perhaps you would like Arcadie to teach you a thing or two?"

I raised my hand. "I'm good, thanks."

Since my training, I hadn't really tried using my gifts. They were still too shaky for my comfort and I felt clumsy and slow when practicing.

"We will work on that," Drew whispered.

A strange quiver tickled my belly at the sound of that promise. I had seen him teach others in the yard. He was quick and precise, and demanded the same from his students.

"Are you looking forward to your union?" asked Khalen, looking directly at me for an answer.

I nodded. "I'm a bit nervous, that's all."

Drew pulled me closer. "What about?"

I glanced over at Skye. Her expression was solemn and unreadable.

Khalen tapped her thoughts, smiled and sat back. "You're worried about the consummation," he said.

My face turned several shades darker and I felt compelled to hide.

"It's best if you talk about it," said Skye.

Here? In front of these men? I thought. God, what was she thinking?

"Khalen is your leader, Elle, and Drew will soon be your mate. They are the best ones to talk to you about such matters.

I looked at her and sent her a few choice thoughts.

"I'm fine, really," I lied. In truth, I wanted to run and never look back.

Drew shook his head. "Avel said you'd be like this."

I moved aside and looked at him. "When?"

He shrugged. "A week ago, maybe less. He interrupted my meditation."

"And what exactly did he say to you?" I asked, my embarrassment now devoured by anger.

"I believe that is between him and me."

I tried to stand. He pulled me back down. "Tell me what worries you," he said, his tone leaving no room for escape on this matter.

"I need to use the privy. Do you mind?"

He growled, releasing my arm.

I hurried off to the private room and slammed the door. When I came back out, Khalen and Skye were serving food to the children who eagerly took it into the next room where they could continue to listen to the audio book they had started.

I looked over at Drew who sat quietly on the loveseat sipping his cognac. He was staring into the flames in the circular hearth occupying the center of the spacious living area.

The embarrassing subject seemed to be dropped for the moment and I sighed a silent relief. Skye refilled my wine and gave me a look that assured me the subject was not forgotten.

Honestly, I wanted to strangle her for bringing it up in the first place.

"Don't be angry with me," she whispered. I wasn't sure why she bothered, really. Not when everyone could read her thoughts and mine. Nothing was private here, which made trying to hide my discomfort nearly impossible.

"I don't want to discuss it," I seethed. "Not here, not now!"

"When then?" she asked. "You join with Drew in two weeks and you cannot bring yourself to discuss something this intimate?"

I said nothing.

"This is not like a human marriage, Elle," she said, pulling the stool out and sitting beside me. "This is a lifetime commitment. You need to know what you have agreed to."

I snorted. "I'm not going to back out if that's what concerns you."

Skye groaned.

"Come, let's eat," said Khalen, carrying the last bowl to the table.

Drew pulled my chair out and waited for me to sit before pushing it in. I was not graceful with such a thing, but he hid that fact very well, making it look unusually easy.

Khalen said a prayer and we ate in silence. They were all waiting for me to bring it up, I just knew it. Well, they could wait all evening for all I cared.

Khalen reached over and filled my glass before serving the others. Drew had switched to wine as well.

"The construction seems to be going well," said Khalen.

"Better than expected. Everything should be complete by the end of this week."

"Excellent."

Drew looked over at me. "I thought you would like to help pick out our furniture. We can head into town tomorrow and make a day of it."

I shifted uncomfortably at the thought of living with him. It was silly, of course, seeing we would be joined in two weeks. I wanted this, didn't I?

"Um, yeah. That sounds great."

"We need to find you a dress as well," said Skye. "Perhaps we can go to Silverdale on Friday with the women? Erika needs to find one too."

"Okay," I said numbly.

All the while, I felt Khalen's eyes upon me, like a laser cutting through steel. I met his gaze and smiled.

He smiled back—smugly.

"I have asked Drew to stay here with us until your home is settled," he said.

Of course, he picked the exact moment I swallowed to say it. That man was a real piece of work. I choked down the bite that stuck to my dry throat with a good shot of wine. It helped, but only a little.

"Really?" I squeaked. "You have an extra room?" I knew they didn't.

"He will stay with you, of course."

Now the food I managed to squeeze down to my stomach threatened to come back up. I drank more wine and then switched to water.

"We are not joined yet. Aren't we jumping the gun a bit?" I looked over at Drew. He was smiling. There was no use in asking him about what he thought of the matter.

"You are merely sharing the room, Elle," Khalen explained. "Your consummation will wait until after the ceremony."

My face blazed red. Did they have to speak of such intimate things as if they were—public?

I laughed inwardly. Here, everything was public. What was I thinking?

I regained my composure the best I could given the subject of discussion. "May I ask why?"

"It was my decision," said Drew. "I want to spend more time with you and Connor before the ceremony."

"And that requires you sharing my room?"

"Is there a problem with that?"

Again, I almost choked. Giving up on the idea of eating anything gracefully, I pushed my plate away. "No— yes—I don't know."

"Good, then the matter is settled."

I blinked a few times. What was I going to say? I couldn't exactly tell my mate-to-be that it was inappropriate for us to share the same room. I wasn't exactly a virgin and we were definitely not children. Come to think of it; I had absolutely no idea how old he was. The subject never came up.

"There are many things you don't know about me, Elle."

True, I thought. I knew little about him or anyone else

in this clan for that matter. I realized now that I had kept to myself, just as I had always done with my biological family. Old habits died hard, I thought.

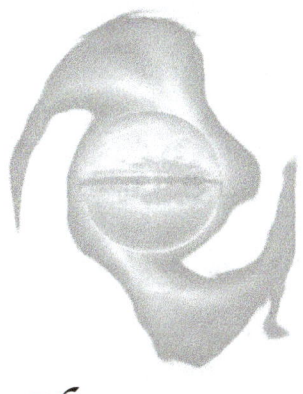

Chapter 25

THE EVENING CAME TO A CLOSE much too quickly for my comfort. Drew had settled into the room comfortably and Skye and Khalen retired to their own room.

I returned from tucking Connor in to find Drew sitting half naked in the bed reading a book.

"Actually," he said, "I'm completely naked."

"Good to know," I replied, refusing to let him rile me. I was an adult. This shouldn't bother me, right?

He patted the spot beside him. I ignored his invitation. Instead, I began gathering my toiletries and nightclothes and stuffing them into a bag.

"Where are you going?" he asked.

"To the shower hut," I said.

"They have a private shower right here," he said, gesturing to the adjoining room.

"I like the ones in the hut much better," I lied. The night was cold and I really didn't look forward to trekking across the camp in the dark with construction debris scattered all over. But I needed some space and it seemed like a good plan for now.

He moved the covers aside and swung his legs off the bed. I turned the other direction, pretending I didn't see a thing.

He chuckled softly. "I'll come with you," he said, grabbing his shirt and pants from the valet in the corner.

"I'm good," I said, my voice higher than normal. Lord, this was awkward.

He came up behind me and placed his hands on my shoulders. "This shouldn't be awkward," he purred into my ear. "It should feel right and perfectly natural."

Don't turn around, I told myself. Don't—

He spun me around to face him. My heart quickened like a rabbit facing down a pack of wolves. There he stood with his shirt unbuttoned. I had seen him without it before as he worked on the cabins. It was no big deal then. Why was it now?

"Breathe, Elle. I'm not going to eat you."

I thought I was breathing until the scent of him wafted up through my nose. Cedar and clove, rough and deliciously masculine.

"On second thought," I stammered. "I think I will use this shower."

His hands dropped from my shoulders as I bent down to fetch my bag.

He took the bag from my hand and tossed it onto the floor. He then led me back to the bed.

"Sit."

I did, my hands wringing together as if I were trying to remove a stubborn stain.

He sat quietly watching me.

"Do you want this?" he finally said, rubbing my

pendant between his fingers.

I pulled it from him, scared that he might try to remove it again. "Yes," I said, starting to stand.

He pulled me back down.

"Stop running from me, Elle. I am not your enemy."

"I know that."

"We have been close before. I have held you, kissed you, snuggled with you. Why are you so nervous about it now?"

"I'm not sure," I said quietly.

"I won't take you tonight if that's what worries you?"

I was suddenly able to breathe again.

He chuckled softly and took me into his arms. "You're worried about our consummation."

I nodded against his broad chest. "Pretty dumb, huh?"

"Not at all," he said.

Tears started to well in my eyes. "I'm not a virgin," I sniffed against him. "I'm just afraid to . . ."

"Love again," he said.

After a few silent moments, he spoke. "You're afraid I'm going to leave you, like Avel?"

He was good—very good. I didn't respond, feeling already too vulnerable and pathetic. I continued to bury my face in his chest.

"Well," he sighed, "I'm just going to have to convince you that I'm here for the long haul. Aren't I?"

"Raphael said that I would live forever. I don't want to be the only one left."

He laughed and forced my head upward to meet his mesmerizing eyes. "Once we join, my love, you will become Spirian. You will age slowly, mind you, but you will become one of us."

"How can you be so sure?" I said. "Not even Raphael

knew if the union would work. What if I'm more human than Angel? What if I don't survive the transition? What—"

His eyes began to glow. They were amazing when they did that; deep purple with metallic shimmers of gold and silver. "You see that, yes?"

I nodded. "The others do it too," I said, "when they use their gifts."

"If you were human, my dear, you would never notice it."

"How is that possible?"

"Humans cannot see the phosphorus illuminate. The vibration is much too high."

"Phosphorus?"

"Along with an enlarged and highly developed pineal gland, we also have an abundance of phosphorus. It is what enables us to communicate telepathically."

"I obviously don't have it."

"You will," he laughed. "After we join, this camp will seem like a concert in your head."

"For how long?" I asked.

He shrugged. "A day, maybe two. You will soon learn to filter it out just like everything else."

I started feeling more comfortable around him again, like it had been between us before all this talk of unions crept in.

"Speaking of age," I said. "How old are you?"

His lips curled into a smile. "I'll make you a deal."

"What kind of deal?" I asked, hesitantly.

"If you guess my age correctly, you shower alone, undisturbed. If you're wrong, I have the right to bathe you."

I swallowed hard. "How about if I'm close, like within

ten years?"

His smile broadened. "Deal."

I sat back and studied him carefully. He looked to be about the same age as Khalen; and Skye had told me he was sixty something. Drew looked slightly younger, not quite as polished, yet strong and more in control of his feelings.

"Stand up and turn for me," I said.

He grinned, stood, and slowly turned clockwise with his arms held out.

Good muscle tone, strong bones, excellent balance. He had to be younger than Khalen.

"Time's up," he said. "Make your guess."

"We never discussed a time limit," I said. "I need time to think, which is best done under the spray of a hot shower."

"Fine, I'll join you."

"That wasn't the deal."

"Make your guess," he said, brow arching with an inviting challenge.

"Ugh," I growled. "Why do I get the feeling you're setting me up?"

His expression didn't change, nor did his posture.

"Fine," I said. "You're fifty-nine?" It came out more like a squeak.

"Try again," he said. "I'll give you three chances."

"Higher or lower?"

He just shook his head. "Make your guess."

It couldn't be higher, I thought. "Thirty-eight?"

"One more."

"Damn it! This is unfair."

"I know your age," he flaunted.

"It was never a big secret," I said.

"Nor is mine," he countered.

"Seventy," I blurted out.

"Nope, sorry lecalla."

"Le what?"

"You're not even close to guessing my age."

"Not even close? Any of them?"

He reached down to grab my bag. "Let's go."

"How old are you?" I said, trying to stall.

He caught on much too quickly. "I'll tell you after we bathe." Grabbing my hand, he led me into the next room, luxuriously equipped with the most unusual shower and bath I had ever seen. I had used it many times during my stay here but my wonderment of it never ceased.

Several shower heads poked out of a stone wall with more than enough room for two people. There were no doors or drapes. The water mysteriously disappeared into a narrow crack in the heated stone floor. Beyond that was a sunken tub that resembled a small jacuzzi.

"You like it?" he asked.

"Very much," I said.

"I designed it."

I ran my hands over the smooth stone walls, finding them to be far more intriguing than before. "What is this stone?"

He started the water flowing and quickly removed his pants.

Suddenly I couldn't breathe. I tried keeping my eyes focused elsewhere.

"It's Jerusalem tile. They formed the streets of that great city for hundreds of years. Each of them is hand polished."

I frowned and then jumped as he began unbuttoning my blouse.

"This," he said, "is something you'll have to get used to, lecalla."

My throat constricted. "What is lecalla?" I said, trying to mimic his accent.

He laughed at my attempt. "In my people's language, it means little cat."

"Right," I said, trying to ignore the fact that my shirt now hung completely open. He slid it off my shoulders and methodically draped it over a hook.

I started undoing my pants before he brushed my hands away. "This is my reward, lecalla. I intend to take full advantage of it."

"Well, I wouldn't want to deny you your reward," I said nervously. God, his touch felt good—practiced, precise, and completely nonsexual. For that, I was grateful.

After hanging the rest of my garments on the hook, he stood back and took a long look at my naked, shivering body. The smile on his face indicated he was not disappointed.

"Why little cat?" I said, needing a distraction.

"Your eyes are the color of a cat's and you banter like a kitten when you are feeling particularly playful."

He stepped closer. "You are very beautiful, Elle." His thumb brushed over my lips before he claimed them with his own. My knees felt ready to buckle.

He laughed, guiding me under the warm spray of water. "This is going to be a very long two weeks."

"How old are you, Drew?" I said quietly, trying not to get lost in his touch.

"Eighty-eight," he said.

I stepped back and found myself against the warm stone wall. "You are not!"

He laughed. "I am."

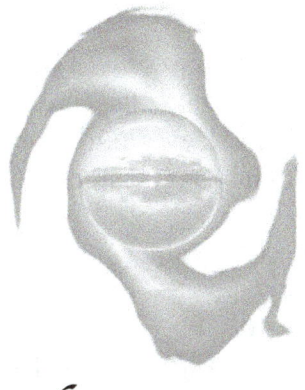

Chapter 26

SKYE, ERIKA, AND I WERE dutifully escorted by Aidan as we ventured through the shops in Silverdale.

I had spent the last few days with Drew, picking out furniture and discussing everything from the audio book we listened to at night to the finer points of weapons fighting. I thoroughly enjoyed spending time with him and found myself missing him as we wandered from shop to shop.

Skye nudged me. "Hey, are you here or somewhere else?"

"I'm here," I said.

"So what did you think of that dress I held up?"

"What dress?"

"Uh huh." She walked over to a rack and held up a white dress that looked like something Barbie would own.

I shook my head. "I want something simple," I told her. "Practical."

She walked over to another rack. "How about this one?"

It was as simple as they come. The fabric was silk with just a hint of lace circling collar. Nothing fancy or frilly. Three-quarter length sleeves ended with a tulip-shaped cuff. The full back and modest hemline was conservative, yet elegantly tailored.

"I like it," I said, allowing the fabric to slide through my fingers. "How did you even see this? Aren't you supposed to be blind?"

She laughed. "The clerk showed me around earlier and told me where to find things."

"Right," I said, walking toward the dressing room. We strode past Erika, who was twirling around in a long gown that ended with a flaring skirt. The strappy sleeves and low-cut bodice suited her and accented her features. The off-white fabric looked great against her dark skin and exotic eyes.

"How does it look?" she asked.

"Perfect," I responded, suddenly feeling inadequate in every way.

"You're not," said Skye from behind. "If you were, Drew would not be so infatuated with you."

"Infatuated? Is that what you call it?" He was more like a possessive mongrel protecting a meaty bone.

"I've never seen him like this with another woman," she assured me.

"Have there been many?" I asked, jokingly.

She quirked her lips. "He's a Spirian male, high status, very gifted, and virile. Believe me, he's had many women."

The knowledge of that made me feel ready to hit someone—primarily the women he lay with in the past.

Skye laughed. "Now who's being possessive?"

I took the dress from her hands and entered the room.

"I want to see it," she said through the closed door.

"You're blind," I reminded her.

"I still want you to come out with it on."

She really knew how to irk me and push me beyond my comfort level. Grant it, that wasn't very difficult, but still, she was supposed to be my friend.

"I am your friend," she said. "That's why I push you."

I didn't respond. There was no need to. She would just read my thoughts anyway.

When I came out, she had dragged poor Aidan over to have a gander at me. Talk about feeling exposed.

He spun his finger. "Turn around."

"Are you kidding me?"

"Just do it," said Skye.

"Ooh," Erika said from the end of the hall. "I like that one."

"Walk out there," said Aidan, pointing toward the showroom.

"Out there?"

"Walk," he said.

I groaned. Spirian men were always so demanding.

"Turn around and walk toward me."

I rolled my eyes and made my way back toward him.

"Now," he said, "do it as if I were Drew and not giving ye an order for somethin' you don't want to do."

Skye giggled. "How about this," she added. "Do it for all the women he's lain with."

My back stiffened. I straightened my shoulders and strutted that dress as if I were Princess Di.

"Beautiful," said Aidan. "That's what I wanted to see."

Skye smirked.

"You're terrible," I told her.

"No," she replied. "I'm very good."

I reminded myself that if I were to find myself in a

strategic game with that woman, I would want her on my side. She had an uncanny way of exposing one's weakness and turning it into effective ammunition.

When it came to finding shoes, however, she was impossible.

"I don't even like shoes," she said.

If Khalen hadn't bought her those strange toe shoes, she probably wouldn't be wearing any shoes at all. He claimed they were the only ones he could keep on her feet long enough to eat dinner at a restaurant.

Skye was convinced that shoes were some kind of residual left over from a medieval torture chamber. I wasn't sure if I shared her opinion on the matter. I rather liked having shoes on my feet, especially when it was thirty-eight degrees outside during the tail end of summer. Whatever possessed me to move up here from California?

"These are cute," said Erika, holding up a pair of gold sandals with several thin straps.

"Those will go great with your dress," I said, not wanting to seem rude. There were so many straps my feet would probably get tangled up in no time.

She rolled her eyes, obviously reading my thoughts. "I have my shoes already, Elle. This is the fifth store we've visited."

Aidan slapped a pair of flats in my hand. "These will do. Let's go."

THE NIGHT WASN'T EXACTLY CLEAR, but the clan was getting edgy after having to eat inside for several days on end. Eve decided to chance having our evening meal by the fires.

The children ran after one another laughing and giggling. Connor and Gabrihen were becoming very close and I worried how Gabrihen's upcoming departure would affect my son.

"You worry too much," Drew said from behind. He held two plates of food in his hand and two glasses of wine. He handled them with the grace and skill of a seasoned waiter.

"I worked at the Chart House for several years when I struggled through college," he said.

"What did you study?" I asked, taking my plate and glass of wine from him so that he could sit.

"Physics and women," he said.

I nudged him. "Yeah, I heard about your plethora of women from Skye."

He sat back and smiled, looking far too proud. "You sound jealous, lecalla."

"They can all rot," I said. "You're mine now." I grinned.

He leaned over to give me a kiss. "Not yet, but soon," he whispered.

Somehow, that deep silky voice of his could send my belly to space, or at least it felt that way.

"So what did you do with your physics degree?" I asked him.

He looked at me as if I were joking. I wasn't, of course.

Finally, after a few bites and several sips of Bordeaux, he said, "I teach the clan to fight."

"To fight?"

"Yes, lecalla, fighting is all about physics—using one force to invoke another."

I remembered how he had planted my keister in the dirt multiple times this morning during practice. It seemed the harder I came at him, the harder I landed.

Connor was very entertained.

Drew smiled. "Yes, now you understand—physics."

I had learned more about self defense from this man than I had during all the years I had studied under Master Mac. God, that seemed like a lifetime ago now. I wondered how Jamie was doing. My memory of her and the others had slowly returned, but my life was so different now that it seemed pointless to try to contact them again. Aidan said that they probably wouldn't remember me anyway.

That thought saddened me a bit.

"You have a new life now, love."

"Yes, I do," I said, planting a kiss on his lips.

I had toyed with the idea of inviting my family to our ceremony but then thought better of it. I couldn't effectively explain the kinds of novels I wrote let alone the life of a Spirian clan.

Drew had agreed to meet them in California after the ceremony so that he could get to know them. I just prayed the subject of his age wouldn't come up.

"How did your shopping go?" he asked between bites.

"I found a dress I liked. I'm not crazy about the shoes, though."

He laughed. "Yes, I heard about the shoes."

I frowned. "Why do I always feel that everyone here knows more about my life than I do?"

"Because they probably do," he answered casually.

"It's very frustrating," I huffed.

He wrapped his arm around me and squeezed. "I have an idea for venting that frustration, if you're interested," he purred.

At least one part of my body was.

"Hmm," he growled. "I think you're warming up to the idea."

"Don't push your luck," I said, sipping my wine, hoping it would calm the butterflies swarming around in my belly.

Across from us sat Ian and Erika. Jazen joined them in conversation, all laughing.

"Look at them," I said, gesturing toward the threesome. "Ian and Jazen were at each other's throats a week ago and now they behave like long-time friends. I don't get it."

"When two men challenge each other for a woman, a strong camaraderie forms between them. They become like brothers built upon the foundation of mutual respect."

I huffed. "I would expect Jazen to feel rejected, angry, and disgusted with himself for losing the fight."

"Immature Spirians would, no doubt, which is why they are forbidden to join when they are young. Jazen respects Ian for stepping up. Both of them know that the victor of a challenge is the right choice for the woman. Jazen accepts that truth and honors it."

"I thought he was going home?"

Drew chuckled. "He was, but then Ian asked him to be Erika's templar."

"He didn't!"

"Yes, he did. It is common for that to happen."

"Ha, weird," I said.

"To be chosen as a woman's templar is a great honor for a man."

I glanced over at Khalen. "I don't think Khalen feels honored at all. He seems more put out with the task than anything else."

Drew laughed. "Khalen would not have accepted the role if he didn't see it as an honor. He takes his promises very seriously. He's a good man—a strong man."

"Once we're joined, will he still be my templar?"

"It is highly unusual for a leader to accept such a role. He is far too busy with other matters. He agreed to Avel's request because he was the only one who could protect you at the time."

"Will I have a templar?"

"Every woman of status is assigned one, yes."

"Have you chosen who it will be?"

"Yes."

I waited. He said nothing. "Well, who is it?"

"You will know soon enough," he said, smirking.

"I have no status, Drew, so I don't really need a templar."

"By joining with me, you do, and yes, you will have a templar."

Perfect, another man to answer to. I saw how Skye had her hands full being under the charge of both Khalen and Aidan—two hard-headed, willful males who openly flaunted their dominance. Why she put up with it escaped me. "I don't have much to offer you. Are you sure you want me as your mate?"

His lip curled, forming that hook at the corner that made my heart skip. "You have much to offer, milah."

"Milah?"

He chuckled. "It means, my love."

I smiled and then frowned, wondering if I would ever be as strong as Skye and Eve.

"You are young, Elle. Your gifts are not fully developed yet. Most Spirian women do not join at your age."

"I'm thirty-three."

"Yes, very young."

I supposed I was young compared to his eighty-eight years. "How old is Erika?" She looked younger than I was. But there again, she is a Spirian by birth.

"She's fifty-three."

"And Ian?"

"He's eighty-one, nearly thirty years older than Jazen."
I smiled, shaking my head. "This is all too weird."

Two elders approached us. The old woman held
something in her hand. They both moved as easily as any
twenty-year-old, but their maturity was obvious. I knew
them both, having had many conversations with them
about the children. Funny how I never asked their names.
The couple tended to mix with the other elders of the
camp, not really socializing with the rest of us. Khalen
spoke with them often and found their company quite
compelling.

The old man spoke with Drew in their native language.
It sounded like a series of mumbles and clicks.

Drew bowed his head, showing respect for the elder
and then kissed the back of his hand. He then stood and
did the same to the woman. In return, the woman hugged
him with such compassion and love, I felt warm just
watching the exchange.

Drew held my hand and pulled me up next to him.
"Elle, I want you to meet my father, Elkinez, and mother,
Aleeza." He placed my hand in his father's first, carefully
closing his father's fingers around mine.

"Honored to formally meet you," said Elkinez.

"Kiss his hand," said Drew.

I lowered my lips to the old man's hand and gently
kissed it. When I looked up, Elkinez looked pleased. He
was a handsome man with a solid build that would put
most thirty-year-old humans to shame. His grip was strong
and true. I felt the hum of his power flow through me.
Like Drew, his eyes were the deep rich color of amethyst
with shards of gold. He definitely had Drew's smile.

Elkinez placed my hand into his mate's hand and carefully closed her fingers around mine the way Drew had done.

The woman smiled. "I'm pleased to see my son settle down with such a lovely female," she said. Though worn a bit from the years, she was a beautiful woman. Silver hair flowed down her back like a waterfall. She stood straight, had all her teeth, and her eyes were the color of tourmaline.

"I've spoken with each of you before but I apologize for not asking your names." My face blushed." I kissed the back of Aleeza's hand the way I had done to Elkinez.

"It would have been rude to do so," said Drew. "Knowing an elder's name requires a formal introduction."

"Oh," I said, my face growing hotter.

Aleeza opened my hand and placed a bracelet into it. It was a simple brown and white leather band that had been hand woven. "My mate and I welcome you into our family, Ellesander Alder, former mate of the Spirit Avel."

I frowned. "You know my birth name?"

Drew nudged me. "Say thank you."

I bowed my head and accepted the gift. "Thank you."

The couple left as quickly as they had approached— silent and mystical.

"Wow," said Caleb. "You must have made an impression on them. They didn't introduce themselves to my mate until sometime after the ceremony.

"They knew my name," I said. "No one other than my immediate family knows my birth name."

"You know it," said Drew.

"How could they have known it? Khalen didn't even know my real name. And how did they know about Avel?" I didn't remember them even being around during that time.

Drew and Caleb laughed.

"Elle," Caleb explained, "our father is two-hundred and twenty years old and mother is one-hundred and eighty three. Believe me, if there is something to know about you, they do. You know how powerful Khalen is, and he is only sixty-four."

I understood that elders held the highest position within a clan, even higher than the leaders. Arcadie would soon delegate his leadership to others and become an elder himself. I wondered if he would remove himself from us like the others had. I hoped not. I would miss his wisdom and charm.

Drew took the bracelet from my hand and slipped it over my left wrist.

"It's beautiful," I said.

"It's a union band," he said, admiring the perfection of the weave. "You must never remove it."

"Why?"

"According to our customs, for each year the band stays on the woman's wrist, another ten years are added to the union. My mother still wears hers, though she's had to remake it several times," he chuckled.

"Isn't that cheating?"

"Hey, they're still together."

"True," I said. "Better tie another knot just to make sure it stays on."

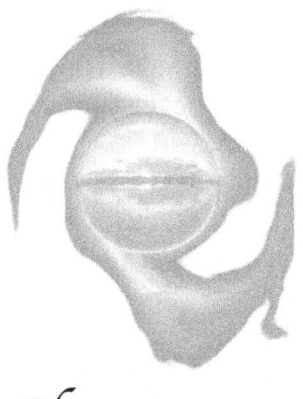

Chapter 27

-Ian-

MY BROTHER'S SOLEMN MOOD WAS getting on my nerves. He and Sunjia hadn't spoken for days, and she had been spending her nights at Case and Eve's yurt. She didn't join the rest of us for meals and her children were starting to feel the brunt of her absence.

Jazen was helping me finish my cabin when I saw Aidan heading to the pasture. I tossed my hammer into the toolbox and started after him.

"No worries, mate. I'll just keep on working here," I heard Jazen mutter.

Take a break, I told him in thought. He wouldn't, though. Once he had a goal in mind, not even a horde of pretty and willing women could distract him. He would, no doubt, rustle up a few of the young to help him finish the cabinets.

The upcoming union had kept me busy enough, and I appreciated his diligence in getting the cabin done in time. His father had been so disappointed in the fact that Jazen lost his challenge against me that the man refused to attend the ceremony.

Jazen didn't take it too well and poured his energy into completing the cabin. Arcadie assured me that he would have a talk with Jazen's begrudging father and convince him to see reason. I was sure he would. Arcadie could be very persuasive when he wanted to be.

Right now, however, I was more concerned about Aidan. I saw him yanking out the fence posts that had been broken during the battle.

His hands were bloody from the splintered wood, and his forehead glistened with sweat. Still he grabbed the next post, grunted, and pulled it free with one swift, anger-powered pull.

"Brother," I said.

He looked up at me. "Now's not a good time, Ian." His voice was gruff and empty of all feeling.

The post slid out of the dirt with a loud swoosh before Aidan tossed it aside. The post weighed about seventy pounds, but he flung it like a rotten branch into the pile. He then set out to conquer another.

I placed my hand on his shoulder. He swung at me and I ducked.

"Easy, lad. I just want to talk with ye."

"I said not now," he growled.

Again I stopped him from gripping the next broken post. He flung himself at me, screaming like a man hungering for blood. This was not the first time he and I rumbled. It happened quite often during our youth.

His fist found my face and blood spewed from my nose and mouth. I countered with a sharp blow to his stomach and then crossed his jaw with my fist. He fell back huffing.

Khalen started heading toward us, but Case stopped him. The rest of the camp stopped what they were doing and watched with concern.

The fight went on for some time before both of us lay panting on the muddy grass.

"Are ye gonna leave me alone, now?" he groaned.

"No," I huffed. "Ye need to talk and we're doin' it now."

He spit blood onto the ground, dragged himself toward me and pounded his fist into my face.

I blocked the third blow, grappled him to the ground and held him there until the fight in him was spent.

My left eye was so swollen it closed shut. The other one wasn't much better. The metallic taste of blood filled my mouth.

"Aye, ye broke m'tooth," I said.

"Ye should 'ave left me alone, fool."

"Talk to me, damn it!" I growled.

His glazed eyes looked up toward the people who had gathered around to watch the spectacle. Khalen stood before them, his lips pulled tight in a straight line. "Get back to work," he told them.

Aidan groaned. "Get off of me, ye lug."

"Are ye gonna talk to me?"

"No."

Khalen pulled us both up and hauled us back to the barn as if we were boys no bigger than a blister.

"I will not have fighting in this camp," he chided.

I rubbed my aching jaw, flexing it to check its function. It still worked, thank God.

Aidan's worked as well; he flexed it now to where the muscles were hard as bone. He pierced me with a look so sharp that it felt like daggers against my skin.

"I will not talk to ye," he growled.

"Ye've been angry long enough," I said. "Can ye not see how it affects the children?"

Aidan launched toward me.

Khalen hit him with an energy blast that dropped him to his knees.

"Enough!" roared Khalen. "Ian is right. Your anger has stewed too long. You will talk about it now, or we can wait just like this until you are ready."

Aidan started to shake. I had felt that energy pulse before and knew the pain of it. Aidan endured, stubborn as he was.

Khalen was patient. Not even he could withstand this pain for long.

Aidan groaned, curling into a ball on the ground.

"Ye're a stubborn fool," I told him. "Just talk, damn it!"

Now he writhed on the ground, the veins in his neck protruding from the pressure.

"Kill me if ye must," he told Khalen. "I won't talk!"

Khalen said nothing. He knew as well as anyone that it was only a matter of time before Aidan would succumb.

Aidan yelled, the sound of it reverberating against the walls. Skye came running.

Khalen raised his hands, stopping her. "You will not help him," he said. "Not yet."

"Ye can help me, lass," I said.

Skye looked to her mate. He nodded. In less than five minutes, my face was back to normal, my ribs stopped aching, and my mouth stopped throbbing.

"Thank ye, lass," I said, kissing her hands.

I stood up and stretched. "Well, I feel better."

Aidan glared at me and groaned.

"Aidan," Skye said. "This anger doesn't do anyone any good. Sunjia made a mistake. You need to forgive her."

"She lied!" he shouted. He squirmed, trying to escape the pain. "Damn it, Khalen!"

"Are you ready to talk?" he asked.

"Yes!" he roared. "I'll talk, rot yer soul."

Khalen ended the pain and hauled Aidan over to a bale of hay where he could sit. Skye made quick work of his injuries as he recovered.

"A good woman does not lie to her clan leader, and especially not to her mate," he said, pain etched in his voice.

"We are not perfect, brother. We all make mistakes. Sunjia did not think this through, that is all," I said.

"No!" he roared. "That is not all. Because of her actions, hundreds of Spirians are dead or in danger. Some, like Skye, are haunted by a darkness few can comprehend." He looked over at Skye. "We almost lost you."

Skye sat beside him and took his hand. "But you didn't. I'm still here, ornery as always."

Aidan pressed his lips to the back of her hand and closed his eyes, still shaking from Khalen's blast. "Thank God for that."

"Sunjia is not responsible for these actions," said Khalen. "She could have let us know sooner, yes, but Tria is responsible for her own choices."

"Sunjia loves ye, Aidan. Her heart is in misery from havin' deceived ye. How long are ye goin' to make her suffer?" I asked.

He clenched his jaw, eyes dark with rage. "I find it hard to trust her again." His voice shook with pain and regret.

"We need her to find Tria," said Khalen.

Silence followed before Khalen continued. "She could help us. Or she could lead us into a trap."

"I've been thinkin' the same," Aidan admitted.

"Do we really have a choice?" asked Skye. "I have been talking with her and she is pure in her intent."

"Like she had been all along?" said Aidan.

"That cannot happen again," Khalen explained. "Unless she has another way to block me, I will know her intentions."

"I'm afraid the woman has many gifts we don't know about, Khalen. I fear what will happen when we discover them."

"We trusted her enough to join our clan," I said.

"And look where it got us?" Aidan spat.

"We can trust her again," said Khalen. "Talk with her, Aidan. We leave on the morrow to find her daughter. I need to know whose side Sunjia's on."

-Aidan-

I LEFT IMMEDIATELY FOR CASE'S yurt to fetch my mate. I feared my actions. Anger ruled my heart now, fueled by deception and heartache. The woman destroyed my trust in her, a bridge that had spanned the width of an ocean. It would take years to rebuild it.

Skye had offered to watch the children as Sunjia and I talked. Without a word, I walked into her temporary room and grabbed her arm.

"Come with me," I said.

She did so without hesitation.

I led her roughly back to our cabin and all but flung her onto the couch. She caught herself and sat in silence, her hands folded in her lap, her eyes down.

"Yer not the mate of a Shadow," I spat. "Ye will meet my eyes and speak yer thoughts. Am I clear?"

"Yes," she said, meeting my gaze. Her eyes were dull and filled with genuine sadness. A part of me felt crushed, but it was a small part.

"I have every right to end yer life," I said.

"Then do it!" she countered, "And be done with it, and with me."

Ian was right. She was suffering and preferred death over the life she had now.

"What are yer intentions, mate?"

She winced at the anger in my tone and then quickly straightened. Always the diplomat.

"To help Khalen find Tria," she said.

"And why would ye do that? She is yer daughter, as ye have so mentioned. Why betray her now?"

"What I did was wrong. I see that. I can't make it right, but I can help end it, Aidan. That is all I can offer."

"Why should I trust ye?"

Her eyes met mine. "Because you have no choice."

"That's not good enough, woman!"

She shrank back. "What do you want from me, Aidan? I'm offering my help. Trusting me is your decision. I pray you make it quick before it's too late."

"We leave tomorrow on Khalen's order."

"I'll be ready."

The crackling of the fire stilled the silence. Her eyes, focused on the flame, were blank inside.

"When this is over," she said. "I want you to sever our union."

My gut fell, threatening to take my heart along with it to the bowels of the Earth. "No," I said, the words spilling out of my mouth involuntarily.

"You do not love me or trust me anymore, and I cannot blame you. But Aidan, I cannot continue living like this. I feel dead inside."

"Me too," I admitted. "Ye have taken my heart, woman, and fed it to the sharks. All that is left is a bloody pulp of anger and mistrust."

"I ask for your forgiveness and the chance to mend our love. If you cannot give that to me, end my life lest I go insane."

My jaw ached from the tension it held. Ian's abuse didn't do it any favors either.

"My trust is shot," I told her. "Yet my love for ye still smolders. Perhaps time will be able to bring back the flame."

"Time is all I ask," she said, reaching out her hand.

I looked at it for a moment, before slowly taking it in mine. She winced as I squeezed her hand more tightly than I had intended. I eased my grip slightly. "Know this, woman. If you ever bring danger upon this clan again, I will offer no mercy."

She breathed deeply and closed her eyes. A tear trickled down her cheek. "I'm sorry for what I've done. I pray you believe that."

"Are there any other gifts ye possess that I should know about?"

She answered without hesitation. "When I tap a person's gifts," she explained, "I assume them. I can block thoughts, feelings and intentions, as you have discovered. I can also control those I have tapped without them even knowing it." Her expression grew dim. "I can make you believe whatever you most desire."

Blimey, I didn't want to hear that. But, I had asked her

and expected her to tell me the truth.

"Have you used those gifts recently?"

"No, not since Tria left with that—Shadow," she spat out.

I continued to hold her hand. "Those are very dangerous gifts."

"I know," she sadly admitted. "Sometimes I think I was born to have a sinister soul. Perhaps I should have stayed with the Shadows."

I squeezed her hand. "I'm glad ye chose not to." It was an honest statement and one that made hope glint in her eyes.

She smiled. "I am loyal to you, Aidan, and to this clan. I swear to you that I would just as soon drive a dagger into my own heart than cause anyone harm."

The words were stated with such virtue that it was difficult not to believe her. Then again, it was one of her many gifts to deceive.

"Tonight, I will expose my gifts to Khalen," she said. "That will give him the ability to know what I am about at any given moment. He will assume my potential."

I arched a brow. Typically, a member of the clan did not have to go through such an act. The leader automatically assumed priority over his charges. My mate, on the other hand, had the unique ability to block that right. Offering to expose herself was a huge step to earning my trust.

"That would honor me," I said, kissing her hand.

WE FOUND KHALEN SITTING BY the fire with his lovely mate by his side. Most of the clan had retired for the evening. There was a bite to the air and the scent of a storm lingered—a promise of wet days to come.

"Khalen," I said, as we approached.

He turned and stood to greet us. "Aidan, Sunjia. Is something wrong?"

"My mate has somethin' to share with ye," I said, moving closer to the fire. I smiled down at Skye. She smiled back.

"Come, sit." He moved a log closer to the fire.

Sunjia took a deep breath before speaking. "First," she began, clearing her throat, "I would like to apologize for my careless actions and deception."

Khalen looked at her intently, holding the silence.

"I did not wish to bring about such destruction, nor did I know it would get so out of hand. Tomorrow, I will help to remedy—the problem," she choked.

I reached over and held her shaking hand.

"Before I ask you to trust me again, I would like to open myself to you."

"You understand what that means?" asked Khalen. Once she opened herself to him, he would assume her strength. Taking her life would be easy and quick.

She nodded. "I do."

Khalen held out his hands. Sunjia released mine and placed hers into the leader's. With a shudder, she opened herself to him, allowing him to see every power, emotion, and intention. The entire process took less than a minute.

Khalen released her hands. The look on his face mirrored my own reaction when she had revealed the sheer force of her gifts to me. She was the ultimate weapon. If Traeger or the other Shadows would have known, she could have single-handedly wiped out the clans. It was no wonder she had kept that truth well hidden.

"Tria is the same," she said, "only worse. The power has consumed her and the Shadows have influenced her soul."

"I will have to take her down," said Khalen.

"You are strong, Khalen, but doing so will end your life. Tria's power is ethereal in nature now. She has joined forces with something far more deadly."

"Azazel," Khalen muttered. "God help us."

There was a resonate hum in the air and a faint scent of sandalwood as Raphael manifested before us.

He shivered, moving closer to the fire. "Excuse my intrusion," he said.

"Always good to see you, Raphael," said Khalen. "Please, tell me you bring good news."

"News is always good, depending on how you look at it," he jibed, rubbing his hands over the fire.

"I thought Angels didn't get cold," said Skye.

"Yes, we're a mysterious lot. Just when you think you know us, we change." His image morphed into an old man in a long black coat. He smiled.

"I assume you know the situation," said Khalen.

"Oh yes. Azazel has created quite a chaos, believing he finally has the upper hand and all."

"You sound doubtful," said Khalen.

"Well, according to Cassiel, the foolish brute has created a quandary. He's forgotten the basic rule of the physical realm. For every action, there is an equal and opposite reaction."

The fire crackled into the silence that followed.

"And for every evil," Skye added, "there's an equal and opposite good."

Raphael clapped his hands. "Excellent!"

Khalen glanced over at Sunjia. "You are the opposite of your daughter."

"The risk is high," Raphael said, looking at Sunjia.

"By annihilating Tria and driving Azazel back to the underworld, you could die."

Sunjia's expression remained aloof. She had known it all along.

"I won't allow it," I said.

"Ah, you have a better solution," Raphael said with renewed hope. "Let's hear it."

Sunjia touched my arm. "There is no other solution, Aidan."

"There has to be," I growled. "I won't risk losing ye."

"Can the Angels help?" asked Khalen.

The glint in Raphael's eye softened. "As you know, young Khalen, the barrier between our dimensions is torn. Once Azazel is sent back to his kingdom, we must seal that tear or risk another more devastating breach. I'm afraid all we can do for now is to stand by."

Khalen bowed his head. "Understood."

"Timing is everything," Raphael said as his image began to fade.

"I'm coming with you tomorrow," said Skye, looking over at Sunjia.

"No," said Khalen. "You will not."

"I can help," she said.

"You can heal from the safety of this camp."

"Not through all the turbulence Azazel will surround you with. Believe me, I know."

"I won't allow him to snag his hooks in you again!" Khalen roared. "You will stay here."

"She's right," I said. "She should come, just in case something happens."

The look he gave me brought vivid memories of the pain he had issued to me in the barn. I shuddered. "She knows this dark one, Khalen. She has seen his mind."

"That's the problem," he said. "He's tapped her before. That makes her more susceptible to his influence."

"It makes me stronger against it," she countered. "Khalen, I can do this. I need to be there."

He snuffed the fire and grabbed her hand. "We'll discuss this come morning." He looked over at me and Sunjia. "Good night."

With that, he turned to leave. Skye glanced back at us and smiled, assuring us that all was well and not to worry. Her mate had a temper. She countered it with grace and practiced skill. He would let her come with us by morning.

"That man frightens me," said Sunjia.

"As well he should." I took her hand. "Come, let's get some rest."

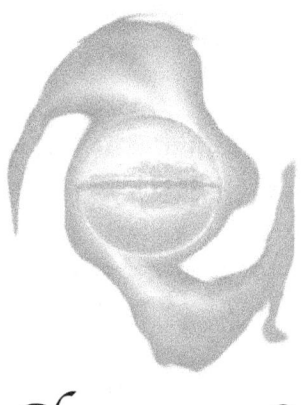

Chapter 28

-Khalen-

IT WAS A MISERABLE MORNING. Rain pelted the windows. The skies were dark with ominous clouds. I stared outside, a hot cup of coffee in my hand.

Skye was in the shower, fully convinced that she would join us. I had no intention of letting her do so. I would bind her to this camp if necessary.

She stepped out of the bathroom, drying her hair. I led her over to the stool at the counter before sliding a cup of coffee in front of her.

"You're staying here," I said.

She remained silent—never a good sign. That meant she was formulating an argument. As expected, her thoughts were closed to me.

Silently, she sipped her coffee.

"Would you like some breakfast?" I asked.

"Yes, thank you," she said. Her voice was calm, calculating. The woman was up to something.

"Did you sleep well?"

"Very," she said. "And you?"

"Deeply," I responded. Idle talk—anything to keep her from thinking.

"How are the union plans coming along?" I asked, gathering eggs and sausage from the refrigerator. I wrapped a few slices of dark bread and set them in the oven to warm.

"As expected," she answered.

Short answer, not good. She was thinking and that was dangerous. "Tell me about them," I said.

She sipped her coffee. "I have a better idea," she said.

I turned around, trying to read her expression. It was calculating, calm, and irritably confident. I sighed. "You're not coming," I emphasized. "End of discussion."

"You had a vision last night."

I stiffened.

"Aidan was hurt. Sunjia was dying. All you could do was watch. It made you sick," she relayed with gut-wrenching accuracy. "If I had been there, you thought, I could have saved them."

I clenched my jaw and continued to whip the eggs into a furious froth. "It was a dream, nothing more," I replied.

"Your call," she said casually. "I will honor your decision, of course."

Clever woman. She had tapped my thoughts the moment I asked her about her sleep. I should have known.

I set the bowl on the counter and leaned down to meet her eyes. "You don't play fair, woman."

She smiled. "You don't live with leaders and elders without picking up a few of their tricks."

I growled.

By ten a.m., we were ready to leave. Tetris agreed to stay at the camp along with the elders. Case, Arcadie, Ian, and Aidan were with me.

Aidan smiled as he opened the door to find my mate sitting beside me. I met his eyes with a warning and his silly grin fell to a straight line. He settled Sunjia next to Skye before joining the others in the back.

"Where to?" I asked Sunjia.

"Bremerton," she said, frowning. "They're on one of the retired ships."

"Makes sense," said Aidan. "Surrounded by water and metal to hide their presence."

"That place is secured," said Ian. "We'll have to arrive as an illusion."

"Sounds good," I said. "Can you maintain it until we find Tria?"

"Oh, aye."

"Once we make ourselves known," Sunjia added, "we'll have to work quickly. Tria will counter my presence. You must take her down the moment she sees us."

"How?" I asked.

"Arcadie and Case will weaken her, Khalen. Then, and only then, can you take her life."

"What happens to you?"

She fell silent.

"Sunjia!" Aidan shouted. "Answer the question."

"To counter her gifts, I must meld with her spirit."

I thought for a moment, playing it out in my head, remembering the vision I had last night. There was a way to do this. There had to be.

GETTING THROUGH THE GATES WAS uneventful and Sunjia was able to locate the exact ship her daughter was on. The ship was teeming with Shadows, most of them young and inexperienced. Their shield kept them out of sight from humans.

I held my hand up, motioning for everyone to stop. "Once this goes down, we need to get off the ship pronto. Understand?" I sent them all an image of the explosion I had envisioned last night.

They nodded and we continued along the docks. I held my mate's hand. She was cold and shaking. I could only imagine the fear she faced right now. The Shadows had nearly claimed her soul and now here she was, walking into the midst of their cold, steely lair. I admired her courage, but silently cursed my decision for letting her come.

She squeezed my hand, ensuring me that my concern was not justified.

Sunjia gestured toward the ship on the right. We followed her up the gang plank, keeping an eye out for Shadows. The shield that Aidan and Ian put up were effective at hiding our presence for now.

Sunjia stopped at a door and took a deep breath. She closed her eyes for a moment and then motioned for me to break through the door.

The moment we entered, Tria's eyes flashed like flint against steel.

"Now!" Sunjia screamed.

Arcadie and Case blasted Tria with enough force to slam her into the far wall. Before she could recover, I added a blast of my own.

"Sunjia, pull back!" I roared over the deafening hum of pure energy.

The moment I felt Sunjia's spirit separate from Tria's, I set the girl's soul free. She collapsed against the floor.

Azazel's roar filled the room. Sunjia lay beside her daughter, unconscious. The walls shook and the air became too thin to breathe.

"Let's go!" I said.

Aidan lifted his mate and followed us out of the room. My head spun as the energy flowed from my body. On numb legs, I followed the others down the long corridor.

Metal screeched all around us. Case and Arcadie made quick work of the young Shadows blocking our exit.

Once on deck, we ran toward the railing. "Jump!" I yelled, hauling Skye over the side. The rest followed, barely escaping the bone-crushing explosion that catapulted us into the depths of the Sinclair Inlet.

I**T COULD HAVE BEEN WORSE.** We escaped with minor injuries that Skye took care of quickly. The hum in the air lingered.

We settled ourselves on an oyster dock, several feet from the shore.

Aidan and his mate were still out cold. He had suffered some broken ribs and a slight concussion. Sunjia's injuries lay much deeper. Skye healed her physical trauma, but could do little for the woman's psyche. Had I waited long enough for her spirit to clear from Tria?

Azazel's presence was like thick black smoke in the air.

"What keeps him here?" said Ian.

Skye frowned. "It's Sunjia. He's trying to get into her head."

"Ian, build an illusion to keep him out," Khalen

ordered. "Skye, get Sunjia to wake up. Everyone else, stay alert."

Ian jumped back. "Agh!" he screamed, shaking his hands.

Case cast a blast of energy toward the dark Angel. The hum of Ian's illusion wavered, but then slowly started to rebuild.

"Okay," Ian said. "The illusion is up."

"Let him get close enough," said Arcadie. "Then we blast him back to hell."

Skye jostled Sunjia. "Wake up!" she yelled. "She needs to hear Aidan's voice." Moving over toward the unconscious man, she shook him. "Come on Aidan, wake up."

"He's breakin' through," Ian said. "I can't hold this much longer."

Aidan started to stir.

Skye shook him. "That's it. Come on."

His eyes snapped open. "Sunjia!"

"She's fine, Aidan," Skye assured him. "I need you to wake her up. Reach her thoughts and bring her back."

The hum quickened. Ian started to shake.

Arcadie, Case and I stood ready. Once Ian released his illusion, Azazel would come in strong and fast. We would need every ounce of our energy to counter him.

"Hurry, Aidan," Skye encouraged. "Do it now. Reach out to her and call her back."

Aidan held Sunjia's hand.

"Agh!" Ian screamed. "He's strong."

Sunjia's eyes fluttered open. Ian dropped to the ground and his illusion shattered all around us, the force of it hitting like a tidal wave, diluting reality.

"Ready yourselves," said Case.

I struggled to regain my bearings.

"Now!" Arcadie yelled.

Our combined blasts rattled the air, drowning out all other sounds. A high-pitched scream cut through the air as the hum reduced to a slow and steady thud, thud, thud. Then, silence so thick it filled the space.

Skye smiled. "It's over. Azazel is gone."

The silence slowly dissolved into the normal rhythm of nature. The barrier between our dimensions had been restored.

"Where's Ian?" his brother asked.

We turned around on the dock.

"Ian?" I called.

No answer. I reached out to him. "He's in the water."

Case jumped in. A moment later, he slung Ian's arm onto the dock.

Aidan and I pulled him up.

"He's not breathing," I said, beginning CPR. "Skye, see what you can do."

"His lungs aren't inflating," she said.

"Can you heal them?"

She shook her head. "I can't get them to open."

Khalen breathed into Ian's mouth, willing his lungs to open.

"They're expanding," said Skye.

After a few more breaths, Ian started to cough.

I fell back, fighting the exhaustion that stripped my strength.

"Um, guys?" Skye said, standing over the lot of us collapsed upon the dock. "How do we get back to shore?"

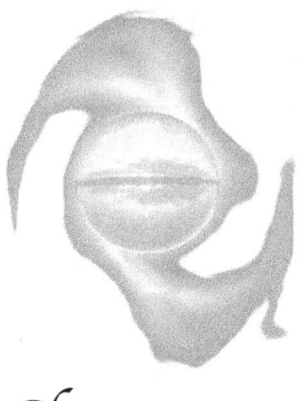

Chapter 29

-Elle-

"OKAY," I SAID TO SKYE, SITTING on our boulder in the meadow. "Tell me again how all this weird stuff can happen without anyone noticing." She told me about the adventure on the boat but I had a hard time believing that none of the human bystanders noticed anything apart from the ship's explosion.

The rain was pouring down, but she insisted that we take a ride in the woods—something about cabin fever.

In answer to my question, Skye just shrugged. "It happens all the time," she said. "Case says that humans don't see certain things because they are not attuned to such frequencies."

"And no one investigated why a retired ship at the shipyard just spontaneously blew into pieces?"

"They may have."

I shook my head. This conversation was going absolutely nowhere. "How's Sunjia doing?"

"Better." She frowned.

"Uh oh," I said. "You have that look."

"What look?"

"The one that says you're worried but don't want to show it."

"If I didn't want to show it, then how do you know I'm worried?"

"Spill it," I said. "What's going on with Sunjia?"

"She lost her daughter. I can't even imagine how that must feel."

I remembered how I had felt the day Avel died. Losing your child must be equally painful. "She's handling it well, though, don't you think?"

"Well enough. Khalen says it will take time for those wounds to heal."

Maiyun leapt onto the boulder, paws muddy and fur slick with rain. She panted heavily, her tongue hanging out of her mouth.

"The men must be back from hunting," said Skye.

"Isn't it a bit early for hunting season?" I asked.

"Elkinez's tribe holds hunting rights all year long, provided they use a bow and arrow."

"Why bother," I said. "I'm sure the men could just zap the poor creature to death."

Skye laughed. "Technically, yes, but that would be unfair to the animal."

"We have plenty of meat here at camp, why go hunting?"

"Arcadie wanted something special for the ceremony tomorrow."

I drew my knees up and started to rock.

"You're not still nervous, are you?" asked Skye.

"No," I lied.

"Just think," she said. "Tomorrow, you will become a Spirian."

"Hmm," I replied. "Metaphysical battles, evil Shadows, rules beyond belief, and absolutely no privacy of thought. Lucky me."

Skye smiled. "You can always return to your life as a human."

"I'm not a human, remember? Archangel? His immortal touch?"

"Would you return if you could?"

I thought about it for a moment. My human life hadn't exactly been uneventful, but then again, it hadn't been all that exciting, either. "Could I take Drew with me?"

"Yes," she said, "but he would be human."

"And Connor?"

"Of course."

"Could I come visit?"

She nodded. "Just like Ember."

I thought about Jamie and the others at the karate school, my life before Avel had found me, and my family with whom I never fit in. How would Drew be as a human? I wondered.

He wouldn't be able to light fires with a thought anymore or read my mind. That could be a plus. He'd still know how to fight.

"I don't know," I finally said. "It sounds intriguing."

Her smiled broadened. "Wait until your union and then answer the question."

"Why?"

"You'll see."

THE EVENING HAD FLOWN by and Drew was getting ready to leave.

"I'll only be gone for a few hours," he said. "I have a few things I need to finish up at the cabin before tomorrow."

"Can't it wait?" I asked.

"Yes," he said, giving me a long and gentle kiss. "But it won't."

"I'll try to stay up."

"Don't," he said. "Believe me; you'll need your rest for tomorrow."

"Why does everyone keep saying that?"

He laughed and walked away.

BY MORNING THE CAMP WAS bustling with activity. The rain hadn't ceased, but that didn't stop everyone from preparing for the big celebration—two unions in one day. I had no idea what to expect. Skye and the other women hovered over me, not allowing me to do a thing other than relax and be pampered.

I stepped outside with a hot cup of coffee in my hand and was nearly floored by what I saw. A tent had been constructed outside—circus tent huge. It was decorated with flowers and lace that kept the rain out and the heat from a central fire in.

Kids ran around, including Connor, with flowers dropping from their tiny hands as they did their best to garnish the tent with color.

I vaguely remember Drew giving me a kiss this morning, but not much after that. He was gone when I rose. I looked around but saw no sign of him. I assumed he was either working on our cabin still, or was forced into a dormant role as was I. Come to think of it, Ian and

Erika were also absent.

Skye walked toward me carrying a bowl of something hot.

"Hungry?" she asked, walking up the stairs.

I breathed in. The nutty scent of grains and fruit made my stomach grumble. "Mmm, what is it?"

"Potlatch pilaf," she said with a beaming smile. "It will hold you over till after the ceremony. Arcadie and Kitta have a huge feast planned."

She stepped inside and placed the bowl on the counter for me, refilled my coffee and then pulled a small loaf of hot bread from the oven. Next, she set out cold goat butter and berry jam that Eve had made.

"Aren't you going to join me?" I asked, frowning at the one-person spread.

"I've eaten already. I'll be by soon enough to help get you ready. After you eat, take a long hot shower and wash your hair. Use the soap I have set out for you and dress in the robe hanging on the door peg."

"Sounds very formal," I said.

"There is no other celebration more sacred than a union."

She left me alone to eat. The fire crackled in the hearth and only the sound of distant conversation and laughter broke the silence.

The potlatch pilaf looked interesting. I stirred in the heavy cream and fresh blueberries before taking a small bite. The texture was soft but not mushy. The flavor was nutty, creamy, and very satisfying. The small loaf of bread had sunflower seeds and bits of rye. Skye had sweetened it with dark molasses—my favorite.

The sweet, creamy goat butter added a subtle salty flavor and mingled nicely with the berry jam. After staying here a few months, eating store-bought food was always a disappointment. I smiled at that thought.

For a short time after Avel's death, I tried reintegrating into my normal life. As much as I tried convincing myself that I was happy, I really wasn't. I missed the clan, the camp lifestyle, and Skye's witty charm and blatant honesty.

I was almost grateful when Khalen came to rescue me that time when the Shadows first approached me. Khalen demanded that I live here. I was angry, of course, not enjoying being told what to do, but deep down I needed this clan to heal.

Now, here I was, facing a union with a Spirian man who managed to wheedle his way into my heart. I still loved Avel, of course, but in a different way. It was hard to explain and even harder to accept.

I smiled inwardly, finishing the last of my cereal. After cleaning my dishes, I meandered toward the bathroom to take my shower.

Candles burned all around the stone room, adding a warm glow and a bit of heat. A bar of sweet-smelling soap with a hint of clary sage sat on the shelf. On the opposite shelf were clear bottles of shampoo and conditioner. They too had the same scent as the soap. Hanging on one of the shower heads was a scrub cloth and a razor for shaving.

I set my coffee down on the counter and began undressing. My thoughts drifted to Drew. Was he also performing this bathing ritual? I smiled thinking about how easy he was with his nakedness. When he had bathed me, he did so with such love, yet there was nothing sexual about it. Did he find me attractive? I wondered.

I decided it didn't matter. I was determined to be a great mate for him with whatever assets I had.

The soap foamed into a rich lather and tingled against

my skin. I scrubbed it with the rough cloth, enjoying how soft it left my body. I finished with the shampoo and conditioner, shaved and then allowed myself the pleasure of standing under the hot spray until my skin began to wrinkle.

The towel Skye had left me was soft but absorbent. The robe was even nicer. It was silky, but almost too revealing for my comfort. I eyed my clothes, hanging on the pegs where I'd left them. They were an inviting alternative to this robe that barely covered my backside. I sighed and thought better of it. Skye would be disappointed if I chose not to stick to her plans.

With the towel wrapped on my head, I padded my way back to the kitchen to refresh my coffee. I heard the voices of Skye, Eve and Sunjia as they ascended the stairs to the yurt.

"Are you ready?" asked Skye, a color of excitement in her tone.

"I feel like a Barbie doll in a room full of girls," I said.

"Come on," said Sunjia. "This will be fun."

Skye sat me down on a stool. Eve started in with my hair, carefully combing it out as it dried. Sunjia worked on my nails while Skye massaged my feet.

"Who's working on Erika?" I asked.

"Dania, Kitta and Ember."

"Ember's here?"

"Yes," Skye chuckled. "She and Liam came in last night. She didn't want to miss your union."

"They're becoming quite an item," I observed.

"It's nice to see," said Eve. "She's been so lonely since her mate was killed."

"Any word on Jade?" I asked.

All of them grew silent for a moment before Skye

answered. "Not yet."

"Ember must be beside herself with worry," I said.

Eve twirled thin strands of my hair around her fingers before pinning the tight curls against my head. "She's handling it well enough."

By the time my hair and nails were done, my nerves hung by fraying threads.

Skye handed me a cordial glass filled with a rich amber liquid. "Here, drink this."

I breathed in its fragrance—chocolate and coffee with a hint of raspberry. "What is this?"

"Khalen's forty-year old Porto Roca. It's a rare tawny port from Portugal. It will help calm your nerves."

"Great," I said. "It's not even noon and I'm drinking alcohol. Doesn't that make me some sort of a lush?"

Eve laughed. "This is a special occasion, my dear. Drink away."

I sipped the dark liquid, allowing it to coat my tongue before it burned down my throat. I nearly coughed it up.

"Easy," said Skye. "That stuff is potent. Take small sips."

"Potent?" I said. "Good Lord, how much alcohol is in this stuff?"

She shrugged. "Enough." She walked out of the room and returned with my dress.

Eve and Sunjia slid it over my head.

"Um," I stammered. "Shouldn't I put some underclothing on first?"

"Drew specifically requested that you don't," Skye said casually, as if this wasn't odd.

"I can't go out there like this," I said. "It isn't—proper."

"It's not like anyone will know," said Sunjia. "Aidan requested the same for our union."

"And you obliged him?"

They all stepped back and looked at me as if I were the one who was crazy.

"What?" I said. "Don't you find this a little strange?"

"No," they all said in unison.

"It's a common request," said Skye.

"Common? So everyone will know that I'm bare-ass naked under this thing."

"Well," she said, "they won't know, but they might suspect it."

"Well," I said, walking toward my bedroom. "I'm not going to oblige Drew's request."

When I came back, the women were smiling.

"Suit yourself," said Skye.

"What does that mean?" I asked.

"Personally," Sunjia whispered in my ear, "I would do as Drew asks."

I frowned. "Why? What will happen if I don't?"

Eve laughed. "Well, either you do as your mate wants or he will have his way when you step outside."

"Meaning?"

"Drew will remove them in front of the clan," Skye explained with a smirk.

"He wouldn't dare!"

All three of them looked at me. Without a word, their expressions announced their thoughts. You bet he would.

"He wouldn't do that," I said.

"Like I said," said Skye. "suit yourself."

"Agh," I groaned, stomping back to my room.

I T WAS TIME FOR THE CEREMONY. Skye removed my pendant and replaced the silver chain with a gold one.

She then slid the pendant into her pocket.

"Okay," she said. "Ready?"

I nodded, unable to speak. My jaw felt clamped shut and my chest struggled with every breath.

"Relax," she said, escorting me out to the large tent. "Try to breathe."

My legs shook as we stepped into the gathering of the clan. Everyone stood. There were no stumps or logs on which to sit. They had all been moved out of the way. The hum in the air was palpable. I felt it deep in my bones.

Ian and Erika stood before Khalen. Drew stood to their right. His eyes glowed that deep amethyst color as he spotted me. Skye urged me forward until Drew reached for my hand.

Skye handed my pendant to him and smiled before stepping back into the crowd.

Khalen nodded to Gabrihen. He was dressed in an ornate robe with several colorful gems sewn into the cloth. He looked more nervous than I felt as he stepped toward his father.

With a quick glance at Tetris, he moved around us, forming a circle and then, with a dramatic wave of his hand, the circle illuminated into a ring of fire with multiple colors. A smile beamed across his face.

"Well done," said Khalen, urging him back to Tetris' side.

The ceremony started out with a prayer spoken in another language—Latin perhaps?

"Gallic," Drew whispered. "The clan's original language."

Khalen continued speaking in Gallic for Ian and Erika's vows. My nerves started to twitch.

"Ours will be in English," he assured me.

I watched in horror as Khalen took Ian's pendant and cut a small line in each of their wrists before tying them together with a red strip of cloth. My stomach twisted. He then slid the pendant over Erika's head, and the chain glowed and shimmered as if it were sprinkled with fairy dust. I blinked a few times, certain I had imagined it.

Khalen turned his attention to Drew and me. Drew's vows came first, preceded by a very long and descriptive family lineage. He repeated each word as if they had been rehearsed for days.

When Khalen looked to me, Drew pressed my palm against the formidable leader's hand. I started to shake.

Khalen's eyes softened. "Ellesander Alder, former mate of the Spirit Avel, do you commit to this union to Drew Hawk, son of Elkinez?"

I opened my mouth to speak, but nothing came out. That, of course, caused my throat to tighten even more.

"Breathe, Elle," Drew said, rubbing my back.

"Yes, I do," I stammered.

Soft laughter rose from the clan. The familiar ring of it eased my nerves a bit.

"Repeat after me," said Khalen. "I, Ellesander Alder, promise to love and honor my mate Drew Hawk throughout our lifetime."

My vows were short, sweet, and to the point, I thought. I can handle this. I took a deep breath and repeated the words with renewed confidence.

Khalen spoke again. "I will obey him, remain loyal to him, and will follow his lead in all matters."

My throat started to close again. I managed to squeak the words out.

Khalen smiled. "I promise to give him my heart completely without falter for the remainder of our days."

I swallowed hard and repeated the words.

When his mouth opened again, my eyes narrowed. My short, sweet vows had turned into a lifelong sentence of obedience and submission. Skye had warned me about this part. I should have listened more carefully.

Even still, I smiled inwardly, I would have said yes to all of it.

Khalen returned my hand to Drew. "May I have the pendant?"

Drew placed my pendant, now strung on a gold chain, in the leader's hand.

I was grateful for the last meal I had several hours ago. If I had eaten anything afterward, it would be coming up about now.

Drew turned my wrist upward to expose the soft flesh. He turned his over as well and presented it to Khalen.

Khalen drew a thin line of blood over Drew's skin and then moved to do the same over mine. The crystal bit into my flesh leaving a stinging hot sensation in its wake.

"Breathe," Khalen said to me.

I hadn't realized I had been holding my breath until the rush of fresh air filled my aching lungs.

He pressed our wounds together and bound our wrists with a red sash, speaking in Gallic again before handing Drew the pendant. He slipped it over my head.

After a quick prayer, drums started beating a rhythm that vibrated in my bones.

Khalen made a final announcement in Gallic, bowed to Ian and Drew and then stepped out of the circle.

Drew pulled me to him and kissed me tenderly at first and then deeply as if announcing his claim on my heart.

"Are we mates now?" I asked.

"Almost," he said. "We must join to make it official."

He urged me forward.

As we approached Seth, his large dark eyes widened. He stepped back a bit and to the side. Drew reached out for his shoulder and then urged me to kneel with him before the young man. I could almost hear him swallow.

"Seth Dunning O'Dougherty, will you honor my mate and me by agreeing to be her templar?"

The clan's endless chatter grew silent. I could feel their eyes upon us and upon the young man who stood there speechless.

"M—m—me?" he asked.

"Yes, Seth. I'm addressing you," Drew said, his voice enticingly silky and confident.

Seth's eyes met mine. When I smiled up at him, his eyes flashed with an obsidian glow that seemed surreal.

"I accept," he said with unexpected confidence. He then removed the sash from around our wrists and tied it to his left arm. When he took my hand in his, I felt a surge of shock ripple through my body. It was the same sensation I had felt from Khalen when he agreed to be my templar.

Seth met Drew's eyes. "Thank you," he said.

Drew bowed to him.

Before we could completely stand, Sunjia came running over and offered me a bone-crushing hug before doing the same to her son. He seemed to be standing taller now; his eyes glowed with a spark that only the older men had displayed.

Drew smiled. "He is officially a man now," he explained.

"But he's so young according to Spirian ways," I said.

"Yes, he is very young to be chosen as a templar. Khalen agreed it would help the boy grow up. He was beaten down so long by his father that he hasn't had much need to grow past it. Becoming a templar for a female he cares about will force him to man up to the task. He will be viewed differently by the men in the clan and especially by the children."

"Aidan beat him down?" That was hard to believe.

Drew laughed and then frowned. "No, Aidan is not his biological father, just as Case is not Khalen's. Khalen had a twin named Traeger. He is Seth's father and was once Sunjia's mate."

"What happened to him?" I asked.

"Khalen killed him." He tugged on my hand. "Come, let's get something to eat."

"Killed him?"

"It's a long story, milah. Traeger was a Shadow, as was their father—a very powerful leader and a heartless man with no scruples. Sunjia and her children came to us for sanctuary. Traeger came to retrieve them and a battle ensued. Khalen won."

"That must have been hard for him," I said.

"It nearly killed him. If it weren't for Skye, we would have lost him."

The vibrant blonde mate of the leader ran up to us and wrapped me in her arms. "You did great!"

"Thank you," I mumbled into her shoulder. I held my arm up to her. "It burns."

Drew lowered my arm. "She cannot heal it," he said.

"Why?"

"It is a reminder of your vows," said Skye. She showed me her scar.

"The burning will continue until we consummate the union," said Drew. His smile broadened. "We can skip dinner if you wish."

My belly did a flip. "That would be quite rude, don't

you think?"

  He and Skye laughed.

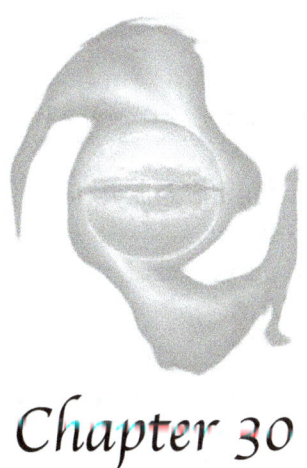

Chapter 30

~ I a n ~

As **Erika and I approached** Jazen, his chin rose up a notch. Erika and I knelt before him.

"Jazen," I said. "It would honor me if ye would agree to be my mate's templar."

"I accept with honor," he said, removing our sash. He took Erika's hand, kissed the back of it and made the connection to her. She almost fell backward from the force, showing just how powerful he could be.

He helped us stand.

"Thank you," I said.

"Be grateful I don't plan your early demise," he jested.

Erika mock punched his arm. "You better not."

Jazen met her smile. "Only upon your request, my dear."

She laughed. "That won't happen."

"Ah, missy, don't shatter my hope."

"I bested ye once," I said, "I c'n do it again."

Jazen held up his hands. "Another time, mate. If I ruin you before your consummation, she'll likely have my head in a vise."

I glanced over at his father, standing with Arcadie, drink in hand and smiling. "I see your father made it?"

"Yeah. We had a long talk."

"A good one, I trust?"

Jazen smiled, but there was still a sadness in his eyes. "Good enough."

We joined the others by the fire. Benches and chairs had been brought in for the evening feast. Afterward they would be pushed back to create ample space for dancing.

The scent of slow-roasted venison filled my nostrils and gripped my belly like a cruel demand. Arcadie was a master at cooking wild game, and I filled my plate with it.

"Don't get sick on me," said Erika, daintily placing a few slices onto her own plate.

"Never," I said, plopping a healthy portion of mashed potatoes over my meat. I added a colorful selection of raw veggies, steamed roots and fresh bread before taking my seat beside Drew.

He and his new mate sat talking to Khalen and Skye. Arcadie and Kitta would join us after they ensured that everyone had enough food. Given the sheer amount prepared for the feast, I was sure we would have enough left over to feed three orphanages.

Khalen served us all a glass of his finest Borolo before raising his glass in a toast. "To the newly joined and their many children," he said.

"Aye," I seconded.

"Hear, hear," said Drew.

Erika blushed making her all the more kissable.

"Many children," I whispered into her ear before

claiming her mouth. My body reacted in kind. Tonight, I would not have to hold back. I could experience her completely the way I had only imagined in the past. She was finally mine.

Drew was still kissing Elle. Her brimming wine glass tipped precariously in her hand.

Khalen reached over and took it from her. "Let her eat, man," he said. "The night will be long as it is."

Drew released a very embarrassed and flustered Elle. She took her glass back from Khalen with a nod of thanks. Before setting it down, she nearly drained half the cup.

Khalen laughed, refilling her cup. He then removed it from her grasp. "Eat. You'll need your strength."

Skye laughed.

"I'm not running a marathon," she stated. "I have joined with a man before, you know."

Skye's laugh deepened. Eve and Sunjia joined in.

"Stop it," Erika said. "You're terrifying her."

"I'm fine," said Elle, lifting her chin a notch. When she reached for her wine, Khalen set it back.

Drew handed her a large plate of food. "Eat up."

She took the plate, glaring at both him and Khalen.

~ Elle ~

JUST WHEN I THOUGHT I couldn't possibly eat another bite of food, Kitta brought out a platter of dark chocolate caramels with a sprinkling of gray sea salt. My mouth watered just looking at them.

Arcadie followed behind with several cordial glasses and bottles of something I was sure would be just as decadent—Black Forest Chocolate dessert wine.

The portions were served and handed to our respective mates, along with a glass of the special wine. The idea, of course, was to feed their women with practiced, teasing perfection.

The clan gathered, banging their glasses as if demanding a show.

It was as if Ian and Drew were in some sort of primal competition with each other.

First, Ian brushed the chocolate against Erika's lips, waited for her to open and then slowly allowed the chocolate to slide into her mouth. He then tipped the tiny cordial glass to her lips and drizzled the wine between her lips. The seductive look on her face made me blush.

The clan applauded with great delight before banging their glasses again.

When I turned to face Drew, he was staring at me and smiled. He brought the chocolate up to my mouth, but when I opened, he pulled it back, shaking his head. "Not until I tell you," he said.

My face heated as the clan quietly chuckled. This was sheer torture. First, I didn't like being looked at, and second, I despised being controlled—something Drew did with practiced ease.

He tilted my head back and brushed the chocolate against my mouth. I could feel it melt upon my lips, tempting me to lick them. I didn't even get them opened a crack.

"Not yet," he said.

The salt mingled with the bittersweet chocolate and creamy caramel, teasing my tongue to want more as it slipped past my quivering lips.

Drew eased my mouth open with his fingers. My heart hammered in my chest, both from embarrassment and excitement. The melted concoction seeped between my lips, flowed over my tongue and delicately mingled with the chocolate wine that soon followed. The combination of flavors erased my awareness of the crowd. Drew placed the rest of the chocolate onto my tongue, allowing his fingers to linger for longer than was necessary. More wine followed.

I savored the flavors before swallowing them down. Only then did I realize that the crowd had become silent. My eyes had been closed. When they opened, Drew hovered over me with such hunger in his eyes, my heart felt devoured.

The clan roared with appreciation, banging their glasses to show their approval.

"Well done," he whispered.

My first breath ached as if I had been holding it too long. "Yes," I said dreamily. "Very."

Music started playing and Drew lifted me to my feet.

"Um," I said, trying to slow him down. "I can't dance."

"We'll see," he said, holding my waist.

The music pounded with a haunting tribal beat. Drew moved my hips to match his. We stepped in time with the beat, his touch and unceasing stare placing me in a state of lustful trance. Nothing else seemed to matter. I moved with the rhythm of the drums and allowed his skillful hands to guide my every step. I gave him complete control and it felt—wonderful.

He laughed quietly. "That's my girl," he said, his voice comforting as a warm blanket on a chilly night.

When the dance ended, my head felt as if I had downed several glasses of wine in one full swallow.

A springy Irish tune started to play. Ian and Erika entered the dance space.

Drew lifted me into his arms and carried me off to his cabin.

"Close your eyes," he said before carrying me through the door and setting me on my feet.

I heard the lights click on. "Welcome home, milah. Open your eyes."

What I saw before tears blurred my vision was something out of a dream. A central hearth occupied the front room, providing ample heat from all sides. The loveseat we had selected fit perfectly against the far wall and played well against the Brazilian Tigerwood floors and cedar walls.

The kitchen sported dark gray granite counters, and a Wolfe range that resembled the one in Skye's kitchen.

"Compliments of Skye and Khalen. He insisted on gifting them to us."

I brushed my hand against the smooth finish. "I love it, Drew."

He held my hand and led me into the bedroom. The king-sized bed we had chosen rested on a rosewood frame with six drawers on either side. The headboard was shaped so that we could sit comfortably in bed. Cleverly, it swooped out to form elegant side tables.

I smiled at the soft and fuzzy purple blanket that draped loosely over the bed.

"Skye's contribution," he laughed. "She demanded that you absolutely had to have it."

I laughed. "I love that woman."

Then he showed me the bathroom, an exact duplicate of the one he had designed for Skye and Khalen, only this one was equipped with embedded lights in the walls that resembled candles.

"Oh, Drew, this is. . ." My throat closed, "Amazing."

"Do you like it?"

"Oh, God, I love it." I wrapped my arms around him and kissed him repeatedly until he lifted me into his arms and carried me back to the bedroom.

"Are you ready for this?" he asked.

I nodded. "More than you know."

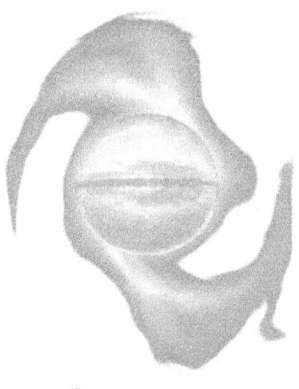

Chapter 31

H E STARTED TO DIM THE LIGHTS and then began
stoking the fire.

"I'm curious," I said.

"About?" He poured us each a glass of cognac.

"Why women are not allowed to wear underwear
under their wedding gowns."

He laughed. "It is done as the first act of obedience."

Obedience. That word stuck in my gut like sticky
weed in the fall. "That sounds barbaric."

"To a Spirian male, obedience is akin to ultimate trust
and respect. When a female follows her mate's lead, it
shows to others that she trusts and respects her mate's
decisions. It honors the male."

I frowned. "What honors the female?"

"The way her mate treats her. She is never without, is
very loved, and should be happy. When a woman is well
cared for, it shows."

I smiled, thinking of how my friends were all very
happy. Looking around the incredible cabin that Drew

had built for me, I figured the exchange was quite fair.

"What would have happened if I hadn't obeyed your first request?"

With a thought, my dress fell to the floor. I gasped. "How did you do that? I had to struggle just to get that thing over my head."

He waved his hand and the dress, or what was left of it, went flying.

The women warned me he could do such things, but I never imagined it was true. "You wouldn't do that in front of the clan, would you?"

His brow arched. "I would." The hard tone in his voice assured me he was serious.

Without saying a word, he handed me my glass and smiled.

I felt a little vulnerable standing there before him, naked. He had seen me naked before, many times, but somehow this was different. The way his eyes roamed over my body felt like delicate feathers kissing my skin.

His smile broadened, obviously noticing how my body responded to his intense attention.

He clinked his glass to mine. "To our union," he said before leaning over to kiss me.

I nearly dropped the glass. Laughing, he took it from me, set it on the table and then carried me to the bed.

His clothes slid from his body and fell to the floor. Though I was shaking, it wasn't from the cold. He had shown me affection before but it was never this intense.

Everywhere he touched made my skin crave more. His kisses were deep and commanding as if he were reclaiming what was already his.

By the time he moved over me, ready to love me, I was desperate. I wanted to touch him, but he held my arms over my head.

"Not this time, milah. I need to stay in control."

His raspy voice nearly drove me over the edge. This felt different, far different than when Avel loved me—inexplicably.

"Open your eyes, milah. I need you to look at me."

I did. His eyes were such a brilliant shade of amethyst, they drew me in. I felt as if I could feel him deep in my belly. The pain was intense, yet I wanted more of it, more of him.

My belly grew warm. I could feel his heartbeat and breath as if they were my own. I experienced his pleasure. His eyes glowed brighter and I felt the merging of our souls. I surrendered everything to him. The momentary feeling of hollowness was quickly replaced by a fullness that words could not describe.

He finished with an explosion of heat, pain, emptiness, fullness and utter delirium.

We rolled over. He wiped the sweat from his forehead with his hand and then gripped my left wrist. The pain that surged through me was paralyzing. I couldn't scream or move.

"It will be over soon," he said.

The pain ceased. His grip relaxed along with the rest of him.

We fell asleep, tangled together. Hours had passed, yet it felt like minutes. Never had I felt so complete, so balanced, satisfied beyond belief.

I smiled, thinking about the question that Skye had posed to me before my union. She had asked if I would return to my life as a human. Now I had an answer for her—no way.

My head hummed with conversation that was not

my own. Thoughts streamed like motion pictures in my head. It had started out dull like background noise but had quickly escalated into a constant chatter.

I tried wiggling free from under Drew's arm. His grip tightened.

"Where are you going?" he grumbled.

"I need to use the privy," I said.

Reluctantly he released his hold. My body shivered from his absence as I padded my way to the privy.

It was separate from the bathroom and did not use running water. It was a compost toilet similar to the one Skye and Khalen had.

My head ached and I was so thirsty. When I came out of the privy, Drew was pouring me a glass of water.

"Thank you," I said, taking a long swallow. The water felt cool against my throat and the minerals in the water were easily detected. It was as if all of my senses were magnified tenfold.

"How's your head," he smiled.

"Pounding, noisy and irritating," I said.

He laughed. "Yes, it's the clan you are hearing now. That will fade in time."

"Agh," I groaned, sagging onto a stool at the counter. "What time is it?"

Drew glanced down at the stove. "Eleven o'clock," he said. "Are you hungry?"

"Starved," I said. My entire body was shaking. "I feel as if I haven't eaten for days."

He laughed. "You haven't. This is Monday morning."

"Monday?"

We had joined last Friday. How could so much time have passed without my notice? Now I understood why everyone said I would need my strength.

He set a cup of coffee before me, perfectly sweetened with maple syrup and a dapple of goat milk. My first sip was heavenly. "Mmm," I murmured. "Everything tastes so different."

He smiled. "Your senses are enhanced. You are Spirian now, milah."

I glanced down at my wrist. It no longer throbbed and ached. A small design looked to be etched into my skin like something between a brand and a tattoo. It was beautifully striking. Very similar to Skye's, only my dragons sported different colors.

Drew traced the mark with this finger, leaving a tingling sensation behind. "It is my mark," he said. "The design represents the clan to which we belong, while the colors depict my family heritage."

"I like it," I said.

He bent down and kissed the mark. "Me too, milah. I love how it looks on you."

He took a plate full of fresh fruit, cheese and meats from the refrigerator and slid it before me. "Eat," he said.

"Shouldn't we join the others outside?"

He smiled. "I'm not ready to share you yet, milah. Eat and then I will make love to you a few more times."

BY THE TIME WE EMERGED from our cabin, it was late into the following day. Khalen was packing a few bags into the back of his Escalade while Skye held Gabrihen, crying.

Tetris stood by and watched. "He'll not be far, mum," he said, trying to reassure her. "You'll come see him often."

Sunjia and Aidan gave Seth a hug after placing his bags in the car.

"Write to us," said Sunjia. "Every day."

"I'll be too busy to write every day," he said, laughing. "But I will write as often as I can."

Kaili came running over and gave Seth a crushing hug. "Don't go, Seth," she wailed.

Seth picked her up into his arms and gave her a squeeze. "I'll be back soon, little one," he said, holding her tighter.

The other children came as well, each hugging his legs.

When he tried to set Kaili down, she clung to him. "I want to come with you."

He laughed and gave her one last hug before setting her down. "No, little one, you must stay here with your mum."

Kaili's eyes welled with tears as she backed away from him.

Connor said goodbye to Gabrihen, trying his best not to let tears form in his eyes.

"You'll come visit me, yes?" said Gabrihen.

Connor nodded.

Tetris squeezed Gabrihen's shoulder. "Come, young apprentice. Let's get this done."

Arcadie, Kitta and Khalen were already in the car and Seth was just stepping into the back seat when he spotted Drew and me.

He approached us with both hands out. "I thought I would have to leave without saying goodbye."

"Where are you going?" I asked, clearly confused.

He glanced back at Khalen and smiled. "I was accepted at Edinburgh. I'm getting my medical degree."

I hugged him. "Oh, Seth, that's great. I'm so happy for you."

"I'll be staying with Shanuk's old clan. You can come

visit if you like."

"Sounds great," I said.

Drew shook his hand and then pulled him into a hug. "Take care, Seth."

"I will."

We watched as he slipped into the car and closed the door. Teary eyes followed the Escalade until it rounded the corner and rolled out of sight.

Connor came over and gave me a hug. "I missed you, mummy."

I picked him up and held him tight in my arms. "I missed you too, pet."

Drew ruffled his hair. "Have you been good for Skye and Khalen?"

Skye smiled. "He's been an angel. He'll miss Gabrihen, though."

Connor buried his face into my shoulder. I patted his back. "We'll see him again soon," I assured him.

"Are you hungry?" Skye asked, wiping the tears from her eyes.

I smiled. "A little."

"Go with the women," said Drew, taking Connor from my arms. "Connor and I need to help Aidan with a few things in the barn," he said, patting my backside.

Embarrassed, I followed Skye to the fire where Eve was chatting with Ember and Liam.

"You look radiant," said Eve.

"I feel exhausted," I admitted.

Everyone laughed.

"Has anyone seen Ian and Erika?"

Skye handed me a tuna wrap and a glass of iced tea before sitting beside me. "They left for Fiji two days ago."

I wondered if Drew had something special planned

for us after the book tour ended in Europe.

You'll find out soon enough, milah, he said in my head. I turned but didn't see him. His words were clear as if they had been spoken directly to me.

Skye laughed. "He can communicate with you over any distance now."

"Can I do the same?"

She nodded. "Just send him a thought."

Can you hear me?

I could feel him laugh. *I always could,* he responded.

Shaking my head, I said, "Everything feels so strange. I'm like a snake that has just shed her skin."

"In a sense, you are," said Skye, turning my arm over to get a better view of Drew's mark. "Very nice."

"You know, if someone were to tell me six years ago that I would be living with a clan of gifted people and mated to a domineering male whose mark I would proudly bear, I would have laughed them out of the room."

"So, do you still want to return to your human life?"

I laughed. "Absolutely not!"

She raised her brow. "Wow, you didn't even have to think about it this time."

A cell phone buzzed. We watched as Case pulled it from his pocket and stared at the screen.

His expression turned pale as he looked to Ember. "They found Jade."

- The End -

A Note From the Author

I hope you have enjoyed reading Illusions. This story, as you may have discovered, did not follow the traditional plot format for a romantic fantasy novel. Straying from the formula, however, was worth the message I wanted to convey.

Ian had to learn how to believe in himself to gain something he thought he didn't deserve. Elle had to learn to love again and believe in the process of her life purpose. It is difficult to weave two completely different plot lines into one. I hope I didn't confuse you too much.

Many of us have a story to tell but are afraid tell it for one reason or another. My goal is to encourage and inspire you all to tell your story, be it as a memoir or as a fictional tale such as this one.

About the Author

Rowena started writing at a young age, feeling an inherent need to tell stories that inspire and reflect aspects of life that are rarely considered.

Being a descendant of James Hudson Taylor, author and founder of the China Inland Mission, Rowena comes from a long line of story tellers, including her mother and father. The tradition of writing continues through her daughter, Erika.

Rowena's goal is to inspire others to tell their stories and share the wonderful gift and adventure of life. She often speaks before groups, sharing her experiences of writing and telling stories. It is a passion of hers that she shares with her mate, Gregg.

Together, they are writing a book entitled, *Finding Peace Among Chaos*, due to be released in Summer 2013.

Though she is over seventy-five percent blind, she doesn't allow that to derail her ambitions. Her husband is deaf, so they make the perfect pair. They live on the Olympic Peninsula in Washington with her guide dog Skye-Bear.

Other Books by Rowena

Protected
Union
Legend
Aeon Pneuma
Fealty

www.RowenaPortch.com

Book a Speaking Engagement with Rowena and Gregg

Rowena and Gregg love to inspire people to tell their story and to follow their passion no matter how unobtainable it may seem.

Both of them have been on their own since age fourteen and have some incredible stories to share. Though both of them are disabled—she's blind and he's deaf—neither of them allow their impairments to deter them from their dreams.

If you want Rowena and Gregg to speak at your next event, please email them at:

Rowena@RowenaPortch.com

www.ingramcontent.com/pod-product-compliance
Lightning Source LLC
Chambersburg PA
CBHW060351260626
47160CB00006B/2270